SPIRIT PATH

"I am going to kill Wolf Who Hunts Smiling."

Touch the Sky's announcement struck everyone dumb, including Wolf Who Hunts Smiling and the Bull Whips. Little Horse gaped; even Arrow Keeper looked dumbfounded.

"You heard me straight," he went on. "His scaffold is as good as built. I will kill this murderer of Cheyenne, this traitor of his own tribe."

Gray Thunder met Touch the Sky's eyes. "I will brook no more talk of traitors and killing our own. Is that clear?"

Touch the Sky nodded once. "As you say, Gray Thunder," he finally replied. "No more talking."

MANKILLER

Touch the Sky felt himself being swung, heaved. Then he hit the ice-cold water. Unable to kick, he swam desperately with one arm, barely keeping his chin out of the water. Another splash nearby told him Little Horse, too, had been thrown in.

"Look at the odd fishes!" a Cherokee warrior taunted. "Are they trout with braids?"

"No, they are Cheyenne warrior fish!"

Over and over he and Little Horse made it close to shore only to be tossed back in. Now his arm was so weak it felt heavy as a stone club, and he was swallowing more and more water. The merciless taunts continued, although by now he heard little in his desperate struggle to stay alive.

As Touch the Sky was lifted and swung, he began chanting his death song. . . .

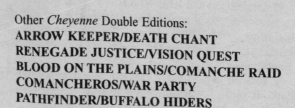

CHEYENNE

Double Edition:
SPIRIT PATH/
MANKILLER
JUDD COLE

LEISURE BOOKS NEW YORK CITY

A LEISURE BOOK®

October 1998

Published by

Dorchester Publishing Co., Inc.
276 Fifth Avenue
New York, NY 10001

ISBN 0-8439-4445-5

SPIRIT PATH

Prologue

In the year the white man's winter-count called 1840, a band of Northern Cheyennes led by Chief Running Antelope was ambushed by blue-bloused soldiers near the North Platte.

When the last cavalry carbines finally fell silent, every Cheyenne lay dead or dying except Running Antelope's infant son, still clutched in the fallen chief's arms. Pawnee scouts were about to brain the child against a cottonwood when the lieutenant in charge interfered. He had the infant brought back to the Wyoming river-bend settlement of Bighorn Falls, near Fort Bates.

The child was adopted by John Hanchon and his barren wife Sarah, owners of the town's thriving mercantile store, which did a brisk business with nearby Fort Bates. The Hanchons named him Matthew and loved him as their own son. From the time he was old enough to be useful, he worked for his parents, stocking shelves and delivering orders to the fort and surrounding settlers.

Occasionally the young Cheyenne encountered hostile stares and remarks, especially from frontier hard cases passing through with Indian scalps dangling from their sashes. But his parents were well respected, and their love was strong enough to smooth the occasional rough places; aware that he was different from other settlers, the boy nonetheless grew up feeling accepted in his limited world.

Then came Matthew's sixteenth year and a tragic love that left him an outcast, welcome neither in the red man's world nor the white's.

Kristen was the daughter of the wealthy mustang rancher Hiram Steele. Surprising the young lovers in their secret meeting place, Steele ordered one of his wranglers to savagely beat the youth. Kristen's implacable father swore he'd kill Matthew if he caught them together again. Fearing for Matthew's life, Kristen lied and told the youth she never wanted to see him again.

To this new grief was soon added a serious threat to his parents. Seth Carlson, a young lieutenant from Fort Bates who had staked a claim to Kristen, delivered an ultimatum to the beleaguered youth: Either he left Bighorn Falls for good, or his adopted parents would lose their lucrative contract with Fort Bates—the lifeblood of their business.

Saddened but determined, Matthew hardened his heart for whatever lay ahead. Then he pointed his bridle north toward the Powder River and Cheyenne country.

Captured by braves from Chief Yellow Bear's band, his hair-face clothing, language, and customs marked him as a traitor. He was sentenced to torture and death.

Lashed to a wagon wheel, he was mercilessly burned over glowing coals. Then, as a young buck named Wolf Who Hunts Smiling was about to kill him, old Arrow Keeper intervened. The tribal shaman, Arrow Keeper had recently experienced an important medicine dream. This vision foretold that an unknown Cheyenne youth, one who carried the mark of the warrior, would soon arrive at Yellow Bear's camp. The long-lost son of a great Cheyenne chief, this youth would eventually lead the entire *Shaiyena* nation in their last great victory against their enemies. Arrow Keeper spotted the mark—a mulberry-colored birthmark in the perfect shape of an arrowhead—buried past the unconscious youth's hairline.

At Arrow Keeper's insistence, the suspicious stranger's life was spared. But many in the tribe were infuriated when Arrow Keeper also insisted the youth must live with them—and even train as a warrior!

Arrow Keeper buried the hair-face name Matthew Hanchon in a hole and renamed the tall youth Touch the Sky. But the wily Wolf Who Hunts Smiling branded him a spy and a white man's dog. By deliberately stepping between Touch the Sky and the campfire, he announced his intention to someday kill his new enemy.

Touch the Sky earned a second formidable enemy in the older cousin of Wolf Who Hunts Smiling, Black Elk. The tribe's war leader, Black Elk saw the long, lingering glances Touch the Sky exchanged with Chief Yellow Bear's daughter Honey Eater. Black Elk planned to send the maiden the gift of marriage horses, and his hatred toward any rivals was great.

At first, up against two enemies covered with such hard bark, Touch the Sky seemed doomed. Only Arrow Keeper and Honey Eater were sympathetic. But neither dared to take his side openly for fear of making his miserable lot even worse. Black Elk led the warrior training, and the youth could not ride a pony, throw an ax, or even sharpen a knife correctly.

Taunted and brutalized by the other braves, he was eventually befriended by a sturdy youth named Little Horse. Through sheer determination to prove himself and finally belong somewhere, Touch the Sky eventually became one of the most able warriors in Yellow Bear's tribe.

But his enemies were clever and constantly turned appearances against him. Acceptance remained elusive, his enemies implacable. Forced by tribal pressures to accept Black Elk's gift of horses, Honey Eater married the war chief. But in her heart she could love only Touch the Sky.

Black Elk's cousin Wolf Who Hunts Smiling has long burned with ambition. He intends no less than a takeover of the tribe and the entire red nation, leading them in a war of extermination against the white invaders and their Indian spies.

Like Arrow Keeper, Touch the Sky has experienced the vision of his great destiny. Now Arrow Keeper has selected him for the long and difficult training as a shaman. For the old warrior knows that victory on the warpath alone will not be enough to save this young warrior from a hard and tragic fate.

Chapter One

"Place these words in your sashes, brothers," Tangle Hair said. "The music you are hearing right now comes from the hollowed-out leg bone of a dead Pawnee. And it is intended to taunt the ears of Touch the Sky and any who would raise their lances beside his."

The Bow String trooper fell silent, and the other braves seated around the fire nodded agreement. The flames sawed sharply in a sudden breeze, tracing the features of Tangle Hair, Touch the Sky, Little Horse, and the youngest among them, Two Twists.

Earlier, distant thunderheads had boiled over the Bighorn Mountains, and reefs of dark clouds had blown in from the north. Now, above the occasional muttering of distant thunder, they could hear the strange music

Tangle Hair spoke of: dull, atonal notes played with a slow precision that never varied. They emanated from the direction of the meat racks behind Black Elk's tipi—a favorite meeting place for the Cheyenne soldier society known as the Bull Whip Troop. Especially when the Whips were planning to do the hurt dance on an enemy.

And everyone in Gray Thunder's tribe knew who their main enemy within the tribe was: the tall Cheyenne who had arrived among them wearing the white man's shoes and the white man's stink. His shoes were long gone. But many still claimed the stink would never wash from him.

"He is playing the tune yet again," Little Horse said. The sturdy little warrior sat crushing coffee beans between two rocks. "It unstrings the horse's nerves and makes the infants cry. I had hoped the headmen would put a stop to it by now."

"They are afraid to," Touch the Sky said. "Many in the tribe are convinced by now that Medicine Flute has strong medicine. This tune, this lifeless thing which sounds like the wind rushing out of the neck when a pony is throat slashed. Wolf Who Hunts Smiling and others claim it can send an enemy running in fear."

Little Horse stopped his labors and glanced at his friend in the flickering firelight. Even seated cross-legged, Touch the Sky was clearly taller than the others. Choosing not to braid his hair, he wore it in long, loose black locks except over his eyes. There it was cut short to

11

free his vision. The warm moons were upon them, and like the other bucks, he wore only a clout and elkskin moccasins when in camp.

"Brother," Little Horse said, "I have seen the medicine you and Arrow Keeper can make. It is strong medicine, true medicine. This Medicine Flute, the warriors of his Spotted Ponies Clan are stout enough. Often one of them has worn the buffalo hat into battle. But tell me a thing. Do you believe Medicine Flute is marked out by the High Holy Ones for a shaman, as Wolf Who Hunts Smiling has begun to insist?"

Touch the Sky remained silent a long time, watching sparks fly up from the driftwood fire. Throughout Gray Thunder's summer camp, located at the fork of the Powder and Little Powder rivers, other clan fires glowed like bright eyes. Indian camps stayed active and noisy far into the night, there being no official bedtime. In the main clearing, young braves placed wagers on pony races, foot races, and wrestling contests. Children with miniature bows and willow-branch shields played at counting coups and taking prisoners. Old men stood in the doorways of the clan lodges, smoking fragrant red-willow bark and making brags about times they had raised the hatchet against Pawnees or Utes or the hair-faced blue soldiers.

"Arrow Keeper tells me that those truly marked for the gift of visions are rare," Touch the Sky finally replied. "Yet, I would be willing to believe that Medicine Flute has magic if Wolf Who Hunts Smiling were not behind the claim."

12

Little Horse immediately nodded, as did the others. "Count upon it, brother. Anything he touches has a bad smell to it. Long ago, before you even knew how to make a war whoop, he vowed to kill you. So did his lackey Swift Canoe when he blamed you for the death of his twin brother. And now Black Elk openly accuses you of wanting to put on the old moccasin with Honey Eater. All three are behind Black Elk's tipi right now. I fear whatever monster is born of this parley."

"Putting on the old moccasin" was a Cheyenne reference to an unmarried buck who desired a married woman. Everyone in the tribe knew how it was: Honey Eater, left alone when her father Chief Yellow Bear died, had been forced by the Cheyenne laws to marry.

But Touch the Sky, the one she loved, had been absent then; he had gone south to fight a battle for his white parents. Believing in her heart that Touch the Sky had deserted the tribe forever, she had reluctantly accepted Black Elk's gift of horses. Still today, Touch the Sky felt a sharp pang in his heart when he recalled riding back to camp to discover Honey Eater living in Black Elk's tipi and wearing the newlywed's bride shawl.

"Little Horse speaks straight arrow," Tangle Hair said. "Soon, I fear, Touch the Sky will once again have trouble firmly by the tail. But though his enemies are many, he no longer stands alone as he once did. I was there when he counted first coup at the Tongue River Battle. And I saw him stand shoulder to shoulder with you, Little Horse, when the white buffalo hiders attacked. They swarmed down on you like angry bees, but I swear by the four directions you two bucks fought like ten men!"

"And the elders," said the youth called Two Twists, who was named for his habit of wearing two braids. "Many of them would die for Touch the Sky. Like my old mother and grandmother, they were present at the hunt camp when Touch the Sky stood alone before an entire charge of Comanche and Kiowa raiders. They saw him make a deliberate target of himself to divert the attack."

All this praise embarrassed Touch the Sky, though it was true. But he held his face expressionless in the Indian way as he said, "It is good if I have these friends. For I have seen the determined glint in the eyes of Wolf Who Hunts Smiling and his cousin Black Elk. Neither buck is a warrior to trifle with.

"Black Elk, a simpler creature than his younger cousin, only wishes to kill me. He is hardened by jealousy, but he will not be treacherous toward his tribe. However, Wolf Who Hunts Smiling has the gleam of a terrible ambition sunk deep into his eyes. He knows that the old grandmothers now often sing the cure songs over Arrow Keeper; he knows our old shaman must soon cross over. He sees the clear division in our tribe between those who follow Arrow Keeper and the hotheaded younger bucks who think like the wild Dog Soldiers of our kin to the south. And in some way, this Medicine Flute will be part of this treachery."

*   *   *

Far across the busy clearing, in the shifting shadows behind Black Elk's tipi, an impromptu council was being held.

The councilors included Black Elk, his younger cousin Wolf Who Hunts Smiling, and the latter's favorite lackey, Swift Canoe. Also present were Lone Bear, troop leader of the Bull Whip Soldier Society, and two highly feared Whips named Big Fist and Snake Eater.

Saying little, but the center of much of the attention, was a slender young buck named Medicine Flute, who had about 22 winters behind him. While the others took turns speaking, he continued to sound the flat, eerie notes of his Pawnee-bone flute.

"You are sure of this thing?" Wolf Who Hunts Smiling demanded.

The Bull Whip named Snake Eater nodded emphatically. "What? Am I suddenly a soft brain in his frosted years? Of course I am sure of this thing."

Wolf Who Hunts Smiling was too preoccupied to take offense at Snake Eater's arrogant tone. A bold scheme was hatching deep in the dark recesses of the young Cheyenne's mind—a scheme that was highly risky, yet potentially devastating to his enemies.

Wolf Who Hunts Smiling leaned closer to the fire, as if seeking clues in its roaring flames. He had an intelligent, wily face that befitted his name, with swift-as-minnow eyes constantly in motion—always on guard, Little Horse once said, for the ever expected attack.

Snake Eater had recently returned from a long visit to his brother, who had married a girl from the Southern Cheyenne living below the Platte. Living among those kinsmen was an Arapaho named Looks Beyond. In his youth he had gone to the white man's school in Denver. He had learned, like the Pawnee, to read the heavens and navigate by star charts.

"Tell us this thing again," Wolf Who Hunts Smiling said. "This thing with the fire-tailed star."

A calumet lay on the ground between Snake Eater and Big Fist. Snake Eater, swollen with the sense of his own importance, picked up the long-stemmed pipe and stoked it to life with a piece of glowing punk. Only after he had smoked and set the pipe back down did he deign to speak.

"This Looks Beyond, he can predict events that will occur in the heavens. He knows that soon, when the dog constellation lines up with the dawn star in the east, a huge, bright star with a flaming tale will shoot across the western heavens. The palefaces call it a comet."

Black Elk scowled impatiently. He was irritated equally by such pointless talk and Medicine Pipe's monotonous music. He looked particularly fierce in the stark firelight. One of his ears was a dead, leathery flap hanging from his head by buckskin thread. It had been severed in battle by a bluecoat saber. Black Elk had sewn it back on himself.

"Only women and old men talk like this merely to hear themselves speak! Of what importance can it be that this Arapaho predicts events in the heavens?"

"Be patient, cousin," Wolf Who Hunts Smiling said. "I will soon crack the shell and dig down to the meat."

Wolf Who Hunts Smiling glanced over at Medicine Flute. The young buck kept his heavy-lidded gaze focused into the flames while he played his eerie music.

"How soon," Wolf Who Hunts Smiling asked Snake Eater, "will this fiery star blaze across the heavens?"

"Within the next few sleeps."

"Good."

Now Wolf Who Hunts Smiling again looked at Medicine Flute. "Brother," he said, "do you believe that White Man Runs Him possesses strong medicine?"

Wolf Who Hunts Smiling had used his favorite name for Touch the Sky. He also occasionally called him Woman Face—after his former white man's habit of letting his feelings show in his face, a trait despised by Indians.

Now Medicine Flute finally lowered his grisly instrument. Still gazing into the fire with his unvarying stare, he suddenly laughed.

"Medicine? Add all his medicine to an arrow, and you will have an arrow. Any fool can put the trance glaze over his eyes, quicken his breathing, and speak in mystic phrases of visions. There are always enough fools to believe."

"You seem to know deception well. Is this what you do?"

Medicine Flute smiled, but wisely said nothing except to repeat, "There are always fools enough."

"Good. Good. For very soon you are going to make an announcement. A prediction about this comet."

"For what purpose?" Black Elk demanded.

"For the purpose of winning the people away from Arrow Keeper and his assistant, White Man Runs Him. Cousin, you have eyes to see. Surely you understand that he who controls a tribe's medicine also controls the tribe?"

Black Elk's scowl softened somewhat as he began to catch the drift of his cousin's thinking. He had failed to understand his cousin's reference to controlling the tribe. All he cared about was the part about winning the people away from Touch the Sky. How many times had he caught Honey Eater crying for the tall buck? How many lingering glances had they traded? Touch the Sky's growing reputation as a shaman made it increasingly difficult to persecute him. If this bold plan worked, the intruder might once again be reduced to the status of a white man's dog.

As for Medicine Flute, this was all much to his liking. He had sniffed opportunity from the very moment that Wolf Who Hunts Smiling had first befriended him. The clever youth was lazy, and though he was a trained warrior, fighting and the hard life of the warpath held no appeal for him. Everyone knew that the life of a respected medicine man, in contrast, could be very pleasant indeed. Never did a powerful shaman lack for meat in his racks or fine buffalo robes.

"Cousin," Black Elk finally said, "I have ears for these words. Speak more of them."

Less than a stone's throw away, at the rear of Black Elk's darkened tipi, the hide cover had been lifted away from the pole. Crouched nervously in the dark, her frightened heart pounding in her throat, Honey Eater took in every treacherous word.

Besides her anger at this latest plot to destroy Touch the Sky, she felt an even stronger emotion gnawing at her: fear. Black Elk and his spies had made it virtually impossible for her to even look at Touch the Sky, much less communicate with him.

But communicate she must. They had sworn their love for each other, and more than once he had shed blood protecting her. His enemies were her enemies—even if one of the enemies was her own husband.

Crouched there in the darkness, trembling at her fear of Black Elk's monstrous rage, she nonetheless resolved to somehow warn Touch the Sky.

Just south of runoff-swollen Bear Creek, about one-half sleep's ride from Gray Thunder's camp, the Quohada Comanche battle leader named Big Tree and a score of his followers had established a cold camp. Not long before they had left behind the pumice plains, flowering yuccas, and low-hanging pods of mesquite that surrounded their permanent camp in New Mexico's Blanco Canyon.

Their magnificent horses were descended from stock introduced further south by the Spanish. Normally, when on the warpath like this, their mounts were kept hobbled foreleg to rear to keep them close. But now they had been turned loose to graze the lush grass bordering Bear Creek.

Big Tree planned to ride out soon for a lone night scout of the area. He caught up his mount, a stocking-footed chestnut, and cinched tight his stolen Texas stock saddle with its bare tree. A roadrunner skin dangled from his horse's tail. It was the good-luck charm of the Comanche tribe.

Big Tree was large for a Comanche, though he was bandy-legged and clumsy on foot like most men of his tribe. Once mounted, however, Comanche warriors could quickly demonstrate why they were called the natural jockeys of the plains—especially Big Tree's Quohada, or Antelope-eater, Band, the famous Red Raiders of the barren Staked Plain.

Several of the packhorses were reserved for hauling huge animal skins filled with pulque, the bitter cactus liquor brewed by the Comanches. One had been untied and liquor-filled gourds were making the rounds.

Big Tree moved easily among his men, accepting a sip here, exchanging a friendly insult there. Because Comanche men admired skill in battle above all else, Big Tree was a respected leader. He alone in the entire Comanche nation could ride 300 yards—and launch 20 arrows—in the time it took a bluecoat soldier to load and fire his carbine. Once, while dead drunk, Big Tree had astounded his fellow braves by launching the last of ten arrows before the first had reached its target.

"Cheyenne guts will string our next bows!" someone shouted, and a cheer rose above the snuffling of the horses.

"*Matanlos!*" came the cry in Spanish. "Kill them!"

"Remember those who can never be mentioned again!" someone else shouted. This was a reference to the braves killed when the tall Cheyenne's band had defeated them and regained their kidnapped women and children—including the slender young beauty Big Tree had been dreaming of bulling. That skirmish had killed the slave trader Juan Aragon and his comancheros. It had also sent many good Comanches and Kiowa allies under. In the survivors' rush to escape, their bodies had been left behind. And by strict custom, any Comanche whose body had not been recovered could never be mentioned by name again.

"Do we attack tonight, Quohada?" the warrior named Rain in His Face demanded.

Big Tree shook his head. No fires were permitted, but a full moon had emerged from the clouds. It limned his features in a stark, silver-white glow like fox fire. He wore a tall shako hat with silver conchos captured from a Mexican officer. Around his neck hung a necklace of dried and blackened human ears. Moonlight reflected from the bits of broken mirror glass embedded in his shield to blind his enemies in the sun.

"Attack, no. Not yet, not now. They are too strong in their main camp, and these Cheyennes, they keep too many dogs trained to bark at an enemy's smell. We cannot hope to surprise them. But I will ride out tonight to study the lay of their camp and the outlying herds. We did not ride this far to die foolishly, but to profit by our enemy's loss. And truly, they are rich in fine ponies."

Big Tree jabbed a stick into the ground and bent it forward. "When the angle of the Dipper matches this stick, I ride. Be patient, stout bucks! Let these scalp-taking fools die for the sheer glory of death. We will not only exact our revenge, but live to enjoy it.

"The superstitious Pawnees claim this tall Cheyenne is a shaman. They say he can summon the grizzly and conjure up insane white men. I say his brain will roast like any other. And I swear by the earth I live on, each of us will taste a piece of it!"

Chapter Two

One sleep after the Cheyenne Bull Whips had met to plan Touch the Sky's downfall, the Renewal of the Sacred Medicine Arrows was held in the central camp clearing.

Arrow Keeper and Touch the Sky presided. Both wore their finest warbonnets, elaborately quilled moccasins, beadwork leggings, and leather shirts. This annual ceremony, involving the entire tribe, was conducted to remind the people of the thought of the Arrows.

The four sacred Medicine Arrows, protected by Arrow Keeper with his very life, symbolized the fate of the *Shaiyena* nation. Whatever fate befell the Arrows would also befall the tribe. One Cheyenne spilling the blood of another, or otherwise violating the Cheyenne laws, stained the Arrows and thus the entire tribe. The High

Holy Ones required that these four blue-and-yellow ceremonial arrows be kept forever sweet and clean, forever protected from enemy hands. And when Arrow Keeper crossed over to the Land of Ghosts, Touch the Sky would become the new Keeper.

The Renewal, also held before battle, cleansed the Arrows of any stains accumulated during the previous moons. Each adult with 12 or more winters lined up to make an offering to the Arrows.

Taking turns, Arrow Keeper and Touch the Sky chanted the long Renewal Prayer while the gifts were piled up around the stump that held the Arrows. Arrow Keeper's failing health required Touch the Sky to lead most of the ceremony. Several times, Honey Eater's eyes met his. She hoped to send him a signal about the plan against him. But each time, before she could attempt to convey a warning, he glanced hastily away. Touch the Sky had learned well the danger to Honey Eater if Black Elk caught them looking at each other.

The last clan had filed by, and Arrow Keeper had wrapped the Medicine Arrows in their coyote-fur pouch. The closing prayer was chanted to the rhythmic backdrop of snake teeth rattling in dried gourds. Arrow Keeper was about to dismiss the tribe, clearing the central square, when a voice rang out.

"Fathers and brothers! Have ears for my words!"

Touch the Sky felt a sharp point of apprehension when he recognized the voice of Wolf

Who Hunts Smiling. Everyone stopped, turned, and stared at the speaker. Huge driftwood fires made the clearing as bright as day.

None could help noticing that Wolf Who Hunts Smiling wore no coup feathers in his bonnet. Though by right of combat he had earned many, the Council of Forty had stripped him of his right to wear them. This happened after Wolf Who Hunts Smiling bribed an old grandmother; he convinced her to claim she'd had a vision requiring Touch the Sky to "set up a pole," to drive sharp hooks through his breast and hang suspended from them all day. Arrow Keeper finally exposed the plot, but only after Touch the Sky had suffered for hours.

"True it is," Wolf Who Hunts Smiling said, "I wear no coup feathers. But I have scalped Pawnees, Crows, Comanches, and Kiowas. I was the first to shed enemy blood at the Tongue River Battle. I have slain hair-faced sellers of strong water and paleface militiamen who would take our land. Never has Wolf Who Hunts Smiling cowered in his tipi when his brothers were on the warpath! So hear me now!"

Touch the Sky and Arrow Keeper exchanged troubled glances. Their faces were painted for the ceremony. Bright claybank reds and yellows and blacks made them look fierce and eerie in the flickering flames.

"I have long been expecting this moment," Arrow Keeper said in a voice meant for Touch the Sky alone. "Now will the ambitious young buck challenge the lead bulls!"

25

"Fathers and brothers!" Wolf Who Hunts Smiling continued. "I will not mince words like a timid girl, but state the case boldly. Our tribe needs new and more powerful medicine! How many babes died of the red-speckled cough during these last cold moons? And what of these white buffalo hiders arriving almost daily to destroy our herds or these blue-bloused pony soldiers building their towns in the midst of our best hunting grounds?

"Is it not as clear as a blood trail in new snow? Our medicine is weak. A tribe with weak medicine is a dead tribe!"

There were certainly some grains of truth mixed up in the chaff of these complaints. All listened. It was Little Horse who first answered.

"Wolf Who Hunts Smiling's sudden interest in strong medicine should be scanned. This from him who bribes addled old grandmothers into making a mockery of true visions and the straight word!"

"I have ears for this," Tangle Hair agreed, and several of his Bow String troop brothers chorused assent. "No one here questions the fighting skill or courage of Wolf Who Hunts Smiling. He is a stranger to fear. But sadly, he is also a stranger to truth."

"A stranger to truth?" Black Elk said. "Do you deny that we have lost many infants to sickness? That the paleface hiders are destroying our buffalo herds? Do Little Horse and Tangle Hair claim the forts cropping up like mushrooms all around us are merely *odjib*, things of smoke? Bad medicine is at work against us!"

26

Now there was a shout of support from the Bull Whips. Their reaction emboldened Wolf Who Hunts Smiling, whose power as a speaker was greatly admired. Even as the young Cheyenne swelled up to speak, Arrow Keeper leaned close and whispered to Touch the Sky.

"Now you will hear me lavishly praised before he sticks his blade deep and gives it a twist."

"Fathers and brothers!" Wolf Who Hunts Smiling said. "I speak only words that you may pick up and place in your sashes. Old Arrow Keeper here is a truly great Cheyenne! He has strewn his enemy's bones throughout the land of the Bighorn Sheep. Count his coup feathers! Once his medicine—like his wisdom—was as vast as the plains, as strong as a winter-rested bear.

"But time is a bird, and that bird has long been on the wing. How many snows has Arrow Keeper seen? How many spring melts, how many greenings of the new grass? He has served his tribe well. But even the mightiest trees eventually lose their sap."

Again many nodded inwardly, if not openly, at the truth of these words. Now Wolf Who Hunts Smiling trained his gleaming black-agate eyes on Touch the Sky.

"The best proof of Arrow Keeper's tangled brain is his selection of our next tribal shaman and Keeper of the Arrows. Clearly this one here is useless. Yes, he knows the words of the ceremonies. But how can a Cheyenne shaman be raised by white men? Would badgers follow a cow or geese fly with the buzzard?"

Arrow Keeper had deliberately held his silence. But Touch the Sky had supped full of this two-faced talk.

"Listen to this Wolf Who Hunts Smiling! How many times has he shed the blood of his own, sullying the Arrows? How many times has he shown open disrespect to our laws and to Arrow Keeper, a shaman whose medicine is feared and respected from where I stand now to the sun's resting place? How many times has this wily Wolf Who Hunts Smiling placed his own narrow ambitions over the good of his tribe?

"And now, listen to this jay's deceptive chatter! Little Horse spoke straight arrow just now. This sudden interest in strong medicine has the putrid smell of a foul plot to it."

"You speak of plots!" Black Elk fumed. "You who plot to steal the women of your betters!"

Everyone present knew he meant Honey Eater, and many present stared at her. Refusing to be shamed by their stares, she boldly held her head high and met all comers fully in the eye—just as she had done when Black Elk once cut off her beautiful braid as a public mark of shame.

"It remains to be seen," Touch the Sky said calmly, leveling an unblinking stare at Black Elk and his cousin, "just who my betters are. On that score, deeds will soon enough speak for words. As for stealing women, they are not blankets or trade knives. Our women have hearts of their own, nor can a man steal that which is his by right."

Spirit Path

At these last words the fury in Black Elk's eyes was frightening to behold. But before he could retort, Spotted Tail of the Bow Strings shouted out, "Wolf Who Hunts Smiling! With one brief speech you have denied the medicine of both Arrow Keeper and Touch the Sky. So then, having stripped your tribe of medicine men, who would you propose for our shaman? Perhaps your loyal shadow, the holy man Swift Canoe?"

His words brought a hearty ripple of laughter. Swift Canoe was a capable enough warrior, given clear orders. But it was common knowledge that his brain was far slower than his name.

His sneer never wavering, Wolf Who Hunts Smiling waited for the laughter to abate. Then he said, "Enjoy your little jokes! Your jests, Spotted Tail, are as faint as your manhood. I, my cousin Black Elk, and the rest of the Bull Whips mark well the faces turned toward me now in mockery! The worm turns slowly, people, but it does indeed turn.

"Now I present the one Cheyenne among us who is truly possessed of strong and true medicine. Medicine Flute! Come forward and tell the people what you have told me."

All heads craned to watch as the slim young buck with the mysterious, heavy-lidded gaze came forward. He glided out from the shadows at the edge of the clearing like a wraith. As always, he carried his odd leg-bone flute.

The tribe fell so silent that nothing could be heard but the wind blowing through the trees, the fires crackling. Medicine Flute already enjoyed a certain status among his clan as a visionary. His odd appearance and manner marked him as different and exotic. And when he spoke, the hollow ghost tone of his voice, combined with his fixed, unvarying stare, commanded the attention of all.

"There is music in the spheres, destiny in a handful of sand. Those who claim to see visions are many, but few ever tread the upward path of the Spirit Way. Fewer still produce true acts of strong medicine. Any fool can clap his hands at the moment a tree begins to fall down and then say he clapped that tree down. But who among you will promise well ahead of the event to set the largest star in the heavens on fire and then trail it, burning, across the sky?"

This claim to such power was so preposterous that many openly gaped or laughed.

"Laugh loud so we can remember the skeptics! You who scoff live in the life of the little day. Within the next few sleeps," Medicine Flute said, "I will do this thing."

"And I," Tangle Hair said, "will make the Powder run backward!"

"I will run atop the wind!" Spotted Tail threw in, and many laughed.

But Touch the Sky and Arrow Keeper did not share in the general mirth. Despite this impossible claim, they knew Wolf Who Hunts Smiling far too well. Serious trouble was afoot.

"How will you do this thing?" someone demanded.

But Medicine Flute was done speaking. Now, he calmly lifted his flute to his lips. A moment later the dull notes of his eerie music drifted out over the people, hushing them.

Only once, as he played, did his eyes move from their ever fixed point somewhere on the horizon. For a few heartbeats they fixed instead on Touch the Sky; a slow, mocking smile divided Medicine Flute's face.

On the morning following Medicine Flute's bold prediction, Wolf Who Hunts Smiling rode into incredible good luck.

He had ridden out alone well to the south, training a new pony he had acquired in a trade with a brave of the Broken Lance Clan. He was practicing turns and reverse charges in a grassy draw north of Bear Creek. Abruptly, two Cheyenne riders appeared, racing toward him from the south with their braids flying out behind them. The red and black streamers tied to their ponies' tails told him they were Bull Whips. When they had come even closer, he recognized Big Fist and Snake Eater. He remembered that both were on scouting duty.

"Brother!" Big Fist greeted him. "Now our warriors are in for some rough sport! Comanches are camped just across Bear Creek. And their faces are painted black!"

"They are led by the trick rider Big Tree," Snake Eater added.

Big Fist said, "Finally they have arrived to avenge our victory against them and Juan Aragon's comancheros."

"How many?"

"A sizable war party, though clearly not enough to attack our main camp."

Wolf Who Hunts Smiling only nodded, holding his own thoughts close. Long had the wily young Cheyenne waited for an opportunity to speak with Big Tree. After all, he had already made a private treaty with the fierce Blackfoot renegade named Sis-ki-dee to the north. Like Sis-ki-dee, Big Tree struck Wolf Who Hunts Smiling as a brave of reckless courage and ruthless ambitions—two traits the power-starved Cheyenne could greatly appreciate.

"We must hurry back to camp with this word," Big Fist said. Wolf Who Hunts Smiling nodded again, watching them resume their hard ride to the north.

But as soon as they were specks on the horizon, he pulled a piece of dirty white cloth from his parfleche and tied it to his lance. Lifting this makeshift truce flag high, he pointed bridle toward Bear Creek and urged his mount to a gallop.

"Look here, Big Tree," the Comanche named Rain in His Face said. "We have been discovered! And our enemy has sent a word-bringer to parley."

The two Quohadas had ridden forward from their trail camp near the creek, scouting for enemies. Sitting their ponies behind a rocky bluff, they watched the lone Cheyenne approach.

Big Tree squinted, more curious than worried. It was not the Cheyenne way to negotiate like this with a sworn enemy.

"It is common knowledge that your mother ruts with Comanches!" he called out in his own tongue when the stranger was close enough to hear. At the other man's blank face, he repeated the insult in Kiowa, Spanish, and finally English.

"Of course," the new arrival responded in the stiff but clear English he had learned while a prisoner of the bluecoats. He added a furtive, cynical smile. "Every brave in my tribe mounts her. Why not yours, too?"

These irreverent and unexpected words made Big Tree's jaw open. He stared at Rain in His Face. Both were surprised. Normally a Cheyenne—haughty and emotional, like their Sioux cousins—was quick to take insult.

A moment later, Big Tree sensed a kindred spirit and laughed with hearty appreciation.

"Load a pipe," he called over to Rain in His Face. "I would smoke with this wily Cheyenne!"

"You are Big Tree. Your skill with the bow is widely know. I am called Wolf Who Hunts Smiling," the Cheyenne said in English.

"A wolf who hunts smiling usually has his nose to a spoor. This is true?"

"Of course. So does a Comanche who rides this far north from his desert home. And perhaps we are both sniffing the same spoor—that of a tall young buck who calls himself a shaman?"

33

So far Big Tree liked the drift of the conversation. But he showed nothing in his face. The Cheyenne's words could all be a piece of clever deception. He slid a Colt revolving-cylinder pistol from his sash. Calmly, in a deliberate show of indifference, he charged the bore and seated a bullet, driving it home. When the chambers were all loaded, he capped them. Only when he was finished did he deign to speak again. He still held the weapon, though it wasn't aimed at the Cheyenne.

"Why should I trust you, scalp-taker? Our two tribes have raised the hatchet against each other since Wolf Creek. Why should I not simply flay your soles?"

This was a reference to a favorite Comanche cruelty: skinning the soles off an enemy's feet, then setting him loose in the wilderness to walk.

"Because you, too, hate this tall buck as much as I do. You must, after what he did to humiliate your warriors. Why deny it? Your braves are good fighters, but you are not enough to attack a strong Cheyenne camp. Together, however, we can defeat this shaman. Then we can form an empire. We can control the plains from the Land of the Grandmother in the north to the Rio Bravo in the south."

Still, Big Tree showed nothing in his face. But he liked the talk more and more.

"What is it you intend?" he said. "To kill him?"

"If possible. But that has proven as difficult as galloping in sand. Almost as good to expose him as a make-believe shaman."

Briefly, Wolf Who Hunts Smiling explained his plan to discredit Touch the Sky's magic, with the cooperation of Medicine Flute and Big Tree.

The Comanche liked the plot even better than an outright kill. It appealed to his warped sense of irony. And it would shame and humiliate the tall young buck, who clearly suffered from an excess of pride.

Besides, no private treaty with a Cheyenne would be binding forever. If the plan failed, another might work.

"How can I measure the depth of your sincerity?" Big Tree finally asked.

"What is it you would have?"

Big Tree held the Cheyenne's eyes with his own. For a moment he recalled the young Cheyenne woman with skin like glistening copper. How cleverly she had pitted the Kiowa leader Hairy Wolf and the Comanche leader Iron Eyes against each other! How cleverly she had driven both men mad with lust and made each feel she secretly preferred him. That division had led to their deaths. And Big Tree also knew she was the woman of the tall shaman.

"What is it I would have? Nothing less than your pony herd."

This was steep. But Wolf Who Hunts Smiling never once flinched. "If I help you gain them, will you then help me?"

"Gladly. Tell me what I must do. But I say to you now, and you may pick these words up and carry them with you, I am not content to merely give the lie to this buck's reputation as a shaman. I intend to roast his brain and eat it."

Chapter Three

"Brother," Little Horse said, "I swear by the four directions, if Medicine Flute plays his tune one more time I will go Wendigo!"

Three sleeps had passed since Medicine Flute made his arrogant prediction. Despite the general feeling that the young buck was merely boasting, each night had seen most of the clan circles gathered in the main clearing, with a close eye on the heavens.

True, the Bull Whip scouts had reported a Comanche war party at Bear Creek. But even blue soldiers with big-thundering wagon guns were afraid to attack Gray Thunder's summer camp. More people were more frightened about this bold prediction than by a few marauding Comanches.

With sister sun only a ruddy afterglow on the

western horizon, the people were gathering yet again. A few called out jokingly to friends and clan relatives, "Tonight will be the night! Eyes to the skies, Cheyenne!"

And during all of it, Medicine Flute sat unperturbed, playing his eerie, monotonous song. His parents were dead, and he had sent the gift of horses to no woman. His tipi stood with those of the rest of his Spotted Ponies Clan directly across the clearing from Touch the Sky's. Now and then, as he played, Medicine Flute lifted mocking eyes toward Touch the Sky.

Little Horse glanced around the camp. "Buck, have you seen Wolf Who Hunts Smiling?"

Touch the Sky shook his head. He knelt to touch spark to a small pile of punk and kindling, starting a tiny fire under the wood of the cooking tripod outside his tipi.

"No, I have not seen him. And do you not find it curious, brother, that he has ridden out so close to nightfall—especially with Comanches nearby? And why now, when he should be in camp to enjoy his moment of glory if Medicine Flute pulls a flaming star across the sky?"

Little Horse watched his friend closely. "Curious indeed, Cheyenne. Is something in the wind?"

For a moment Touch the Sky interrupted his labors to gaze out toward the hostile shadows lengthening beyond the camp. A light tickle, like an insect crawling, moved up his spine.

"Brother," he said, "tell me this. When is something not in the wind?"

He fell silent, and the flat notes of Medicine Flute's tune reached them once again.

Wolf Who Hunts Smiling had no idea when the white man's comet was due to pass. He knew only that Big Tree was growing impatient to strike. So they had settled on this night, when herd guard duty was the responsibility of Wolf Who Hunts Smiling's rivals, the Bow String troopers.

The main pony herd, nearly 200 head of excellent mustangs, had been captured during long and difficult spring hunts in the high rimland of the Little Bighorns. The horses had been broken in and marked by their various owners. He himself had three on his string besides the paint he rode. All would have to be lost or he risked exposing his treachery to his own tribe.

But ponies could be replaced. If the raid that night indeed won Big Tree over to his cause, three ponies would be a small price to pay for destroying Touch the Sky. His destruction was assured if Big Tree cooperated now and in the near future.

Wolf Who Hunts Smiling's plan for tonight, as always with him, was simple and bold. He had already described the location of the herd to Big Tree. They were grouped north of camp in a natural sink where forage was good and fresh water covered a rock bed. There was no corral, only four mounted guards—one riding each flank.

It was critical that no shots be fired during the raid, or the main camp would be alerted.

So Wolf Who Hunts Smiling had based his plan on simple treachery.

He approached the herd on the south flank. He was immediately challenged by the vigilant Bow String sentry, Born in Snow. Wolf Who Hunts Smiling identified himself.

"Why are you here?" Born in Snow asked suspiciously. There was no love lost between the Bow Strings and Wolf Who Hunts Smiling's Bull Whip troop. "Everyone in camp is watching the heavens to see your new shaman count coup on the stars."

"Mock all you wish. They will not be disappointed, buck. Nor will you. As for me, I am indifferent to shows of magic. I have come to cut out my new buckskin and ride him. The strong one with the yellow mane. Have you seen this one?"

Born in Snow frowned in the silver-white moonlight. His pony started and pricked her ears toward a line of nearby sandstone shoulders. Born in Snow glanced in that direction.

"When did you develop this love of night riding, Bull Whip? Do you have foolish plans to count first coup on the Comanches?"

Wolf Who Hunts Smiling scowled. "If you know my name, Bow String, then you also know I am not one to play the big Indian with. I asked if you have seen my pony, and I expect a civil answer."

Born in Snow scowled back. But despite his suspicions, he did not wish to force Wolf Who Hunts Smiling up onto his hind legs. He tugged on his pony's hackamore, turning it away from the sandstone shoulders. He pointed off toward the far side of the natural sink.

As Born in Snow started to speak, Wolf Who Hunts Smiling slid the Colt Model 1855 rifle from its scabbard. Gripping the muzzle, he swung the wooden stock hard into the side of the guard's head. Born in Snow grunted once, then slumped, sliding to the ground like a heavy bag of grain.

Wolf Who Hunts Smiling imitated the hoot of an owl. A few heartbeats later, several shadows slid forward from the deeper darkness behind the sandstone shoulders.

Big Tree and his warriors had smoked their ponies and their clothing in cedar-and-sage fires to cover their unfamiliar smell and avoid spooking the mustangs. While they slipped around the fortified Cheyenne camp, silence was also critical. So the Comanches had muffled their horse's heads with blankets. Now they removed them.

"Wait here," Wolf Who Hunts Smiling told the war leader. "I will send the others back one by one. If you value your scalp, do nothing to scatter the horses."

But Big Tree barely nodded. He was busy watching as Rain in His Face and another brave dismounted. To conserve ammunition and kill without noise, the stealthy Comanches wore deadly rawhide-wrapped rocks looped around their wrists with thongs. There was a fast, hollow thud, then another and another, as they beat the fallen Cheyenne's head to a bloody pulp. When they finished, Big Tree met the eyes of Wolf Who Hunts Smiling. The Comanche grinned wide.

"We are killing your own, Cheyenne. Will you beg us to stop?"

Wolf Who Hunts Smiling had indeed flinched at the first blows. But he hardened his heart until it was all stone with no soft place left in it. Loyalty to his tribe had finally given way completely to his ambition and his long-seething hatred for Touch the Sky. Truly, Touch the Sky was marked out as an obstacle to his destiny. The business tonight was not pleasant, but was necessary. A weak man, Wolf Who Hunts Smiling reminded himself, had no business trying to be a leader of men.

"The day I beg for anything," Wolf Who Hunts Smiling replied, "is the same day a grizzly will mate with a horse."

Wolf Who Hunts Smiling urged his paint toward the west flank. The guard there was Stands on His Sash.

"Brother, lower that rifle. I am no enemy!" Wolf Who Hunts Smiling greeted him. "We have trouble! I came to cut one of my ponies out of the herd, and I found Born in Snow lying hurt on the ground. Evidently his horse threw him and he struck his head. He is still breathing. You ride back to him while I bring help from camp."

Stands on His Sash nodded and chucked up his pony, racing for Born in Snow's position. Then, his heart hard as flint, Wolf Who Hunts Smiling proceeded to send the rest of the herd guards to a hard death among the waiting Comanches.

Night had descended over the Powder River Valley like a dark cape unfurling. Touch the Sky and Little Horse lingered over the last of juicy elk steaks dripping marrow fat. They spoke of inconsequential matters.

Suddenly a cry rose from the center of camp. "Look! Look to the sky! Maiyun protect us. Look!"

Touch the Sky did look. He craned his neck and stared up toward a star-spangled sky dotted with thousands of glittering pinpoints. A falling star, he told himself, nothing more. But at first, looking at the wrong quadrant of the heavens, he noticed absolutely nothing out of the ordinary, not even a falling star.

Then his eyes scanned in another direction, and suddenly his blood seemed to reverse its flow in his veins.

A huge, magnificent, bluish-green ball of fire trailing a long and brilliant tail arced through the heavens. It seemed so close that Touch the Sky almost believed he could reach up and pluck it from the dark dome of the sky.

"Look! Look!"

"Medicine Flute spoke straight arrow! Look, only look! He has moved the very heavens with his great medicine!"

"This time Wolf Who Hunts Smiling spoke from one side of his mouth. This is truly big medicine. Even old Arrow Keeper never set a star on fire!"

Comments such as these flew through the camp. Some of the more superstitious Cheyennes even became hysterical and fell upon the ground, stupefied. Children bawled in fright, dogs howled, and old grandmothers sang their ancient prayers.

"Brother," Little Horse's voice said beside him, amazement clear in his tone, "how can this thing be? How?"

Slowly, still watching the wondrous spectacle blaze across the sky, Touch the Sky shook his head.

"Buck, I know not. But count upon it, the Cheyenne winter-count will call this The Time When Medicine Flute Burned A Star."

Touch the Sky was referring to the pictographs that Indian elders made to record the major events of each year. A moment later, with shouts still ringing throughout camp, Arrow Keeper moved up next to the two youths.

"Father," Little Horse said, "how did Medicine Flute perform this amazing magic?"

Arrow Keeper, too, glanced overhead as the miraculous vision cleared the last part of the visible sky.

"What we are seeing is indeed amazing," Arrow Keeper said. "So, in its own way, is the weaving of a spider's web or the foaling of a mare. However, that it is also magic, I am not so sure."

"But, Father, you heard Medicine Flute predict this thing before it even happened."

"I did, little brother. I also heard the worst liar in our camp call him forward to announce it. When a Pawnee raises one hand in friend-ship, ignore it. Instead, watch the hand hidden behind his back."

"Speaking of liars and hands hidden behind the back," Touch the Sky said, glancing around, "where is Wolf Who Hunts Smiling? What could be so important that he would miss his new brother's great triumph?"

At that same moment, the sound of horses whinnying reached them from north of camp, where the herd was bunched. Perhaps, Touch the Sky told himself, it was only the horses reacting to the strange celestial phenomenon.

Then his eyes met Arrow Keeper's in the firelight. And when the old man nodded slightly, Touch the Sky realized that the senior shaman felt the same hunch his apprentice did.

Touch the Sky had not yet returned his best pony, a tough little bay with a white blaze on her forehead, to graze with the others in the herd. Instead, she was tethered behind his tipi, cropping the bunch grass.

"Brother," he said to Little Horse, "keep your eyes open for Wolf Who Hunts Smiling. I want to know when he returns and from what direc-tion."

"As good as done, buck. But where are you going?"

Again Touch the Sky glanced at Arrow Keep-er. "To check on the ponies."

Before he caught up his pony, he lifted the hide entrance flap and slipped inside his tipi. He stirred up the embers in the firepit. By their light he slid his Sharps percussion-action rifle from under the buffalo robe that protected it from dew at night. He made sure there was a bullet behind the loading gate and dry powder in the charger. He capped the piece and stepped outside.

The blazing wonder had finally cleared this section of the sky. But still the people stood in groups, clamoring at the amazing feat. As he grabbed his pony's mane and swung up onto her, Touch the Sky again saw Medicine Flute across the way, calmly playing his leg-bone flute.

Touch the Sky had just cleared the sandstone shoulders when he recognized the sound of pounding hooves. Ahead, in the ghostly moonlight, he saw the pony herd racing to the west in a tightly bunched group—Comanche warriors pointing them!

He had been riding with the butt plate of his Sharps resting on his thigh. Now he raised the piece and fired a warning shot to summon warriors from camp, then slid his rifle into the rawhide scabbard sewn to his rope rigging.

A moment later his pony nearly stumbled on a grisly sight: the four Cheyenne herd guards heaped together on the south flank of the natural corral. They had been savagely brained, their heads cruelly battered so hard they looked like squashed melons. Nor had the Comanches, who scorned scalp-taking, neglected their penchant for horrible mutilations. Each brave wore his genitals crammed into his mouth, and the coiled white ropes of their intestines had been pulled through slits in their bellies.

Spirit Path

Hearing the thud of a hoof, Touch the Sky looked up even as he slid an arrow from his fox-skin quiver and notched it in his bow.

Wolf Who Hunts Smiling sat his pony only an arm's length away. He held his Colt rifle aimed at Touch the Sky, who in turn aimed his arrow at the other brave's chest.

"You! Why are you riding this way, braggart warrior?" Touch the Sky demanded. "You and your cousin Black Elk tire me with your endless boasting about how you will grease your enemy's bones with war paint. And now, under your nose, Comanches escape in the opposite direction with our ponies!"

But Wolf Who Hunts Smiling had seen the comet pass. And now he knew that Touch the Sky's glory—as well as that of the old soft brain, Arrow Keeper—would soon be as dead as those Bow String troopers. In fact, he thought, a little more pressure on his trigger right now, and—

"If you do it," the young shaman said, easily reading his enemy's face, "my dead fingers will let fly this arrow. Look at it! I hardened it twice in fire and filed those points on pumice. This arrow would drop a black bear."

Wolf Who Hunts Smiling loosed a long, harsh laugh. He slid his finger outside the trigger guard.

"As you say, shaman. Why should I waste a good bullet? Soon the people will worship Medicine Flute. Arrow Keeper already totters on his own grave. Once he crosses over, you will make no more he-bear talk. If you do, perhaps Medicine Flute will hint to his worshipers that an enemy within us must be executed."

"Buck, are you chewing peyote? Why do you make speeches and taunt me now while our enemy escapes with our—"

And then, reading the mocking glint in Wolf Who Hunts Smiling's eyes, Touch the Sky finally understood.

"You traitor," he breathed softly. For a moment he recalled his brave Apache friend Victorio Grayeyes, who had watched Mexican soldiers slaughter his entire family after a turncoat uncle led them to their hidden cave. "You treacherous, low-crawling, double-tongued dog! You have just shed the blood of your own and helped our enemy steal our ponies!"

"See? Once again, just like a woman, you show your feelings in your face."

"I do, and this time with no shame! This crime defies a stoic. A warrior with a heart has to show his hatred when a Cheyenne helps Comanches butcher fellow Cheyennes."

By now the braves who had kept their ponies in camp were pounding closer, the war cry sounding.

"It is my word against yours, White Man Runs Him," Wolf Who Hunts Smiling said. "And after Medicine Flute's great miracle this night, your word is worth less than a spent cartridge!"

Chapter Four

The lightning raid by the Comanche shifted attention away from Medicine Flute's apparent miracle. An official council of all the adult males was called on the morning following the tragedy of the stolen herd and murdered guards.

But in truth, informal councils had been held all night, warriors remaining vigilant and meeting with their clan or soldier troops to discuss this new emergency. Although some ponies had been safe in camp, all of the well-rested animals had been among the grazing herd. Some braves had tried to follow on tired mounts. But they were quickly left behind. Only River of Winds, the best scout in camp, was ordered to keep trailing them.

Almost every clan had lost ponies, some braves losing every pony on their string. And throughout the night, everyone heard the keening wails of the wives, mothers, and sisters mourning the four brutally slain guards.

While listening to the cries, Touch the Sky agonized. How should he handle this new and dangerous situation with Wolf Who Hunts Smiling? Once again the tall young warrior had no witnesses to confirm the other brave's treachery. In fact, he himself had no proof that could be picked up and examined. Yet, he knew the truth deep in his innermost core.

Before reporting to the council lodge, Touch the Sky cut short his hair to mourn their new dead, as was the custom. Then he joined Tangle Hair and Little Horse and filed into the hide-covered council lodge. Arrow Keeper, Chief Gray Thunder, and the clan headmen occupied one side of the huge lodge; the other was quickly filled with braves who counted 16 winters or more.

A clay pipe was stuffed with a mixture of rich tobacco and fragrant red-willow bark. When all who wished to had smoked the common pipe, Chief Gray Thunder laid it down between his leg and Arrow Keeper's, signaling the beginning of discussion.

"Brothers!" Gray Thunder said. "All you who are gathered here now know what has happened. Who could not? We are now pony warriors without ponies! We must discuss our battle plan. We must quickly make plans to acquire a few more ponies immediately.

"Once again, Cheyennes, we have cut short our hair because of Comanche treachery. First they took our women and children, now they have our ponies. Our women and children are back with us now"—here Gray Thunder recognized Touch the Sky with a nod in his direction—"thanks to the bravery and skill of our warriors. What Cheyennes have done, Cheyennes will do! Once again our ponies will graze the lush grass of the Powder River country."

Gray Thunder was still a vigorous warrior despite having some 40 winters behind him. Only now were the first streaks of silver showing in his hair.

"Black Elk," he said, "you are our battle chief. How do you counsel?"

"Father, these drunken thieves from the south country are as wily as any Pawnees. This raid, it could well be an elaborate ruse to lure all the warriors from camp so our enemy might capture the women and children. We made this mistake once before. I say, never again!

"First, we must quickly visit True Bow's Lakota village at Elbow Bend. They will give us more ponies. Then, a small but deadly band chosen from our best warriors must ride south under the raised hatchet."

Black Elk frowned as some memory returned.

"This Big Tree, the one who ties a roadrunner skin to the tail of his pony. When did Black Elk ever hide behind his tipi? Yet, I freely admit I have never seen a more dangerous foe! Once, near Blanco Canyon, several of us thought we had trapped him. We were fools! Fathers and brothers, he sat backward on his pony while

51

it galloped. He held a great fistful of arrows and fired them so rapidly that he emptied two quivers in the time it takes a hungry man to eat a handful of cherries."

Gray Thunder nodded. A quick voice vote of the headmen approved Black Elk's plan. Among those selected to ride out were Black Elk, Wolf Who Hunts Smiling, Little Horse, and Touch the Sky. Because his own coup feathers reached nearly to the ground, Gray Thunder was not voted down when he insisted on riding with the war party.

When this business was completed, Wolf Who Hunts Smiling rose to his feet.

"Fathers and brothers! Hear me! The raid this past night naturally has the thoughts of all red-blooded warriors set toward revenge against the cricket-eating marauders. But let us not forget what may, after all, have been the most important event of all."

The Cheyenne paused and carefully stepped around his brothers, making his way to the back wall. He took up a place beside Medicine Flute. This brave sat cross-legged, his leg-bone flute lying across his lap.

"You have, all of you, eyes to see. Who can deny that Medicine Flute set a star on fire, then sent it flaming across the sky?"

"He did," someone said.

"I saw it," another said.

"All of us did!"

"At first glance," Arrow Keeper said quietly, not bothering to stand as the younger men did, "what appears to be an elk may turn out to be a

Cheyenne dressed in buckskins. What we see is not always what we shoot at. Appearances are seldom reliable."

At these words the lodge went stone still and silent. All eyes turned toward Black Elk. By now all had heard the story about how Black Elk had once fired at Touch the Sky, supposedly mistaking his buckskins for an elk's hide.

"Elks?" Wolf Who Hunts Smiling injected a condescending tone into his voice, as if he were indulging a slow-witted child. "Old Grandfather, no one is speaking of elks. But of course, the power of Medicine Flute's magic has understandably rattled you. And do not forget, Medicine Flute described this event before it passed. But of course, at your advanced age, many things are easily forgotten."

This was the first time Wolf Who Hunts Smiling had ever called the shaman grandfather instead of father, and Arrow Keeper had noticed it.

"Truly," he said, "I have forgotten more than you will ever learn. And still I am the wiser."

"As you say, Grandfather." Wolf Who Hunts Smiling winked for the benefit of some of his Bull Whip brothers in the last row. "But what I wish to say is this. We will need strong medicine to achieve success on this mission. Therefore, I say Medicine Flute should ride out, too!"

"You will have strong medicine," Arrow Keeper said quietly. "The strongest. For Touch the Sky is riding with you."

"We will have a stout fighter in Touch the Sky," Wolf Who Hunts Smiling said. "That much no man disputes. But who, besides Arrow Keeper or Little Horse, claims to have truly witnessed any magic? Yes, yes, we all know the story from Shoots Left Handed's band up north in the Bear Paw Mountains. How Touch the Sky supposedly turned bluecoat bullets to sand. But why is it that we ourselves have never seen the miracles?

"In contrast, Cheyennes, only think on what Medicine Flute did in front of the entire tribe, as he predicted. I say, let him ride with us!"

This brought a loud chorus of support, and Touch the Sky realized that the moment he'd been waiting for had come. He rose to his feet.

"I am going to kill Wolf Who Hunts Smiling."

His announcement struck everyone dumb, including Wolf Who Hunts Smiling and the Bull Whips. Little Horse gaped; even Arrow Keeper looked dumbfounded.

"You heard me straight," he went on. "His scaffold is as good as built. I will kill this murderer of Cheyennes, this traitor to his own tribe."

Gray Thunder frowned, the furrow between his eyebrows deepening. "Buck, I have long been weary of the feud between you and Wolf Who Hunts Smiling. These are strong words. Both this talk of murdering Cheyennes and this talk of traitors."

"Yes, they are strong words, Father, for they must match the crimes. I do not speak them lightly."

"Why speak them at all?"

"Because, Father, they are true words and truth should be uncovered." Touch the Sky made the cutoff sign. "You all knew Born in Snow. He was no warrior to be taken by surprise. Every one of the murdered Bow String guards was an honor to Spotted Tail's troop! Count upon it, Big Tree did not steal our ponies or kill our herd guards without valuable help. Help from one inside our own tribe."

Arrow Keeper and Little Horse knew, better than any other brave present, that Touch the Sky never gave the name of truth to any statement unless it flew straight arrow.

"What proof do you have?" Gray Thunder demanded.

Touch the Sky shook his head. "Nothing I can place in your sash. But I swear by the four directions this one conspired with Big Tree. If he did not actually draw the blood of our dead companions, he at least allowed it to flow."

By now Wolf Who Hunts Smiling realized Touch the Sky had no more surprises to spring. He again flashed his furtive smile, dark eyes mocking the taller Cheyenne.

"He is driven by desperation. This is choice jesting indeed, this business of accusing others in the tribe of being spies. This one drank whiskey with the same murdering whites who killed our people! Now Medicine Flute has exposed his magic for what it truly is, a thing of smoke, and he attempts to turn me into a traitor to disguise his own treachery."

This set the lodge buzzing. Gray Thunder

frowned again and folded his arms, the signal for silence.

"A good chief does not dictate to the people. But, brothers, this is no time for a clash of ambitious young bulls! We must paint our faces and make ready our battle rigs. The tribe must come together as one to retrieve our pony herd. The others want him, so Medicine Flute will ride with us. The tribe has spoken with one voice."

No one disputed this. Now Chief Gray Thunder met Touch the Sky's eyes.

"I will brook no more talk of traitors and killing our own. Is this thing clear?"

Touch the Sky nodded once. He saw Medicine Flute and Wolf Who Hunts Smiling exchange a triumphant glance. Again Touch the Sky recalled his dead companions lying mutilated on the ground and recalled that glint in Wolf Who Hunts Smiling's eyes and his taunting words: *It is my word against yours, White Man Runs Him.*

"As you say, Gray Thunder," he finally replied. "No more talking."

By the time the council ended, rain clouds had blown in from the Bighorn Mountains. Touch the Sky was among the first to exit the lodge. His thoughts were skittering around inside his skull like frenzied rodents. Right then he did not feel like facing any of his friends and explaining his bold words in council.

He hurried across camp and untethered his bay. She nuzzled his shoulder, glad to see him.

He would have to prepare his battle rig since the war party would ride out soon. But for now the confused thoughts warring inside him made him desire solitude.

He knew a peaceful spot downriver from camp where, toward sunset, the young, unmarried bucks sometimes held the girls of their choice in their blankets for love talk. It was a sheltered glade, lush with lavender, vines of blue morning glory, and wild orchids. During the day it was almost always deserted. Several times he had visited the spot when, following Arrow Keeper's advice, he wished to stop all thought and simply listen to the language of his senses.

Thunder muttered in the distance, and dark clouds obscured the high rimland to the west. He slipped the hide headstall on his pony and rode out. He looked neither right or left.

During a brief ride along the grassy riverbank, he watched the cottonwood leaves turn their undersides out, a prelude to the coming storm. He reached the glade and left his bay on a long tether in the lush grass. He stepped past a wall of hawthorn bushes and immediately felt the presence of another person.

Thinking of the Comanche raiders, his hand went to the beaded sheath of his knife.

"No enemy here, Cheyenne warrior. So the council is over? But I am so glad to finally see you!"

Although it startled him, Honey Eater's voice also tugged his lips into a smile. A heartbeat later he spotted her. She sat in the shelter of a weeping willow. The low-hanging branches formed a soft green curtain around her.

"Yes, it is over, little one. And soon Black Elk will be raging throughout camp, searching for you. I should leave, or you had best return."

He was right, but neither of them moved. The wind whipped up, fluttering the leaves. Muttering thunder gathered into a sudden clap that made Honey Eater wince.

He moved closer, parted the willow branches, and knelt beside her. She was fragrant from the fresh white columbine petals braided into her hair. A soft doeskin dress molded itself to the delicate curves and hollows of her body.

Normally, on the rare occasions when they met alone like this, they could not help touching and embracing. But lately there was a curious tension between them, and they avoided such closeness. Touch the Sky knew why. It had not been so very long since Honey Eater, whose simple heart was guileless, had frankly told him that in her heart she was his wife. And if he sent for her, then somehow, some way, she would lie with him as his woman.

Touch the Sky wanted her with a passion that sang in his blood. But asking her to meet him like an animal in the forest and exposing her further to Black Elk's jealous, murderous wrath—that and the strict Cheyenne taboo against adultery gave him pause. It was as if they both sensed that one touch between them could lead to a storm of dangerous passion.

But now she clearly had something more urgent on her mind—something she had been impatient to tell him.

"Touch the Sky! Two Twists told me you sometimes come here. I have been coming to this place each day, hoping to see you. You are no stranger to unfair suffering. But this time you are up against it! Wolf Who Hunts Smiling and his Bull Whip brothers are determined this time to either kill you or destroy you."

Quickly, she told him what she had overheard when the Whips had met behind Black Elk's tipi and planned the ruse with the comet.

"Black Elk is in it, too, of course," she said bitterly. "But now I clearly understand a thing. Black Elk is mixed up in his cousin's schemes only to get at you. Jealousy long ago destroyed his sense of fairness. He is only a dangerous pawn.

"But Wolf Who Hunts Smiling, he is surely the Red Man's devil! I see now that he is driven by the base impulse for power. Nothing, not the thought of the Arrows nor the welfare of his tribe, will come between him and his brutal ambition. And this Medicine Flute, he is well suited to such treachery!"

"Clearly you know both of them well," Touch the Sky said, nodding. "Wolf Who Hunts Smiling missed his opportunity to kill me when he might have. Now he does the next best thing by giving the lie to my medicine—and thus Arrow Keeper's."

Honey Eater glanced around them at this peaceful spot where the purling of the river and the soft warbling of the thrush so often lulled couples in love. A huge crystal tear formed on her eyelid and zigzagged down her cheek.

"My father was right," she said bitterly. "Happiness is a short, warm moment; suffering is a long, cold night."

Another rolling crash of thunder. A far-flung spider web of lightning electrified the sky.

"How much must you suffer, brave Cheyenne warrior? How much? Enemies outside, enemies inside. Is there no end to this hating and killing and base plotting? On the night you first vowed your love for me, when we were both trapped in the whiskey traders' camp, even as you spoke your love, they were torturing you!

"Look around us now. This place where happiness normally reigns. You, too, should be strolling down here nights to meet a pretty maiden. Where is your life, your happiness?"

"Here I sit," Touch the Sky replied, "beside the prettiest girl in our tribe. And the only one I love. You are my life and my happiness, and I desire no other."

Another tear chased the first down her cheek. "And you are mine, Touch the Sky. But how can I be as cruel as your enemies and deny you your life?"

He shook his head, banishing all such talk forever. "Know this, little Honey Eater. I would rather have you this tortured and painful way than any other woman I might have freely."

"My father—" She hesitated. But he touched her hand, encouraging her to give word shapes to the feelings troubling her. Now soft tendrils of rain lashed at their faces.

"My father, just before he crossed over, he rose up from his deathbed and spoke startling things to me. One thing he said was that you were meant to be a great chief. He told me, 'Love him, my little daughter, but know that his way will be hard.'"

She looked long and hard into Touch the Sky's eyes. "I must go. You are right. Black Elk will scour camp for me, and we are both at risk. But first, tell me a thing. Do you believe there is a destiny already in the stars for us? Touch the Sky, will we ever live openly as husband and wife? Will we have a child? None of these things did my father tell me."

His pulse throbbed in his palms, and cool sweat broke out on his back. For these questions were the very same ones that often plagued the peace of his sleeping hours. They rose and, hand in hand, walked slowly to the edge of the glade.

He said, "Arrow Keeper's teachings have indeed convinced me that every human destiny is already written in the stars. However, even Arrow Keeper has no magic to tell exactly what that destiny will be."

"The song the young girls sing in their sewing lodge," she said timidly. "It is about us. And according to the song, we will be married and have a child."

He nodded. "I have heard it." Indeed, hearing that very song had stopped him once when, discovering that Black Elk had whipped Honey Eater, he had been on the verge of killing his rival. Such violence would have banished him forever from the tribe and, thus, Honey Eater.

"But now you ride out again," Honey Eater

61

said. "And this time, you face the loathsome Big Tree. His very glance makes my skin crawl! He is a sick Indian, crazy in his eyes. As if he were not danger enough, Black Elk, Wolf Who Hunts Smiling, and other tribal enemies will surround you during this mission. Touch the Sky, I am frightened like never before. May the Holy Ones ride with you!"

With that she rose quickly on tiptoe and did what Indians seldom did—she kissed him. A moment later she was gone, leaving Touch the Sky alone with his aching heart and troubling thoughts.

Chapter Five

Big Tree and his Comanche warriors drove their stolen pony herd hard to the southwest, stopping only to graze them in the lush grass near the rivers.

These ponies, like all wild stock, were much sturdier and better able to survive harsh conditions than the coddled, overbred horses ridden by white men. Paleface horses were bigger and clumsier, spoiled by diets of good grain and forage. Indian ponies, in contrast, could survive a hard winter by nibbling on cottonwood bark and twigs and stunted brown grass trapped under the snow.

Mustangs were also used to covering great distances at a run. With the braves riding at the fringe of the herd, the Comanches set a grueling pace. Their riding skills were second to none on the plains. The braves seemed mere extensions of their horses, bouncing along on top of them with seemingly effortless ease. A Comanche could ride without holding on, freeing his hands to load and fire weapons. Indeed, many of the braves, copying their leader, wore two quivers to accommodate all the arrows they could launch in a short time.

Big Tree knew the Cheyennes would eventually follow them. They could trade with neighboring tribes for a few replacement ponies. But it would require the rest of the warm moons to again track and capture so many magnificent animals. Besides, no Plains Indian tribe would abide such a strike without revenge. Not to avenge it was as good as an invitation to terrorize their homeland yet again.

Yes, the Cheyennes would eventually follow them south. And once the Comanches reached the dry plains of Southern Colorado, the pace would become much slower as the rivers—and thus, the grass—grew more sparse. Then the Cheyennes might catch up to them.

Big Tree circled the herd and selected the brave named Stone Club.

"Ride our back trail," he told him. "Wolf Who Hunts Smiling will soon be sending a word-bringer ahead to us. Relay the message back to me."

Stone Club filled his parfleche with parched corn, then pointed his pony toward the north again. After the brave's departure, Big Tree found himself smiling again. This Wolf Who Hunts Smiling—what sort of treachery against his own tribe was he planning? Clearly, this renegade Cheyenne hated the tall shaman nearly as much as Big Tree himself. Perhaps even more, if such were possible.

Again Big Tree thought of the honey-skinned maiden who had driven the leaders Iron Eyes and Hairy Wolf giddy with loin heat. How cleverly she had brought about their downfall by driving a wedge between them. Big Tree had vowed to top her himself—perhaps someday he would make good on his vow. After all, Wolf Who Hunts Smiling had vowed they would share the fruits of power.

But for now, one thing at a time. Soon his wily Cheyenne ally would send word of the next move to destroy this haughty shaman.

"Brothers," the Lakota chief named True Bow said. "We knew these Comanche dogs were riding north. But our scouts were sure it was a raiding party aimed at the hair-face settlements. We Lakota drove them out once, and they fear us. For unlike them, a Sioux warrior is not afraid to die!"

True Bow paused and took stock of his Cheyenne visitors. The two groups looked distinct in the clear, early morning light of the Sioux camp. True Bow and his braves wore their hair long, tightly braided, and wrapped around their heads. Their Cheyenne cousins, in contrast, wore their hair roughly cropped short in honor of their slain companions.

Judd Cole

"True it is," True Bow said, "that I signed the hair-face talking paper. I have pledged this Lakota band to peace with all red men and white men alike. I have pledged neither to raise my battle-ax nor assist those who do."

The old chief fell silent, thinking. The Lakota Sioux and the Cheyennes had fought as one people from their earliest days on the plains, even intermarrying with little fuss. Now they spoke in the easy mix of Sioux and Cheyenne words understood by both tribes. His Cheyenne visitors included Touch the Sky, Little Horse, Black Elk, and Wolf Who Hunts Smiling and his new companion, Medicine Flute. All stood a respectful few paces behind Chief Gray Thunder.

"I respect your pledge," Gray Thunder said. "You do not keep it out of cowardice. Your camp includes the best warriors on the northern plains. And I was there at Hanging Woman Creek, True Bow, fighting in my first battle, when you led combined Sioux and Cheyenne warriors against Roaring Bear's Utes."

True Bow's face divided in a wide smile. "The fish eaters!" he said with contempt. "Well, buck, did we give those big, lumbering fools a war face? Now it is said the Ute are a mountain tribe. You young bucks, pin my words to your sash. They live in the mountains only because Sioux and Cheyennes drove them there!"

"I have ears for this," Black Elk said, and his younger cousin nodded, too.

Again True Bow fell silent. He gazed out

across the neat clan circles. Sioux tipis were taller and more narrow than those of their cousins, with no hide flap over the entrance. The Sioux were not nearly so modest as Cheyennes, and couples often made love in public.

But True Bow was gazing at the wild mustangs gathered in a buffalo-rope corral near the river.

"True, I have pledged not to assist any war party. But this here today, it is not strictly war. You are a horse tribe. These insect eaters from the desert, they have taken the very lifeblood of your people. It is a question of getting back what is rightly yours."

The old chief's brow was furrowed with age and worry. Now he hunched his shoulders under his blanket and said, "Take what you need, brothers. You can pay us back from your own herd when you recover them. Had I not pledged my people to the peace road, our lances would be raised beside yours."

"With your good ponies," Black Elk said confidently, "we will be enough to do the hurt dance on them."

But Touch the Sky and Little Horse were watching Wolf Who Hunts Smiling. The wily young brave exchanged a long glance with Medicine Flute. Both braves traded a knowing half smile.

Medicine Flute saw Touch the Sky watching. He raised his leg-bone flute by way of mocking salute.

* * *

The Sioux ponies were wild mustangs not yet broken to human riders. They had been driven into captivity with plans to divide and break them later.

Each man in the Cheyenne war party was permitted to select one pony, giving each a remount for the long chase. Touch the Sky rode the perimeter of the corral until he spotted the pony he wanted: a pure white mare with a silky gray mane.

Little Horse, flicking a light sisal whip to control his pony, was moving to cut out a claybank he liked. The other braves, too, had made their selections.

It was in their differing styles of breaking green horses that Touch the Sky had truly learned the vast differences between the white man and the red man. The white man, consistent with his belief in ownership of land and animals and even people, deliberately broke a horse's wild spirit and dominated it. The red man, in contrast, saw his pony as an equal companion in the struggle for survival. And the animal's wild nature must be respected in order to gain the survival edge.

White men began by beating, blindfolding, and starving a horse. They shoved iron in the animals' mouths, nailed iron to their hooves, and strapped cumbersome saddles and headstalls to them.

Red men, in contrast, simply jumped on and rode the horse. If the Indian was still clinging to the pony when it finally quit running, it was his.

The mare veered out of his way when Touch the Sky nudged his mount closer. He tugged his hackamore right and circled again, trapping the mare between him and the buffalo-hair ropes. The bay surged closer, and Touch the Sky leaped.

He landed on the mare solidly enough and caught a good grip on her mane. But with a suddenness that shocked him, she hopped violently to the right, then bucked hard. A heartbeat later he was flying through the air. He landed hard in the deep grass and had to look sharp to avoid being trampled.

"Woman Face shows his surprise!" Wolf Who Hunts Smiling taunted him.

Touch the Sky ignored him, rising to his feet. This time he didn't even bother with his bay. His mouth a grim, determined slit, he simply charged the white mare.

She saw him coming and fled. But he had guessed her direction of flight. Now he leaped that way as she moved, landing hard on her back and wrapping his arms about her well-muscled neck to hang on.

Several Sioux observers whistled and shouted, untying one of the ropes. The white mare tore out across the short-grass plain. Touch the Sky hung on for dear life, bouncing from side to side, always on the feather edge of being tossed clear.

On and on the sturdy little mustang raced, infuriated by this human beast clinging to her.

Touch the Sky could hear Little Horse and the others all around him, likewise pitting their wills against the animals' struggles. Occasionally the pony would suddenly halt and hop, bucking hard and trying to shake him again. But Touch the Sky clung tightly despite the battering to his ribs and groin.

Sister Sun was well through her journey across the sky when the pony and Touch the Sky, both bone weary, returned to the Sioux village at Elbow Bend.

"She is yours, brother!" Little Horse greeted him triumphantly. His own claybank now grazed quietly, submitting as Little Horse scratched her withers.

Touch the Sky nodded. The ponies would still have to be halter broken. But since Indian headstalls included no iron bits, the ponies would not rebel so severely as mounts broken by hair faces.

Time was critical, so the Cheyennes moved out that same day. It was no problem to cut sign on the Comanches—not when they were driving an entire pony herd before them.

"Our enemy travels by night, too," Touch the Sky told Little Horse. "See all the rocks turned over? Rocks they would have avoided by day."

Little Horse nodded. Earlier, they had gone through the painstaking process of estimating how many Comanches they were trailing. This was done by starting at the very edge of the tracks to sort out the individual riders. The depth of the print separated mounted horses from mustangs.

They counted some 20 riders. "Twice that number," Little Horse said, "if you count Big Tree's true battle worth."

And through all of it, whether riding or snatching a quick rest before resuming the grueling trek, Medicine Flute quietly mocked Touch the Sky.

Knowing they were safe from their fleeing enemies that first night, the Cheyennes made a meat camp with a cooking fire. Earlier Little Horse had shot an antelope near the Trinidad River. They butchered out the hindquarters and roasted them over blazing driftwood.

After the meal, when sentries had been posted and the braves had rolled into their buffalo robes for the night, the eerie flute music began.

"Brother," Little Horse said in a low voice beside Touch the Sky, "count upon it. This journey is not merely to regain our ponies from the Comanche. Your enemies within the tribe also plan to challenge your shaman powers. So far they cannot kill your body. So now they plan to lay your powerful spirit to rest."

"Straight words, brother, though I am not so sure as you just how powerful my spirit is."

"Deeds speak louder than words, tall buck. Did I not stand beside you, unarmed, while an entire unit of bluecoat soldiers shot at us from less than a stone's throw away? And did one bullet hit us? To me, this is power and nothing else. You have strong medicine."

Touch the Sky lay on his back, watching countless stars glitter in the black dome overhead. He heard the horses snuffling, frogs croaking, cicadas sounding their monotonous rhythm. Arrow Keeper's words drifted back to him from the hinterland of memory: *For every war path, there is a spirit path*.

But always mocking him, challenging him, setting his nerves on raw edge—the dull, monotonous notes of Medicine Flute's hollowed-out leg-bone flute.

Chapter Six

The Cheyenne war party rode hard throughout the next day, stopping only to water their mounts. They ate on horseback, subsisting on the pemmican and jerked buffalo in their legging sashes. They switched often to their new remounts and used this opportunity to learn the ponies' personalities, their individual strengths and weaknesses.

Touch the Sky's new mare showed ideal traits for a warrior's pony: inexhaustible stamina, reckless courage, surefooted agility. The Cheyenne learned how to sense, with his knees and thighs, the mare's subtle muscular contractions that signaled a jump or turn; in turn, the mustang learned to sense the precise meaning of Touch the Sky's nudges and tugs.

All day long Wolf Who Hunts Smiling and Medicine Flute mocked Touch the Sky with their eyes. Meantime, their Comanche enemies' path did not alter: a bead-straight line toward the dusty canyons, arroyos, and mesas of their arid Southwestern homeland.

River of Winds, the only Cheyenne sent to trail the Comanches on the night of the raid, had not yet returned with a report. But the Cheyennes—despite many personal differences—agreed to the last man on one point: If the Comanches reached their beloved Blanco Canyon, the herd was lost. Not even heavily armed bluecoats dared attack this Comanche stronghold.

Touch the Sky knew the Blanco well—the way a survivor knows a horrible disease. True, he and a small band had managed to infiltrate the canyon. But once within, they were fortunate to have escaped with their lives, let alone mounted an attack. The canyon could not even be approached safely. It was stuck in the middle of the notorious *Llano Estacado* or Staked Plain, where the only ground cover consisted of the bones of dehydrated men and animals.

No, the Comanches must be caught even before they reached the Texas Panhandle and New Mexico Territory. The fight would be hard enough, even if they were caught. But Touch the Sky and Little Horse both realized something else. Wolf Who Hunts Smiling's new plan represented as serious a threat as any official enemy of the Cheyenne.

That night they camped in a sheltered canyon lined with traprock shelves.

"Brother," Little Horse said quietly when the two friends had separated themselves from the others. He made the cutoff sign. "I cannot stop seeing the dead faces of Born in Snow and the other guards. You have said Wolf Who Hunts Smiling had a hand in their deaths. Since you said it, I believe it. But I confess, though there is little I thought him incapable of doing, never did I expect him to nail his colors to a Comanche lodgepole. He has sullied our Arrows!"

Touch the Sky nodded, his mouth held in a grim, determined slit. "He has, buck. They are dripping blood even now."

"And listen. There it is again. Medicine Flute and his eternal tune. I have always wondered if a buzzard can vomit. I shall find out if one hears this music. They are goading us, buck, and I confess, since Wolf Who Hunts Smiling's treachery a few sleeps ago, I am keen to meet them."

Touch the Sky shook his head. "Do not rise to their bait. Only keep your eyes and ears sharp, stout buck. Even now Wolf Who Hunts Smiling and his shaman have their heads bent together. Count upon it, another monster is being bred."

"Do it this night," Wolf Who Hunts Smiling told his new medicine man. "You know what to say. Earlier today, when I rode out to scout our flanks, I met with the Comanche word-bringer Stone Club. Now they have their instructions.

All will be ready when we arrive. Then White Man Runs Him will feel heat in his face."

Medicine Flute only smiled his heavy-lidded smile, nodding slightly. He didn't miss a note of his eerie fluting.

"This music," Wolf Who Hunts Smiling said. "It would make the Wendigo himself tear out his hair. Gray Thunder is on the verge of ordering a halt to your playing. But play on, play on, buck. Woman Face and Little Horse hate it more than I do."

Wolf Who Hunts Smiling studied the shadows and decided the time was right. He rose and strode to the middle of camp.

"Chief Gray Thunder! Brothers! Have ears for my words."

"Now the snake drives home his fangs," Little Horse told Touch the Sky.

"I have a sporting challenge," Wolf Who Hunts Smiling said. "A friendly challenge. We have two shamen with us. I do not believe both of them can possess the true shaman's eye. Therefore, I ask this thing in the name of the tribe. Give the rest of us proof one of you has the true shaman's eye."

"A friendly challenge from you," Little Horse said, "is no better than a bullet from a bluecoat rifle. This is more treachery."

"Of course, speak up for your master. White men run him, and he runs you."

"Your mouth is like the back end of a horse," Touch the Sky said, "and produces the same thing."

"You two," Gray Thunder said, "still fighting between yourselves even as we pursue an enemy. Why not just join them and fight on their side against us?"

"Yes," Touch the Sky said, his eyes boring into Wolf Who Hunts Smiling's. "Why not just join them, indeed? You are as good as on their side now."

"Of course you ignore my challenge and try to veer the talk onto me. For Medicine Flute stands ready to expose your deceit! Just as you are a pretend Cheyenne, so are you a pretend shaman. If you truly have strong medicine, why fear my challenge?"

Touch the Sky ached to expose the recent treachery involving the comet. But to do so would put Honey Eater at great risk.

"You are a fool, Panther Clan. Do you think the Great Medicine Man gave magic to mortals for frivolous sport? To perform tricks on command, like trained ponies?"

Black Elk joined his cousin in the fray. "This is not frivolous sport! We are up against a powerful foe. My cousin speaks straight; our tribe's medicine has grown weak. This challenge my cousin proposes, it may help us decide which brave truly has medicine. All of us saw Medicine Flute send a burning star across the heavens! No wonder Touch the Sky is reluctant to lock horns with such a powerful bull!"

Touch the Sky felt the noose tightening again as he realized that his refusal to demean the magic taught to him by Arrow Keeper would

77

be held as a confession that he was a pretend shaman.

"This gets out of hand," Gray Thunder said. "I am no shaman. Never have I experienced a vision. But Touch the Sky spoke right. Matters of the spirit are not meant for such a show."

Many sitting in a circle around the fire nodded agreement.

"I always have ears for our chief," Wolf Who Hunts Smiling said. "But my cousin speaks straight. We are on an important mission. Never mind my suggestion for a challenge. Is it not fair to ask at least this of our two shamen. Has either one sensed or felt anything since we rode out? A sign about this mission?"

This struck the listeners as reasonable. Many nodded, including Gray Thunder. As if on signal, all stared at Touch the Sky.

After a long silence, listening to wind whistle through the nearby canyon walls, Touch the Sky shook his head. "I have experienced nothing."

Now everyone turned to look at Medicine Flute. Unperturbed, the slender youth laid his leg-bone flute across one knee. "Certainly I have seen things, though still the reason for seeing them is not clear. Sometimes we must wait for the wind to abate before we can see patterns in the snow."

"What things have you seen?" Wolf Who Hunts Smiling encouraged him.

"Things not meant for the faint of heart, buck! Visions that portend a great sadness. I saw a Cheyenne pony, screaming in pain as it floated on a river of blood. I saw a charred circle within a vast clearing, I saw bloody entrails, and I saw a rack of charred rib bones protruding from the ground."

A long silence greeted these disturbing, mysterious words. Little Horse glanced at Touch the Sky, but the taller Cheyenne only shrugged helplessly. He could not fake a vision simply to rival this so-called shaman.

The silence was finally broken when Medicine Flute raised his leg-bone instrument to his lips and began piping his eerie notes.

River of Winds rode a fresh mount and was unencumbered by heavy equipment. He caught up with Big Tree's Comanches just north of the white soldiertown called Fort Pueblo. This was Southern Colorado plains country, semiarid and hilly, with plenty of buttes and redrock canyons to offer shelter.

The canyons and blind cliffs kept the Comanches vigilant as they guided their stolen herd. Carefully avoiding their outlying flank riders, River of Winds managed to ride within hailing distance of the herd. He was well hidden behind the rimrock when the Comanches grouped the herd for the night in a grassy draw near a stream.

As dark descended, River of Winds moved in closer. Carefully he picked his way over a talus slide, fearful of dislodging a rock. The noise of a rider approaching from the north sent him quickly to the ground. He watched Big Tree confer for some time with the scout he had sent out earlier to cover their back trail.

River of Winds knew that his tribe would have sent out a war party by now. No doubt this scout had ridden back to check on their progress. Whatever it was he reported, it made the fearsome Big Tree grin like a skull.

Big Tree barked out a command and two of his braves, carrying braided horsehair ropes and a hackamore, crossed toward the grazing pony herd. They cut out a magnificent ginger stallion, leading it by the hackamore and bringing it back to camp.

It was a fine pony, one River of Winds had admired when Tangle Hair claimed it and put his clan mark on it. Perhaps Big Tree was selecting it for his own string.

The Cheyenne watched Big Tree admire the fine animal. He scratched its withers and stroked the finely muscled flanks. He nodded several times, praising the pony.

River of Winds felt his face flush with apprehension when Big Tree slid the Colt pistol from his sash.

Big Tree set the hammer at half cock and spun the cylinder, inspecting the load. A heartbeat later he lifted the weapon and planted a slug in the pony's brain.

River of Winds winced as an arc of blood shot out and the pony's knees buckled like sticks snapping. Casually, Big Tree set his pistol at half cock again and cleared out the spent cap. He reloaded the cylinder.

To a Cheyenne, ponies were almost as human as his fellow Indians. So River of Winds was forced to choke back retches of nausea as he witnessed the rest of it.

While the cactus-liquor *pulque* flowed freely, the drunken Comanches butchered the pony. Its coiled entrails were pulled through slits and roasted in the hot embers. Meaty steaks were cut from the haunches. The skull was cracked open with rocks and the brains roasted, then mixed with a soup made from the blood and organs.

A huge fire was built in the center of the camp clearing. Remembering his instructions from Wolf Who Hunts Smiling, Big Tree directed that the pony's ribs be set up on end as a cooking rack for the steaks. Far into the night, the Comanches feasted on the Cheyenne pony.

But River of Winds felt his smoldering rage nearly give way to helpless tears when five more ponies were shot. These were not eaten. But each was savagely gutted, its entrails spread in greasy heaps for the Cheyenne pursuers to discover.

Chapter Seven

"Only look! You have eyes to see. It is just as Medicine Flute described it!"

Wolf Who Hunts Smiling's voice was smug with triumph. He sat his paint at the head of the long, grassy draw where their enemy had camped. The scene, as they rode upon it late in the afternoon, had shocked them to the core of their souls: the pony guts strewn everywhere, even dangling from tree limbs; the hollowed-out, decapitated carcasses and the heads left on stakes; the gnawed bones left over from this barbaric feast.

And reigning in the middle of this macabre tableau was the blackened-ribs cooking rack, rising from the ground just as Medicine Flute had described it.

"They are eating our ponies!" Tangle Hair

said bitterly. "Though game is plentiful. And look how many were slaughtered for no reason."

"There is a reason," Black Elk said. "They do this thing to taunt us. They know that no tribe on the plains respects ponies more than we. But they make one mistake. Such as this does not make true men wring their hands in fear. It only goads them to a war cry."

Wolf Who Hunts Smiling aimed a sly glance at Touch the Sky. "It is grisly. But at least we know we finally have a shaman whose medicine is powerful indeed."

Touch the Sky rode out ahead, then turned his pony to address Wolf Who Hunts Smiling and the rest of the group.

"We know nothing, Panther Clan. Our tribe has an official shaman already. His name is Arrow Keeper, and his medicine is respected throughout the red nations. The Council of Forty decides who our medicine man will be, not a power-starved Bull Whip who speaks from both sides of his mouth."

"I have no ears for this, Woman Face! Our own chief has witnessed this thing. You were trained by Arrow Keeper. Yet do you deny that you could see nothing, while Medicine Flute told us a vision that came true?"

"True, I saw nothing because Maiyun chose not to reveal it. And, yes, I do deny that Medicine Flute had a vision."

"You fool!" Wolf Who Hunt Smiling glanced from Chief Gray Thunder to Black Elk. "Here is the scene, just as Medicine Flute foretold.

How else could this thing be, if not ordained by a vision?"

Touch the Sky felt a tight bubble of helpless rage swelling inside his chest. This thing was awkward. Even Little Horse was clearly impressed by the apparent vision.

"How else could it be? Simple, low-crawling wolf. You have conspired with our enemies! You had a bloody hand in the death of our guards, and you now play the fox with Big Tree against us."

This charge struck most of those present as preposterous. True, all knew that Wolf Who Hunts Smiling was ambitious. All knew, too, that he hated this Touch the Sky with a belligerent passion. But to play the turncoat against his own tribe and with such an enemy as this?

It was a serious charge. Long had Wolf Who Hunts Smiling and others likewise accused Touch the Sky of being a spy for the palefaces. But they did not level specific charges for specific crimes, as Touch the Sky was doing now.

It was Gray Thunder who spoke.

"Touch the Sky, you are a warrior unlikely to die in his sleep. I was told how you stood shoulder to shoulder with Little Horse and fought off the white hunters at the Buffalo Battle. And never will I forget the time when you rallied the junior warriors and saved our women and children from Comanche and Kiowas. Unlike some in the tribe, I no longer question your loyalty to your people.

"But, buck, these are serious words you speak against Wolf Who Hunts Smiling. You call him a traitor, an offense which, if proven, means sure death. Twice now have you said this thing. All right then, Cheyenne. Where is your proof—proof I can pick up and examine?"

Touch the Sky felt the weight of their stares. His gaze met the mocking eyes of Wolf Who Hunts Smiling, the inscrutable gaze of Medicine Flute. One by one, he looked at the other warriors.

Only Tangle Hair and Little Horse did not avert their gazes. True, they were confused and did not understand how their friend Touch the Sky could know these things. But they had decided to stand with him no matter what.

Touch the Sky longed to reveal what Honey Eater had told him: the details explaining Medicine Flute's miracle, a miracle which in fact came straight from the white man's sky charts.

Then his eyes met the fierce, hateful stare of Black Elk. And those burning eyes reminded him that he could not say too much and let Black Elk suspect that Honey Eater warned him after overhearing the plan. For truly, Black Elk was already on the verge of killing her.

"Father," he finally answered, seeing which way the wind must set for the moment, "I cannot give you proof now. Perhaps later, but not now. So I promise this thing. No more will I publicly accuse Wolf Who Hunts Smiling of this crime."

"Good," Gray Thunder said, nodding. He cast a stern glance at Wolf Who Hunts Smiling. "And you, buck. You, too, are very free with your accusing mouth. I ask both of you to remember that only through the tribe do we live on. And a tribe divided cannot defend itself."

Wolf Who Hunts Smiling wiped the grin from his face. But his eyes still mocked Touch the Sky as he replied.

"Of course, Father. We are up against a powerful and clever foe. I shall do my part to keep my thoughts bloody against only them. I care only for the welfare of my people."

Big Tree and his Comanche warriors continued to drive their stolen ponies south. But the relentless pace had slowed. Grass was more sparse now, water holes fewer and farther between. Some of the water was alkali tainted, and great care had to be taken to keep the herd from drinking it.

Stone Club, keeping a constant eye on the swift-moving Cheyennes, reported that the war party must soon catch up with them. This news did not cause Big Tree undue concern. True, he was not eager for a fight, not against fanatical Northern Cheyennes. These north-country men knew only one style of battle—fighting until either they or their enemies were all dead.

The Comanches, in contrast, fought for the spoils of war. They did indeed glorify warfare, but dying in battle was not glorious. It was just death. They were indifferent to taking scalps or counting coups. Although revenge was sweet to them, as to most Indians, they placed little value on honor. An enemy killed in his sleep was just as dead as one killed on the battlefield.

Therefore, Big Tree planned to continue cooperating with Wolf Who Hunts Smiling. Of course, he would do so only insofar as such cooperation benefited him. But he differed from the wily Cheyenne on one important score. Wolf Who Hunts Smiling had apparently despaired of ever killing the tall shaman. Now he was content merely to destroy his standing as a medicine man, and thus his power as a leader.

Big Tree, in contrast, meant to kill Touch the Sky.

Well did he recall that night in a little canyon outside the shanty-and-sod hovel known as Over the River. The Comanches and their Kiowa allies were all set to trade their Cheyenne prisoners for a group of kidnapped white businessmen. But the businessmen turned out to be well-armed, disguised soldiers friendly to the Cheyennes. In the ensuing bloodbath, Big Tree had seen the Kiowa and Comanche leaders slain. And he himself had been knocked from his pony by the arrogant young Cheyenne shaman.

About midday, one sleep after the slaughter of the Cheyenne ponies, Rain in His Face rode up beside his leader.

"The ponies are tired. Gall has scouted forward and reports good grass near the Rio Mora. It would be smart to graze the herd there. Else we will arrive at the Blanco with skeletons."

Big Tree nodded. "Graze them. Then camp for the night. But move out even before the sun and make the best time you can. You are in charge until I return."

"Return? But, Quohada, where are you going?"

A grin split Big Tree's dust-coated face. Like his brothers, he wore his hair parted in the middle and just long enough to brush behind his ears. He was still a young man, but the sere Southwest sun had lined his face like the clay bed of a dried-up river.

"I am going to backtrack, brother. I am going to infiltrate the Cheyenne trail camp. And I am going to kill this tall Cheyenne who has left us the names of many dead who may no longer be mentioned."

It was a bold enough plan. But Rain in His Face showed little surprise. After all, next to their superb horsemanship, Comanches were best known for stealth. Like the Apaches, they were masters of concealment and subtle movement. It was said that not even shadows moved as smoothly as Comanches.

"Then kill him, Quohada."

Big Tree nodded. "I said I would. And when Big Tree speaks a thing, it is already done."

Trouble was in the wind. Some new threat was very close at hand. Touch the Sky sensed it.

Forward scouts reported they must soon overtake their enemy. That night, in their camp, the warriors attended to their battle rigs. As he tested the sinew string of his new bow, Touch the Sky constantly kept glancing out past the flickering tips of the fire.

"What is it, brother?" Little Horse said.

Spirit Path

Touch the Sky stared into the blue-black maw of the night. The fine hairs on the back of his neck stood up.

"Nothing, buck," he finally replied. "Only a thing of smoke."

"It is this infernal flute playing," Tangle Hair said, staring past the fire toward the spot where Wolf Who Hunts Smiling sat with Medicine Flute. The flat, eerie notes of Medicine Flute's playing hovered over their camp like annoying birds.

"Straight words," Little Horse said. "This music would disturb the sleep of a dead man."

Touch the Sky nodded. But again a little tickle of premonition moved up his spine like an icy fingertip. He stared into the orbit vastness surrounding them, unable to shake the sense that tragedy loomed nearby.

Big Tree halted and dismounted well back from his enemy's camp. He hobbled his pony foreleg to rear with a short piece of rawhide. Then he prepared for the final and most dangerous leg of his journey.

He stripped completely naked and wallowed in a nearby muddy swale until his body was coated dark. Using short leather whangs, he tied broken-off bushes to his upper arms, legs, and back. Then, leaving most of his weapons with his mount, he selected only his osage-wood bow and one special Comanche arrow especially designed for victims sleeping on the ground.

The bow was so powerful it could drive a normal arrow through a buffalo's left flank, the arrow exiting cleanly from the right before falling on the ground. But this arrow Big Tree carried now was intended for cruelly pinning victims to the ground. The arrow point was cut from white man's pressed tin—a jagged, barbed point designed to tear and rip on its way through the victim, before biting deep into the ground under him.

He slipped the bow over his right shoulder, gripped the arrow in his mouth. Then he waited until the wind picked up, rustling the leaves in a ghostly whisper. Under cover of the noise he began creeping toward the Cheyenne camp, silent and smooth as the night shadows surrounding him.

Sentries had been posted and Medicine Flute had finally given over with his maddening music. The Cheyennes had drunk much water to ensure that aching bladders would wake them early. Now the fire had burned down to embers that glowed like eyes in the night.

As usual Touch the Sky had unrolled his buffalo robe near those of Little Horse and Tangle Hair. Soon he heard the steady, rhythmic breathing as they settled into sleep. But still, rest eluded him.

Beyond the silent camp circle, a coyote howled. An owl hooted, and far off in the distant foothills of the Red Hawk Mountains, Touch the Sky heard the ferocious kill cry of a mountain lion.

Nearby, a twig snapped, and Touch the Sky started up, his knife in his hand. But he relaxed when he saw it was just a fox sniffing at the scraps of meat from earlier.

But the snapping twig reminded him of a trick he had used to good effect in the past. Quietly, not disturbing the others, he gathered dried sticks and dead, crisp leaves, forming a little ring around his sleeping robe.

Still uneasy, but exhausted from the grueling pace of their mission, he finally settled into a fitful, uneasy sleep.

As the half-moon began to creep down from its zenith, Big Tree strung his special skewering arrow for the kill.

Slipping through the Cheyenne camp had been a risky business, and his heart was still pounding in his throat. But now his enemy lay on the ground before him, barely more than an arm's length away.

Big Tree pulled his bowstring taut, felt the long, sturdy bow give under the pressure. He aimed the longer-than-usual arrow and moved slightly for a better angle.

A stick crunched.

A heartbeat later, simultaneously, Big Tree launched his arrow and the barely alerted sleeper rolled hard to the right. But just before he bolted, the Comanche had the satisfaction of seeing his barbed-point arrow punch hard into his enemy's chest.

Chapter Eight

Little Horse thought, at first, that he must be dreaming.

Through thick cobwebs of deep sleep, he heard a gasping rattle that sounded like teeth being shaken hard in a gourd. It was the Sun Dance ceremony, he thought. Arrow Keeper must be keeping time for the high-kicking dancers.

But who was calling his name in that weak voice—a weak voice made tight and urgent with severe pain?

His eyes blinked open. Overhead, the star-shot heavens were vast and undisturbed. The camp was quiet except for the rhythmic cadence of the snoring Indians, the snuffling of their ponies tethered nearby under guard.

He heard again, faintly, the words charged

with horrendous pain. Someone calling his name.

He pulled his buffalo robe aside and sat up. Tangle Hair lay to his left, Touch the Sky on his right. He reached over to shake Touch the Sky awake, and his fingers brushed something warm and wet and sticky.

Then a breeze stirred, and he recognized the familiar odor of blood.

At that same moment a raft of clouds floated away from the moon, and Little Horse spotted the arrow that pinned his best friend to the ground like a stake.

Instinctively, his heart leaping into his throat, Little Horse raised the wolf howl, which to Cheyennes anywhere meant that their enemies were right on them. The next moment, dread heavy in every limb, he leaned over his friend to see if he was still among the living.

The fierce Black Elk was the first warrior to his feet, followed immediately by Tangle Hair.

"Who raised the alarm?" Black Elk demanded. He kicked up the embers.

"I did," Little Horse replied grimly. He had bent low over his friend and felt faint, warm breath on his eyelids. "Touch the Sky still lives, but he has been pinned by a Comanche long arrow!"

By now all the braves were awake, weapons to hand. All knew well what it meant to be pinned by the dreaded Comanche long arrow— almost certain death if the jagged-metal tip had gone through or even near vitals.

Touch the Sky's last-second roll spared him

from instant death, the pressed-tin point missing his heart by a hair. But his situation, trapped flat on the ground, was nearly hopeless. The buried point could not be snapped off behind him. This meant the arrow would have to be broken just above his chest. Then he would have to be lifted off the arrow. With the shaft—also notched to cut and tear—so close to the heart, this was as good as a death sentence.

"Never mind that," Black Elk said when a brave headed out beyond the circle of the fire. "These Comanche dogs may avoid open battles, but they are no cowards. This was the work of a lone brave. He has done it as a message of contempt. No attack is coming."

Wolf Who Hunts Smiling gaped in open astonishment. Could this thing be possible? Could the one man he hated more than any other possibly be treading the Death Path even now? This Big Tree—he had acted on his own, clearly, for this was not in the plan. Yet, it was a bold, rash, reckless act of courage. Thus it earned the wily Cheyenne's admiration.

He exchanged a secret glance with Medicine Flute. This brave, too, was fighting back a smirk of celebration. Both sensed that soon power would shift into their hands.

"New light is rimming the east," Gray Thunder said. "Black Elk, you are our battle leader. How do you counsel?"

"I am not one to stand about wringing my hands," Black Elk said. "Better to get them bloody! I say we ride out now."

He, too, was gloating as he listened to Touch the Sky's hard, uneven breathing. Black Elk recognized the early stages of the death rattle. This was the randy stallion who would mount his mare! Perhaps he had already topped Honey Eater. If so, surely he would never do so again.

"Ride out?" Little Horse stood and looked at the others. "Has a rabbit been wounded? Or is it the best warrior in the Cheyenne Nation?"

"I have ears for this," Tangle Hair said. "I would need to live two lifetimes to believe that Cheyenne warriors will coldly turn their backs on their own. Especially one who has bled for his tribe like this one has."

"Turn our backs?" Black Elk repeated scornfully. "Tangle Hair, I have never seen you hide in your tipi. With ten braves like you and Little Horse I could destroy ten times as many bluecoats.

"But, bucks, only use the eyes Maiyun gave you! Look there, how the pink bubbles flow from Touch the Sky's lips. He is hurt in his lights. And look at that long shaft. This one has been skewered by a Comanche long arrow. The metal point has torn his guts like bluecoat canister shot. If there is breath left in his nostrils, he had best sing the death song with it."

"This one," Wolf Who Hunts Smiling said, "is smoke behind us. The world belongs to the living, Cheyennes! Let us ride. Little Horse, all you have left for your grief is revenge. Ride with us, stout brave, and we will dangle Comanche scalps from our coup sticks."

"The world belongs to the living," Little Horse repeated with contempt. "You speak from two mouths, Panther Clan. Touch the Sky once told me a thing. He told me how your cousin Black Elk sent you and Swift Canoe to murder Touch the Sky while he was on his vision quest at Medicine Lake.

"And indeed you tried. Even so, Touch the Sky saved you when, on your way back to camp, Pawnees attacked you. And now you would leave him like so much dressed-out meat!"

Chief Gray Thunder knew nothing of this story. Now he stared at Black Elk and Wolf Who Hunts Smiling, waiting for a denial.

But they both wisely held their silence. For the murderous anger in Little Horse's eyes would brook no more slighting of his friend. If any warrior could fight as an equal beside Touch the Sky, it was surely Little Horse. No one present was eager to cross lances with him when he had blood in his eyes as he did now.

"While we talk," Black Elk said, "our enemies drive our ponies closer to the impregnable Blanco Canyon. This is a war party. Therefore we are not guided by rules of council, but by my commands. And I say we ride."

"Do as you will." Little Horse had knelt beside his friend again. "I stay with this fallen warrior, the man I consider our tribe's best."

"We could use you, buck," Black Elk said. "But despite your insolence, I will not hold you in violation of my orders. I admire you too much."

And for a moment, just a few heartbeats, Little Horse saw Black Elk's face soften a bit as he looked at the supine Touch the Sky.

"And as you say, this is a warrior. I trained him. I confess, he was so mired in white man's ignorance that I was sure the training would kill him within five sleeps. But Cheyenne blood will eventually out, and he has since covered this tribe in glory more than once. Now he must soon cross over to the Land of Ghosts. But I promise that he will be carried to his scaffold wearing new moccasins and with all his weapons about him."

"One world at a time," Little Horse said grimly, turning his back on the rest as they prepared to ride. "He has not left this one yet."

The war party rode out, faces blackened with charcoal. And once again Touch the Sky's fate was in his best friend's hands.

Little Horse knew that his companion's life was balanced on the edge of a feather. Just as his own had been when the bluecoat Seth Carlson shot him near the Milk River. And hadn't Touch the Sky pulled him back from the very jaws of death into the world of the living?

Little Horse dreaded what had to be done immediately. Lifting Touch the Sky off that arrow would be one of the hardest acts Little Horse had ever performed. And not just because his friend was big. That long shaft had been deliberately barbed and notched to rip and tear. The damage already done might have been fatal.

How could the unconscious warrior possibly survive another pass through his body?

Although morning light streaked the eastern sky, Little Horse built up the fire. He said a simple battle prayer to focus his courage. Then, working with great care, he used his knife to cut through the shaft of the arrow where it protruded from Touch the Sky's chest.

His friend still breathed, but barely—the rapid, shallow panting of a dying animal. Little Horse knelt, opened his parfleche, and removed several twists of fine white man's tobacco. He scattered it to the directions of the wind as a gift to Maiyun, the Great Medicine Man.

Little Horse owned a beautiful Indian saddle, recently obtained in a trade with one of Chief Bull Hump's Dakotas. It was flat, beautifully embroidered with Sioux beadwork, his favorite possession and the envy of his clan. Not once hesitating, he now uncinched it from his horse and completely shredded it with his knife. Thus, he hoped, his sacrifice would give wings to his prayer for Touch the Sky.

Finally, it was time. He knelt, slid both arms carefully under his friend, and planted his feet firmly. He inhaled a huge breath, expelled it, then took another. His heart pulsed hard in his ears.

"Today, brother," he said out loud to his companion, "is not a good day to die!

"Hi-ya, hiii-ya!"

Screaming the fierce war cry of his tribe, Little Horse strained to rise. His well-muscled thighs and calves went taut, but at first the arrow refused to let go of its victim.

Summoning strength he never realized he had, the short but stocky warrior gasped with supreme effort. Veins in his neck swelled up like fat blue nightcrawlers, his arms trembled, and he felt a slow giving away of tension. Then, just as he was sure he must collapse, he felt his friend slide up and off the arrow.

But Little Horse felt little elation even as he gently laid his brother in his open buffalo robe. True, his friend's harsh grunt of pain proved he was still alive. But he had glimpsed that shaft—what remained of it—in the new light. And it was covered with bloody gobbets of gut and flesh.

For two full sleeps Little Horse tended to his friend, doing his best to confound death.

He heated his knife blade in the embers and cauterized the entrance and exit wounds. He made a paste of river mud, gunpowder, and balsam, binding the wounds with strips of cypress bark. Touch the Sky alternated between burning fevers and bone-numbing chills.

At first he could take no nourishment except sips of water. Everything else he vomited up. Little Horse stole wild peas from the caches of field mice. These he cooked and then mashed with his knife, mixing it with bone marrow. Touch the Sky was able to hold this concoction down.

Though he passed in and out of consciousness, his talk was wild and dreamlike, that of a man gone Wendigo. Then, on the third day after the long arrow pierced him, Touch the Sky's eyes opened wide.

"Brother," he said weakly to his friend, "cook some meat. I would eat like a living man!"

Later that night, over Little Horse's objections, Touch the Sky decided they would ride out next morning. The sun was still rising, Touch the Sky moving slowly and carefully, when they cut sign on the others and set out.

Chapter Nine

"Cousin," Black Elk said, "I regret that a Comanche arrow did what we could not. Still, Woman Face has been sent under. I could not wish the deed undone."

"I have ears for this, Cheyenne. Long have I dreamed of burying my tomahawk in his skull. But he has been sent under. This is one kill I do not begrudge our enemies."

Black Elk, leading his war party, had dropped back to ride beside his cousin. The land was more barren—buttes and mesas and redrock canyons with grass sparse away from the rivers. The pace had been considerably slowed for the fleeing Comanches and their stolen pony herd. Now the Cheyennes could spot their dust trail far out above the horizon.

"A thing troubles me," Black Elk said.

Wolf Who Hunts Smiling had prepared for this. He had noticed his cousin brooding more and more, and he knew what was coming.

"Then speak this thing," he said.

"It concerns Medicine Flute. I was present when plans were made to play the fox with this miracle of the burning star. It was a good plan and worked well. Only, tell me a thing. Tell me about this business with the pony ribs sticking from the ground. How could he have had this vision without cooperating with our enemies? Surely he is not truly blessed with big medicine. A true shaman would never have lied about the burning star."

Black Elk's face was stern. Though he had gone so far to make Touch the Sky's life miserable—even sullying the Sacred Arrows by trying to kill him—he could never be a traitor to his tribe. Nor would he tolerate such behavior in any Cheyenne.

Wolf Who Hunts Smiling knew this. Now he said, "Cousin, I could tell you it was Medicine Flute's magic. But I will not. Only think. Do you know where Swift Canoe is?"

Black Elk's face was blank. "No. Nor do I care. Why should I? He is back at camp, I would wager. But—" He cut himself off as his cousin's meaning dawned on him. "You had him secretly scout ahead?"

Wolf Who Hunts Smiling grinned. "I did. I confess I played the fox on my own. Medicine Flute had a good description, indeed."

This evoked a rare smile from the stern war

leader. "So that is the way the wind sets. Good work, buck!"

Relief surging through him, Wolf Who Hunts Smiling congratulated himself for this successful deception. Black Elk, never one for schemes, had been readily fooled. This was important. For truly Wolf Who Hunts Smiling found himself walking a fine line. Granted, Touch the Sky was no doubt dead or dying. This was a source of great personal pleasure as well as essential to his plans for someday leading his own red nation in a war of extermination against the palefaces. Touch the Sky had been the greatest obstacle to those plans.

But Touch the Sky aside, Wolf Who Hunts Smiling still needed Big Tree as an ally. The young Cheyenne's ambition was as wide as the plains themselves. He wisely understood, however, the one great weakness of the red man: any real lack of unity. Tribe warred upon tribe, weakening their potential to combine and deal the bluecoats a massive death blow.

Big Tree was the key to gaining an important southern plains ally. But that meant Wolf Who Hunts Smiling must purchase the fierce Comanche's loyalty. To his own tribe, Wolf Who Hunts Smiling must appear eager to defeat these Comanche raiders; but, in fact, he knew he must subvert his tribe so their enemy might escape. That was his agreement with Big Tree.

Black Elk chucked up his pony, resuming his spot at the head of his war party. But several times Wolf Who Hunts Smiling saw his cousin turn to stare back toward him.

Then he realized that Black Elk was looking well beyond him—staring farther behind, as if he still could not believe that Woman Face was worm fodder.

"Brother, this hard pace is making fresh blood flow from your wounds," Little Horse said. "Let us make a camp for the night."

The two friends had stopped to water their ponies in a small runoff stream. Their sister, the sun, had gone to her resting place, leaving the vast night sky to Uncle Moon.

Touch the Sky shook his head. "It is only a spot of blood. The moon is full, the stars many. Light is good, so let us keep riding."

"Buck," Little Horse said, impatience creeping into his tone, "I admire your stout heart, surely. But what good is it to kill yourself playing the hero?"

"I play at nothing. We must hurry. Wolf Who Hunts Smiling and Medicine Flute have become dogs for these Comanches. If we let the grass grow under us now, our pony herd is lost. Perhaps our comrades are, too."

Little Horse narrowed his eyes, watching his tall friend closely in the generous moonwash. Yes, his face was drawn and pinched with pain, dust-streaked from the grueling pace. Touch the Sky was still weak from loss of blood. But there was also an odd, determined glint in his eyes—a look Little Horse had seen before. Better to bait a grizzly, he told himself, than defy that glint.

"Brother," he said quietly, "I have seen the

mark of the arrow buried past your hairline. Arrow Keeper has spoken to me about the meaning of this mark, about his vision that foretold you would be a great leader.

"I have also seen this light like fox fire in your eyes. The hand of the supernatural is in this thing. That Comanche arrow should have killed you, but Maiyun willed otherwise. So if you say we ride, then, Cheyenne, we ride!"

Medicine Flute's eerie music finally fell silent. Wolf Who Hunts Smiling feigned sleep until all of his comrades were snoring around him. Then, silent as the stalking wolf for which he was named, he slipped from his buffalo robes.

Earlier they had met up with River of Winds. According to the scout's report, they would overtake their enemy on the morrow. But Wolf Who Hunts Smiling had no intention of letting this happen.

The ponies were tethered in a grassy draw just north of camp, under guard as always. Wolf Who Hunts Smiling now took a lesson from the Comanche. He found a fist-size rock and wrapped it tight in rawhide.

The guard was Tangle Hair. But Wolf Who Hunts Smiling had no intention of killing him if he could avoid it. His faith in the Medicine Arrows was weak. However, the Cheyenne taboo against slaying fellow Cheyennes was strong and affected him, too. He did not consider Touch the Sky a true Cheyenne, so the taboo did not apply to him. But letting Comanches kill the herd guards, on that night of the miracle, was as far as he cared to go.

Now he told himself that a good tap to the skull would suffice to silence Tangle Hair for a bit. He would then drop the rawhide-wrapped rock beside him as proof Comanches did it.

The land here was sandy. So Wolf Who Hunts Smiling was careful to walk on his heels. He wanted no telltale prints leading back to his sleeping robes.

He waited for gusts of wind to cover the sound of his movements. Tangle Hair was no brave to be taken lightly, one of the best of the Bow String troopers. But the brave would not be looking for trouble from the direction of camp.

Finally Wolf Who Hunts Smiling spotted him. Tangle Hair was seated at the crest of a small hill, his vigilant eyes directed toward the south. Wolf Who Hunts Smiling stopped breathing through his nose—this was too much noise around a brave as sharp as Tangle Hair.

He crept closer, raised the rock, and swung it into Tangle Hair's left temple. There was a sickening thud. A heartbeat later, Tangle Hair lay sprawled on the ground.

Grinning with elation, Wolf Who Hunts Smiling glided smooth as a shadow into the midst of the ponies. Familiar with his smell, they only snorted in friendly greeting.

He stooped and quickly began removing their tethers.

It was Little Horse's keen sense of smell that first told them they were about to overtake the camp of their companions.

He had stopped his mount to carefully sniff the wind.

"Ponies ahead," he said. They had already cut sign on their comrades and knew from the number of riders that it must be the Cheyennes.

"Brother," Touch the Sky said, "I have no desire to rouse the entire camp when they are painted for battle. There will be a pony guard out. Let us slip up on the camp and give him the owl hoot so he will not wake the rest and get us killed for Comanches."

Little Horse nodded. He sniffed the wind again. Then he led them up a long bluff. Below, in the silver-white moonlight, they saw the grazing ponies. However, they could not yet spot the guard.

Touch the Sky imitated an owl hoot, the Cheyenne way of signaling the approach of a friend. At first, nothing. But after he did it again, the signal was returned.

"Good. He knows we are here," Touch the Sky said.

"Give me your hackamore, brother," Little Horse said. "You are so tired even your voice is weary. Go roll into your buffalo robe while I tether our mounts. Get what little sleep remains for this night."

Touch the Sky was indeed too exhausted to argue with this. His wounded chest throbbed mightily. He was halfway down the draw, threading his way through the ponies, when he noticed that several of the ponies were drifting away from the group, farther than normal tethers would allow. Before the meaning of this could sink in, he almost tripped over something.

He glanced down and recognized Tangle Hair in the moonlight.

Blood matted the left side of his forehead, but fortunately his breathing was still strong. Wincing at the pain in his own chest, Touch the Sky knelt to take a closer look. Satisfied his friend would live, the Cheyenne rose again and prepared to raise the wolf howl of alarm. But who, he thought, had answered his signal?

That was when he spotted a lone figure off to his right. The intruder had knelt and was staring back toward the camp.

No doubt another Comanche. Clearly this was a lone raider. Now Touch the Sky understood why there had been such a long pause before his owl hoot was answered. This wily enemy had given the response, not a Cheyenne.

Touch the Sky knew the interloper might well escape if he raised the wolf howl. His mind calculated quickly. He was armed only with his obsidian knife, having left his other weapons in his pony rigging for Little Horse to carry. Touch the Sky knew he was too weak for a sustained battle. But if he could capitalize on the element of surprise. . . .

He slid his knife from its beaded sheath and moved in closer. He was perhaps a double arm's length from striking range when his foot suddenly startled a fat gopher snake. It streaked off, rustling the grass, and the crouching figure suddenly rose and whirled around.

"You!" Wolf Who Hunts Smiling gaped in wide-eyed astonishment. It was he who had answered the owl hoot, unsure who had made it. But in the clear moonlight, there was no mistaking his enemy's broad shoulders and the grim, determined slit of his mouth.

Touch the Sky, fully expecting a Comanche warrior, was equally surprised.

"Once again, White Man Runs Him, you have outfoxed death. Notice, this time I do not tremble as I did when you outwitted the grizzly. I see from that blood on your chest that you are a man of flesh and bone."

This was a reference to the time when Wolf Who Hunts Smiling and Swift Canoe had lured a ravenous grizzly to Touch the Sky's cave at Medicine Lake. Convinced his foe must be dead and returned as a spirit, Wolf Who Hunts Smiling had begged for his life when his enemy appeared before him.

"You still had some decency left in you then," Touch the Sky replied. "You could have killed me. But you didn't because you still respected the Sacred Arrows. That decency you once had is gone, as this further act of treachery against your own tribe proves. You know these ponies are still wild and will run when the tether is slipped."

"I know many things, Woman Face! I know that I only spared your life because there was still a soft place in my heart. But it is all rock now, buck."

"No, you are wrong there. For a rock cannot be a traitor to its own, Comanche dog!"

In a moment Wolf Who Hunts Smiling's knife was in his hand. Clearly, his enemy was exhausted, weakened, in no condition to fight. And had Woman Face not already boldly announced, at council, no less, that he intended to kill him?

Reading Wolf Who Hunts Smiling's eyes close, Touch the Sky also gleaned his enemy's thoughts.

"Yes," he said, "I announced I was going to kill you. For after all, it was you who first walked between me and the campfire, saying to all that you would send me under. And now you play the dog for those who stole our women and children, killed our elders. The Cheyenne way does not permit murder of our own. But it also decrees that a traitor ceases to be a Cheyenne. Your blood cannot stain the Arrows."

"I have no ears for you. You have knocked Death from his pony more times than I can count. And I chafed, thinking Big Tree had deprived me of the pleasure of killing you. But now, like the ponies I just set free, your luck has reached the end of its tether!"

A heartbeat later, his blade glinting cruelly in a shaft of moonlight, Wolf Who Hunts Smiling leaped on his enemy.

Chapter Ten

Wolf Who Hunts Smiling was small. But he was hard knit, quick, and surprisingly strong, and once he bridged the gap, his every instinct led straight for the kill.

Knowing he was too weak to overpower Wolf Who Hunts Smiling in his present condition, Touch the Sky did not try to resist. Instead, he fell in the direction of the attack. Pain jolted through his wounded chest as he hit the ground. But the unexpected lack of resistance sent Wolf Who Hunts Smiling tumbling head over heels behind him.

Touch the Sky scrambled to his feet, slower than usual. Just in the nick of time he managed to spin around and meet the second assault.

He twisted sideways, feeling his enemy's blade slice his ribs as it ripped through his leather shirt. Already Touch the Sky was breathing hard from his exertions. Desperate, he swept his left leg in a wide arc and hooked it behind one of Wolf Who Hunts Smiling's legs. A moment later, the smaller brave crashed to the ground on his back, literally swept off his feet. He grunted in surprise.

By now several of the ponies, agitated by the commotion, were nickering in nervous fright. Touch the Sky's chest wound bled freely. He raised his knife and fell on top of his enemy, seeking warm vitals and a final end to this long rivalry. But the powerful brave instantly arched his back hard, rolling Touch the Sky clear.

With a snarl of wild triumph, Wolf Who Hunts Smiling leaped atop his weakened adversary. Touch the Sky barely managed to grab his opponent's arm in time to stop it before the knife sank deep into his neck. Now the razor-sharp edge of the blade was poised only a few hairs away from his throat as Touch the Sky pitted his brawn against Wolf Who Hunts Smiling's.

At first it was a standoff, death held at bay but only an eye blink away. But then slowly, inexorably, the blade began to press into flesh as Touch the Sky's exhausted reserves of strength rapidly gave out.

"Die, Woman Face!" Wolf Who Hunts Smiling taunted him as a line of blood appeared on his victim's neck. "Perform your strong medicine now, shaman!"

Pain was a white-hot crease across his neck.

Touch the Sky felt the blade sinking deeper. A few more heartbeats and his trembling arms would collapse. Then his throat would be ripped open like a second mouth. But a moment later, Wolf Who Hunts Smiling was lifted off of him.

"Buck," Chief Gray Thunder said with angry authority, "you are on the feather edge of murdering your own! Had the ponies not woken me, you would have the putrid stink of the murderer on you for life. Do you sully the Arrows even as we pursue an enemy? Do you risk Maiyun's wrath at a time when we need His benevolence most?"

The powerful chief's face was hatchet sharp in his anger.

"But," Wolf Who Hunts Smiling said, "you do not understand! I caught Woman Fa—Touch the Sky scattering our horses! Do you not see? Clearly this is an act of revenge. He is angered because Medicine Flute's true magic has exposed his sham medicine. This act of treachery was meant to suggest that Medicine Flute cannot protect us."

By now, alerted by the noise, the rest of the braves had formed a circle around them.

"Touch the Sky," Gray Thunder said, "are these words straight? You were hurt deep in your lights and we gave you up for dead. Perhaps we did wrong in leaving, but we had an enemy to pursue. Is this how you exact revenge?"

"Father, I have exacted nothing. Once again this wolf lives up to his name. He was scattering the ponies! I say it again. Wolf Who Hunts Smiling is drinking from the same pond as Big Tree and his Comanches."

This set the warriors buzzing. Many found both stories hard to believe.

Little Horse edged his way through the circle and spoke up. "Touch the Sky speaks straight arrow. We had just arrived in camp. I was turning our ponies out to graze, and he was heading toward the camp to sleep."

"Did you see Wolf Who Hunts Smiling turning loose our ponies?" Chief Gray Thunder demanded of Little Horse.

Reluctantly, the sturdy little brave shook his head. Touch the Sky watched Wolf Who Hunts Smiling and Medicine Flute exchange a knowing glance.

"Tangle Hair has been hurt!" a brave named Battle Sash called over. "He is coming to now. I think he will be all right. He has been hit with a rock."

A few moments later, Battle Sash led a stumbling Tangle Hair over to join the others.

"Brother," Gray Thunder said, "did you see who hit you?"

Tangle Hair shook his head. "Whoever it was came from the direction of camp."

Tangle Hair had turned accusing eyes on Wolf Who Hunts Smiling. "I suspect this one! He is a Bull Whip, and they are not close friends with honor."

"I, too, am a Bull Whip," Black Elk said hotly. "Would you insult my honor?"

"Enough of this clash of bulls," Gray Thunder said. "What has this tribe come to? Our enemy lies just ahead, with the best pony herd we have captured in recent memory. And here we stand, making war faces against one another. You"—he turned to Touch the Sky—"once again you have accused Wolf Who Hunts Smiling of traitorous behavior. And once again you cannot prove the charge. Do you offer even one bit of evidence we may pick up and examine?"

Touch the Sky bit back his words and merely shook his head. The only course open to him was to explain what Honey Eater had told him—how she had overheard the plot hatched that night behind Black Elk's meat racks. Honey Eater was greatly respected. If she swore to these things on the Arrows or the Buffalo Hat, she would be believed. But her life would be forfeit, for Black Elk's jealous pride would never brook such behavior from her.

"And, you," the chief said, whirling to stare at Wolf Who Hunts Smiling. "You are no better. You say Touch the Sky was freeing our ponies, and you, too, lack any proof. Now your chief says this to both of you. There is no council present. This is not a matter for Black Elk, as battle chief, to decide. So now your peace chief speaks, and you had both best have ears for my words.

"I have my eyes on both of you. For truly, one of you is a traitor. And I swear by the sun and the earth I live on, when I discover which of the two it is, he will die a dog's death!"

* * *

"Quohada, are you telling me my long arrow did not kill the tall young buck?" Big Tree said.

Stone Club nodded. The secret messenger had just returned from a hasty conference with Wolf Who Hunts Smiling.

"He is weak but alive. The Cheyennes are divided now. Some follow the thin shaman with the bone flute; others are loyal to the tall one. According to the Wolf Who Hunts Smiling, their chief knows not what to believe. And even now they are riding hard to meet us."

Big Tree was so incensed that his nostrils flared. He sat his stocking-footed chestnut on a long, rocky spine south of the Smoky Hill River. They had paused briefly to graze the ponies for the long haul across the barren panhandle country of Texas. Now his band was pointing the herd to resume the trek.

How, Big Tree wondered yet again, had the Cheyenne survived? It had been a good hit with a deadly arrow. Could the stories be true? Was his life charmed, protected by magic? But, no, it must have been when he rolled at the last moment. Somehow that fateful roll kept the arrow from striking to the quick of him.

"Wolf Who Hunts Smiling has sent a message," Stone Club added. "He has a new plan. When we reach the Red River, we are to select six more of the ponies, slaughter them, and leave them by the trail. He said to be sure that their eyes are gouged out. He promises that this time his tribe will turn against the tall one."

Slowly, Big Tree nodded. The silver conchos on his tall shako hat reflected in the bright sunlight, as did the bits of broken mirror embedded in his rawhide shield. Gradually a grin replaced his frown as he realized his wily Cheyenne ally was up to yet more treachery.

"Good," he said. "We will do it. I have no desire to waste good horses. And yet, if it hurts us, how must it make those pony-loving fools feel?"

Big Tree had no respect for a tribe that permitted its men only one wife each. And unlike the Comanches, Cheyenne braves were not permitted to slaughter their wives for cause—even if the woman was caught lying with another man! No wonder they practically worshiped their horses; they were sentimental fools. Cowards, no, but sentimental fools. And Big Tree had learned long ago that the more things a man loved the more ways he could be hurt.

"Now we ride hard," Big Tree said. "They will catch up to us soon enough. But when they reach the Red River and see what we have left for them, they will certainly pause."

Despite the loyalty of Little Horse, Tangle Hair, and a few others, Touch the Sky could feel the hostility of many in the war party.

Their slanted glances and quiet remarks showed that many had accepted Wolf Who Hunts Smiling's story that Touch the Sky had attempted to scatter their ponies. Many had made a great show of expressing friendship toward Medicine Flute, a brave hitherto

117

mostly ignored. Only the hard pace across the barren plains kept them too distracted to act on their suspicions—that and Chief Gray Thunder's clear desire to remain neutral and let the truth uncover itself.

"Brother," Little Horse said, riding beside his friend, "keep your senses stronger than your thoughts and your weapons to hand. Tangle Hair and I have already discussed this thing, and we are sworn to death beside you if it comes to that. We both agree that it is better to die like men, free warriors, than to play the dog for the likes of Wolf Who Hunts Smiling and Medicine Flute.

"Certain others agree with us. But they will not speak out now and encourage dissension. Not now, as we are closing for battle against a tribal enemy. But the fight is finally at hand, brother. I feel it."

Touch the Sky nodded. He rode the tough little bay, his new white mare with her silky gray mane following on a lead line. "It is closing fast upon us. Wolf Who Hunts Smiling and his Bull Whip brothers have set things in motion, things that cannot be undone. The tribe as we know it will soon be no more. And those who survive the bloody battles to come will be forced to choose not just a leader, but life or death."

Even as he spoke, Touch the Sky spotted Black Elk and Wolf Who Hunts Smiling staring at him.

"But for now, brother," he added, "I follow your advice. The future of our tribe is not the matter. I listen to the language of my senses, not to thoughts. And you must do the same, for they now understand that an attack against either of us is a fight with both of us."

Forward scouts confirmed that the fight would be soon, probably soon after the next rising of the sun. The Cheyenne warriors planned to rest their ponies well when they reached the Red River, then mount a classic running battle—the type of warfare they excelled in.

Though they knew Comanche scouts had an eye on them, they made a cold camp on the night before they reached the Red River. Black Elk chose a site just east of the rolling region whites called Purgatory Hills, a grassy flat in the lee of a mesa.

The guard was doubled, the rest of the braves tending to their battle rigs. By now hardly anyone bothered to notice when Medicine Flute's eerie music began.

But all did notice when it abruptly halted in midnote.

And all stared, jaws dropping in astonishment, when the young shaman's eyes went wide in terror. He no longer blinked, but seemed not to focus his gaze on any scene in this world. He sat cross-legged and rigid in the last of the sun's weak rays; the leg-bone flute had rolled from his fingers and dropped unnoticed to the ground.

He did not have to request their attention, as braves normally did. When his words rang out, they had the force of supernatural authority commanding them.

"Had I the choice, I would never have been born to see what I must see now for the sake of my people!"

"Hold fast, brothers," Touch the Sky whispered to Little Horse and Tangle Hair. "More wolf barks."

"Our tribe has blindly followed a false shaman!" Medicine Flute called out. "Now Maiyun is sending us a sign that we must pay for that blindness. What I have just seen, I have no heart to describe. Only wait until we reach the Red River, brothers, and you will see what our blindness has done!"

Chapter Eleven

The Cheyenne warriors rode out from their cold camp well before the sun had risen. Black Elk sent out point and flank riders, each equipped with a fragment of mirror for communicating with the main war party.

The rolling plains had given way to flat, unvarying country with only the occasional redrock butte or sandstone formation to break the monotony. Ahead, they could see the lingering, yellow-brown columns of dust raised by their stolen herd.

There was great excitement—tinged with dread—about Medicine Flute's cryptic and dramatic prediction. But by now Touch the Sky knew full well the prediction would indeed come true. He had no doubt that Big Tree and

Wolf Who Hunts Smiling had secretly teamed up to ensure this.

River of Winds had been sent forward on point. Soon after sunrise he returned, his face a grim mask. He spoke privately with Gray Thunder and Black Elk. But he only shook his head in mute refusal when the rest asked him what he had seen. He made a point, however, of avoiding eye contact with Touch the Sky.

"Notice, bucks," Little Horse said to Touch the Sky and Tangle Hair, "that Wolf Who Hunts Smiling has not troubled to speak with River of Winds as the rest are doing. He is not even curious to know what he saw."

"Why should he be?" Touch the Sky said. "River of Winds can only tell him what he already knows. Arrow Keeper was right. The red man's faith in visions can too often be cruelly exploited. Soon, I fear, we will be up against more trouble.

"Therefore, look sharp, Cheyennes! You have chosen to cast your lot with mine, and now my enemies are yours, too. We three must ride close and cover each other; we must watch for the attack. This vision has been devised in hopes of finally turning the rest against us. We must make it clear we will sell our souls dearly."

Finally, with the morning still young, the war party spotted the scattered cottonwoods of a river valley ahead. They crested the last long rise and saw sunlight glinting off the quick-flowing water of the Red River.

"There!" Black Elk called out grimly. He

pointed to the left of the trail they were following.

The gleaming, mutilated pony corpses had already drawn a swarm of flies, and the first carrion birds had quit circling and were beginning to land.

"Look!" Wolf Who Hunts Smiling called out when he had ridden closer. "Only look, brothers! Their eyes have been cut out. Did Medicine Flute not say that our blindness in following a false shaman has caused all this trouble? Now, look how the eyeless ponies themselves give powerful testimony to this same fact!"

"Brothers!" Black Elk called out. "How much proof do we need of Medicine Flute's powerful magic? Touch the Sky has not described one vision to us!"

"Because he is a pretend shaman!" the Bull Whip named Snake Eater called out. "Just as he is a pretend Cheyenne."

This time, with the eyeless ponies lying in mute accusation, more braves spoke out against Touch the Sky.

"Our mistake was in listening to Arrow Keeper. That one dotes on this tall one. He said this Touch the Sky would train for a medicine man. Once he spoke, all critics were silenced!"

"How much harm has it cost us? How many times has this pretend shaman led the Renewal of the Arrows, and we believed there was medicine in it?"

"How angry have we made the High Holy Ones?" Wolf Who Hunts Smiling shouted. "Is it a thing to wonder at, that we have lost our fine ponies? And how can we expect to get them back when we ride into battle with no medicine? Indeed, with the bad medicine of white men and their dogs?"

This was a serious thought, indeed, and every warrior was silent. A typical Cheyenne brave would face any danger—even certain death— if he were properly dressed and painted, if his shield and lance were blessed with strong medicine. But stout warriors were not considered cowards when they ran away from battle because they had no medicine. For dying without medicine meant eternal darkness and solitude in the Forest of Tears. And no Indian feared anything more than he feared solitude.

Chief Gray Thunder was about to speak up, but Wolf Who Hunts Smiling sensed blood in the wind, and he took a bold chance.

"Brothers, have ears! This is three times now that Medicine Flute has proven his strong medicine. Do you realize what we have done? We have been following a false shaman! We have let a white man's dog touch our Sacred Arrows! This White Man Runs Him, he has the stink on him that scares off the buffalo herds. Yet, we have let him chant the cure songs and lead the Animal Dance!"

Quietly, as they had arranged, Touch the Sky, Little Horse, and Tangle Hair maneuvered their ponies until the three braves formed a sort of triangle. With the river running before them, Touch the Sky faced the right flank, Little Horse the left, and Tangle Hair covered the rear. They knew what was coming, and it did.

"Cheyenne brothers!" Wolf Who Hunts Smiling shouted. "We have no choice but the honorable deed! This Touch the Sky, aided by his allies, has destroyed our tribe's medicine. We ride to certain death against the Comanches unless we appease the High Holy Ones. We must execute this pretend shaman, or else we are lost!"

He thrust his streamered lance high overhead, and many braves followed suit, raising the war cry. But even as they turned to face the trio, Touch the Sky spoke up.

"Hold, and have ears for my words now! This Wolf Who Hunts Smiling, what manner of leader is he? Does he wear the Buffalo Hat? Has he been elected a headman? Is he your war chief or the leader of a soldier society? No, he is none of these things. Yet, you all listen to him as if his words had authority behind them.

"His words are lies, as black as his heart. A Cheyenne can put nothing before the welfare of his tribe. Yet this ambitious young liar, lusting for power and a bloody, senseless war against the hair faces, has made a mockery of the Cheyenne way. He speaks of a false shaman. Yet you who follow him follow a false god, for truly he has set himself up as a god.

"And now I say this. Things are the way they are. Look close, all of you, and notice that three of the best warriors in your tribe are now prepared to sing the death song. We have defeated hair-faced soldiers, Pawnees, Crows, Comanches, and Kiowas. Our coup feathers, trailed together, would stretch from where I stand now to the Land Beyond the Sun! We challenge any brave to bridge the gap, for we are ready. Perhaps you will kill us. But tuck these words in your sashes. Many will cross over for each of us you kill, and the widows will wail for many moons after we three have done our bloody best."

These sobering words took the blood out of more than one warrior's eyes. Now Gray Thunder spoke before Wolf Who Hunts Smiling could retort.

"Now your chief is speaking! This decision to execute a Cheyenne has nothing to do with our present battle. Therefore, it is not a matter for Black Elk or his hotheaded young cousin to decree. Black Elk, as war leader, makes all battle decisions. But I, as your peace chief, decide other matters in the absence of the Council of Forty.

"Look at those three! Look at their faces! Are those white-liverd cowards or are they warriors to be reckoned with? Touch the Sky spoke well. A dear price will be exacted for their blood. Now stop all this foolish talk of killing our own. We came to rescue our ponies. Those who are thirsty for blood will find plenty to drink when we catch up with Big Tree. But so long as we stand here, fighting among ourselves, the Comanches have nothing to fear.

"Black Elk, be a man! Take charge of your warriors and let us raise our battle cry as one tribe!"

This speech met with a rousing cheer from almost every Cheyenne present except Wolf

Who Hunts Smiling and Medicine Flute. Black Elk nodded once, approving his chief's wisdom. Then he led his men in fording the river, and the chase was on.

Big Tree was seething with rage.

Wolf Who Hunts Smiling—had he not assured Big Tree that the tall one would be worm fodder by now? And yet the report from Stone Club was as clear as a blood spoor in new snow. The Cheyenne war party was closing upon them fast, and the arrogant young shaman rode with them.

"Truly," Stone Club added, "this tall warrior is a difficult one to catch by the throat. Some of our men, Quohada, are saying things. They are saying this shaman truly is the Bear Caller of Pawnee nightmares, his vitality beyond the power of mortal weapons."

Stone Club stopped short, but Big Tree understood his hint clearly enough. A Comanche war leader was respected most for ability in combat. His braves had a right to expect him to demonstrate that superior ability in a contest with the best warrior the Cheyennes could send out. Comanches loved entertainment, be it a torture session or a good duel to the death between well-matched bucks.

Big Tree knew his power as an Indian leader lay in his seeming invincibility. He must confront the Cheyenne dog in single combat.

"Stone Club, next time you hear the men saying these things, tell them this. Tell them the Bear Caller may indeed be beyond the power of mortal weapons. But ask them if mortal weapon has yet brought down their leader, Big Tree?

"Say this, Stone Club. Many Comanches were there when the Bear Caller killed our leader and then tried to kill Big Tree. He gave it his supernatural best, yet only knocked Big Tree from his horse. Big Tree falls from his horse when he is drunk! This is nothing.

"And finally, do certainly say this. Say that no red man on the plains can outride or outfight Big Tree. Say that a word-bringer has been sent back under a truce flag to meet with the Cheyennes. Say, too, that Big Tree challenges this tall Cheyenne shaman to mounted combat with battle lances and war clubs only. The winner keeps the pony herd."

It was the brave named Rain in His Face who took the message to the Cheyennes. He spoke enough Sioux words to make himself understood, using sign talk when all else failed.

Black Elk turned to Gray Thunder when the message was delivered. But their chief only shrugged. "This is a warrior's decision, not a peace leader's. However, we came to get our ponies. We must get them if possible, but not forget that we also came to avenge the blood of our dead herd guards."

Black Elk and the rest understood Gray Thunder's meaning. In agreeing to the contest, he was not also promising to ride the peace path. Big Tree had not demanded that. Their word of honor would mean, of course, that they would surrender the herd if Touch the Sky lost. But they would be free to attack at any time afterward, for blood vengeance was a separate issue.

Black Elk looked to his cousin and Medicine Flute. At first, this unexpected move left Wolf Who Hunts Smiling as surprised as the rest. This Big Tree, his new ally—he was turning out to be as unpredictable as the Blackfoot warrior Sis-ki-dee, who called himself the Contrary Warrior. Unpredictable men could be dangerous.

But it was Medicine Flute who changed his thinking.

"Panther Clan, why do you fret so?" he said quietly so the rest couldn't hear. "Why not champion this duel? If Big Tree kills Woman Face, all the better. If not, if Woman Face kills him, so what? We can form a new alliance with the next Comanche leader."

Wolf Who Hunts Smiling nodded. "I have ears for this." He turned to face his cousin, his spirited little paint prancing first left, then right. After all, it was Black Elk himself who had said that no red man on the plains could outride Big Tree.

Wolf Who Hunts Smiling met Black Elk's eyes. He nodded once.

Black Elk turned his pony to address Touch the Sky.

"Do you accept the challenge? I cannot and will not order you to do it."

"Tell me, war leader. Would you do it?" Touch the Sky demanded.

Fire sparked in Black Elk's eyes. He scowled fiercely, not hesitating a heartbeat. "If I were the buck he challenged, yes, I would. I would expect to die, of course, for I have watched this Big Tree ride and fight. Indeed, he sent me and my men scrambling for cover. But I fear no man."

"Brother," Little Horse said in a voice just above a whisper, "leave this challenge alone. Big Tree has deliberately limited the fight to riding skills, and you know no man has a chance against him on that score. What good is it to die by his terms? Better to live by yours."

"Good counsel, brother," Touch the Sky said calmly. "As always. You always speak straight arrow to me. Sadly, I do not listen as often as I should."

Touch the Sky faced Black Elk. Then he shared a long glance between Medicine Flute and Wolf Who Hunts Smiling. A sudden impulse made him grin at them and inject bantering sarcasm into his tone.

"Though I know it will break many hearts to see me dead, tell Big Tree I accept his challenge."

Chapter Twelve

After accepting Big Tree's challenge, Touch the Sky took on a different status among his comrades in the Cheyenne war party. He was still alive, yet, in the eyes of most, as good as dead.

Few disputed that he was the best warrior to send out. True, Black Elk and a few others were more experienced riders, and still others had the necessary courage and fighting spirit. But Touch the Sky was that rare warrior whose cool cunning increased with the desperation of his plight. He could unleash a mad war whoop and charge with the best of them, and yet, he was just as likely to win a fight by burying his enemies in a rock slide or by disguising a naked white boy as an evil spirit.

Still, this time, he was up against a foe the likes of whom he had never met before. To the Cheyennes, especially those who had seen him in action, this sneering Comanche in the tall shako hat was not a mere man, but some terrifying spawn of the Wendigo. And even those few skeptics who did not consider him in league with the Wendigo agreed he was the most dangerous mortal warrior on the plains.

For these reasons, all taunting and disparaging of Touch the Sky had ceased as if by silent order. Where he walked, braves stepped respectfully aside. Voices were not raised in his presence. Even his worst enemies recognized this new respect and left their foe alone. They simply avoided his eyes, as if he were already dead.

Little Horse had tried in vain to stop his friend. But once the challenge was accepted, he reacted as a warrior must. He assumed victory was theirs to earn if they acted like men.

"Brother," he said, early on the morning appointed for the crucial contest, "will you ride your bay? The new mare you acquired from Chief True Bow's Sioux is powerful. She snorts pure fire! But you are still training her. The bay is well trained, and she knows your touch."

Touch the Sky had been wrestling with that same question. The two Cheyennes were watching Touch the Sky's ponies graze with the rest in a hastily strung rope corral. To avoid surprise moves by either war party, both groups had agreed to meet in the wide-open flatland near the melon-shaped Pueblo Mountains.

"The bay knows my touch, and I hers," Touch the Sky agreed. He could pick the bay out easily by the pure white blaze on her forehead. "But the mare, her wild blood is still running closer to the surface. She trembles with the urge to break free and soar."

Little Horse was cautious. "Yes, clearly. And for this very reason, you will find her less predictable."

Touch the Sky nodded. "But so will Big Tree."

Little Horse narrowed his eyes, studying his friend closely.

"Sometimes," he said slowly, "a man gets a feeling that runs against the grain of good sense. My uncle, Roaring Bear of the Crooked Lance Clan, fought at Washita Creek. When a fellow warrior lost all his weapons, my uncle chose to give him his good new rifle instead of his pistol.

"His clan brothers chided him, saying he had sacrificed a good pony for a lame dog. But that night, they were attacked in their sleep. My uncle had his pistol to hand and killed a blue blouse only a heartbeat before he himself would have died. Never could he have fired his rifle so quickly."

Little Horse was thoughtful, watching the white mare impatiently stamp in protest at the pesky flies. "Ride her then, brother, if you have a feeling."

Tangle Hair had joined them. Cheyenne warriors were allowed great leeway in the matter of choosing weapons. He knew that Touch the Sky did not normally carry a war club. But all of the Bow String troopers did, and now Tangle Hair held out his. Not the fearsome, solid-stone skull cracker of Comanche fame—this was a wooden mallet carved from solid oak. The striking surfaces were cruelly tapered to concentrate and focus the power of the blow. It was carved with the magic totems of Tangle Hair's clan.

"It has killed before," Tangle Hair said solemnly as he handed it over.

By now Touch the Sky had learned the ritual when accepting a borrowed weapon.

"And it will kill again," he promised just as solemnly when he accepted it.

The war clubs would be a roughly even match. As for the second weapon permitted by Big Tree's challenge—lances—here Touch the Sky was at a clear disadvantage. The Cheyennes, valuing mobility in battle above all else, opted for lighter weapons. This one was made from sturdy but lightweight osage wood, tipped with sharp flint. Comanche lances, in contrast, were longer, made of heavier wood and tipped with heavy stone heads chiseled to lethal points.

"He will have the reach on you," Little Horse said, watching his friend carefully examine his red-streamered lance for weak spots. "Best have one of your famous tricks to hand, brother."

Even as he finished speaking, the shout was taken up from those on the south flank of camp. The cry was repeated over and over, a menacing refrain:

"Here come the Comanches!"

Big Tree's superbly muscled chestnut with the stocking feet was the strongest, swiftest pony on the Comanche string. As was customary in such a duel, Big Tree had stripped off his saddle to reduce weight and targets—a good hit to the saddle could throw a man from his mount.

Touch the Sky, too, had left his blanket and rope rigging off his mare. Both braves would ride bareback, holding onto and directing the pony with their tight-gripping legs.

The Comanches lined up on one flank of a huge clearing, the Cheyennes on another. All were armed, their weapons at the ready. Insults were freely exchanged, though few understood what their enemies said.

"Look!" the Comanche named Rain in His Face shouted out. "These northerners have all cropped their hair off for their dead! How noble! They make shows of grief like women! No doubt they cried like puling babies over their dead ponies."

"Look here, brothers!" the Cheyenne named Snake Eater countered. "These Comanches mate with dogs. See their plug-ugly faces, how the nose and mouth are so like a snout? Indeed, they lick their own crotches and eat their own droppings!"

Stone Club had been chosen as the Comanche referee; Black Elk as the Cheyenne's. The two braves met in midclearing, on foot and unarmed. Touch the Sky and Big Tree joined them for the drawing of the reeds. Touch the Sky drew the short reed—meaning Big Tree got to choose the direction from which he would ride.

"I have nothing to fear from this Cheyenne. So I will ride into the sun," he announced in English.

When Wolf Who Hunts Smiling translated this, many of the Cheyenne warriors were puzzled. Why would the fierce warrior wish to have the sun facing him, rather than in his opponent's eyes? This was indeed a brave show of contempt.

Big Tree lowered his voice, still speaking in English. His eyes mocking Touch the Sky, he addressed a final comment to his enemy.

"Know this, haughty one! They say you are a shaman. And perhaps they say straight, for I am staring now at the wound that should have killed you. But all your medicine could not keep me from bulling your honey-skinned woman when she was my prisoner in Blanco Canyon. And she enjoyed it, Cheyenne! She howled like a hot coyote and told me she had never been mounted by a man until she had a Comanche. Think, in these final moments left before I kill you, of me topping her."

Touch the Sky was beyond rising to such obvious bait.

"Certainly I can see you rutting on a pig, for such are your own filthy women," he replied. "Though everyone knows that the Comanche men are more likely to bull each other in their drunkenness. Indeed, the men take turns playing the squaw for each other."

This was a capital hit, and for a moment rage flashed in Big Tree's eyes. But he caught himself in time and only grinned. As he turned to take up his position, he spoke almost fondly.

"You are a man among men, with no cowardly bones in your body. I am going to enjoy killing you, tall Cheyenne."

The mare felt like a tightly coiled spring under him as Touch the Sky trotted her to his starting point and turned her to face his opponent.

The sun was well up behind him, casting his slanting shadow before him. Still he was puzzled. Why had Big Tree opted to face the sun? Touch the Sky did not believe it was merely a gesture of contempt. It was a sacred Comanche habit to attack from out of the sun.

But he had no luxury for examining the motivations of his enemy. The mare, sensing excitement in the air, was rebellious and required constant attention to keep her in position. She bucked several times, sidestepped, and hopped before settling down.

When the riders were set, lances balanced on their thighs, Black Elk suddenly thrust his arms into the sky. With a whoop, both riders were off.

Divots of dirt were flung into the air by the ponies' hooves; both riders gripped hard with their thighs and raised their lances and shields. Touch the Sky spotted sudden bursts of light, then abruptly squinted when blinding flashes forced him to avert his face. His pony, too, faltered, and Touch the Sky suddenly understood why Big Tree had chosen to face the sun. The fragments of mirror embedded in his shield were blinding the Cheyenne and his pony!

The two warriors thundered closer to each other, Touch the Sky desperately trying to orient himself in the brief pauses when the reflection missed his eyes. He saw Big Tree grinning behind the heavy stone point of his lance. When they were almost upon each other, Touch the Sky made his move.

He shifted right and forward, lying low over the pony's neck. This threw the sun out of his eyes. Big Tree's first lance thrust missed him by inches. Touch the Sky, off balance, only managed to strike his enemy's shield a glancing blow. Then, a heartbeat later, they had passed each other and were turning for the next attempt.

Now Touch the Sky rode into the sun, and Big Tree could not use his mirror fragments. Touch the Sky had been fighting his pony to control her. Now, on an impulse, he decided to give the feisty little mare her head.

Big Tree, still grinning, bounced with perilous ease atop his chestnut. Again he raised his lance, preparing to skewer the tall Cheyenne. The ponies drew closer, manes flying. Big Tree drew his arm back, ready to strike.

But now Touch the Sky's white mare showed her wildness.

With a hard shudder, she deliberately threw herself against the chestnut, taking a good nip out of its flank. The impact made the beast stumble, and Big Tree had to scramble wildly for a hold.

A cheer rose from the Cheyennes. Surely the Comanche was doomed now!

But in an amazing show of balance and strength, man and horse avoided going down. And now Touch the Sky was turning for the third pass.

Again these two implacable foes bore down on each other; again Touch the Sky had to keep glancing aside as mirror flashes blinded him. Before he even had time to think, Big Tree's lance point was flying straight at his heart.

In a skillful move, Touch the Sky got his lance up in time to parry the blow. Then, tragedy. As Touch the Sky's parry knocked Big Tree's lance aside, the tip of his own lance punched into the side of his pony. She shuddered once, then blew pink foam from her punctured lung. The mare slowed to a walk, staggered, and collapsed under him. Suddenly, Touch the Sky was standing on the ground beside his dying pony, and Big Tree whirled around to deliver the death blow.

The Comanche had tossed aside his lance in favor of his stone skull cracker. The ground thundered and vibrated as he closed the distance, sure of the kill this time. A cheer rose from the Comanche spectators as they sniffed blood in the wind.

Best have one of your famous tricks to hand, brother.

Little Horse's words taunted Touch the Sky. He had no medicine to help him. Only the words of old Arrow Keeper. During the short white days of the cold moons, as they huddled near the fire pit in the old shaman's tipi, Arrow Keeper had told his young apprentice

139

many stories about famous Cheyenne battles. One of those stories was about the Cheyenne warrior named Running Antelope—the same warrior who Arrow Keeper claimed was Touch the Sky's father.

This warrior, Arrow Keeper had claimed, once faced a mounted Ute warrior on foot and brought his horse down with a daring move invented by Cheyenne warriors in the days before they had acquired horses to fight their mounted enemies.

Big Tree bore closer, his skull cracker raised high. He was leaning far out from his pony, balanced for the blow that would send Touch the Sky across the great divide. Now the Comanches were cheering wildly, knowing it was only a matter of time before the unmounted Cheyenne dog was brained.

The pony was nearly upon him when Touch the Sky feinted to the left. But he checked his movement and dropped to the right, spinning his body as he fell.

Timing was everything, and Touch the Sky had timed it perfectly.

As the chestnut flashed past, and the skull cracker whipped by his head so close that Touch the Sky felt the wind from it, he wrapped his body hard around the pony's left foreleg.

For a moment his grip was precarious and he was almost thrown free. Then he found purchase and clung on for dear life, feeling the powerful pony shudder, then trip. Touch the Sky knew it might well fall on him, crushing him to death, but he had no other choice.

Spirit Path

The chestnut crashed hard to the ground, tossing Touch the Sky in a hard tumble across the open field. And the last thing the Cheyenne saw was Big Tree crashing with his pony. Then the Cheyenne's head struck a rock hard, and Touch the Sky's world shut down to darkness.

Chapter Thirteen

Both groups, Cheyenne and Comanche, had fallen silent at this unexpected outcome. The two warriors now lay less than a stone's throw apart, and for all anyone knew, both were dead.

On the Cheyenne side, Little Horse and Tangle Hair had started to run forward to check on Touch the Sky. On the Comanche side, likewise, braves started out to check on their fallen leader. But Black Elk and Stone Club quickly ordered them back. The fight was not over until they declared it so.

On the Cheyenne side, even Touch the Sky's enemies were clearly impressed by the amazing tactic he had just employed to bring down Big Tree's horse. Neither luck nor magic had anything to do with it. The courageous, agile brave had timed his move perfectly and shown the fighting courage of a she-bear defending her cubs.

Even the Comanches—who measured all men by their fighting skill—showed a certain respect in their faces. Big Tree had done well, they all agreed, and need not feel shame that he was on the ground. But this tall, brazen Cheyenne, clearly he was the victor—if he were still alive.

At almost the same moment, both men moved. And then all the spectators realized that whoever got up first would surely kill the other.

"Get up, Cheyenne!" Little Horse urged, his face grim and tense. "Stand up, buck! Today is not a good day to die."

"Quickly," Tangle Hair said. "Quickly, Touch the Sky! Stand and live!"

A moment later, as if obeying them, Touch the Sky slowly sat up and shook his head to clear it.

A mighty cheer rose from the Cheyenne side. Even those who had lately turned against the tall young buck—with the exception of Wolf Who Hunts Smiling, Medicine Flute, and a few of the Bull Whip troopers—showed loyalty to their tribe and pride in this *Shaiyena* victory.

Touch the Sky saw the dead mare, his lance still protruding from her bloody chest. And he saw Big Tree lying nearby, out cold but still breathing.

"Kill him, Touch the Sky!" a Cheyenne shouted. Several others chorused support.

"Remember the herd guards, Touch the Sky! This one led their slaughter. Kill him!"

Tangle Hair's war club was still lashed to Touch the Sky's legging sash. Touch the Sky untied the rawhide whang securing it. He felt the solid osage wood filling his grip as he slowly stood up and crossed to the supine Comanche.

By the rules of the fight, Touch the Sky was permitted a kill, so long as it was done with one of the weapons agreed upon. He assumed a wide stance over his downed foe and raised the club high, preparing to brain him.

He hesitated, some inner revulsion filling him. This was not a kill, he thought. It was simply slaughter, as one might thump a half-dead rabbit against a tree to finish it off.

"Kill him, Touch the Sky! Kill the Comanche dog!"

"This pig's afterbirth killed our elders and children and kidnapped our people. Kill him!"

Touch the Sky's muscles trembled. Still the revulsion filled him, for a true warrior disdained to kill a sleeping or unconscious foe.

He glanced over at his people. His eyes met Little Horse's. And quite clearly, Little Horse shook his head no. For in that moment, he, too, realized the same truth Arrow Keeper had spoken all along. Touch the Sky was marked out for a special destiny. He was bound by a higher code than most others. The words of old Arrow Keeper came back now to both of the youths, guiding their decision: *If gold will rust, what then will iron do?*

Touch the Sky was meant to someday lead the entire Cheyenne nation. The code of the warrior required more than courage and skill at killing. It also required magnanimity and compassion. It mattered not who Big Tree was. He was on the ground, defeated, and no more violence was required.

There was yet another consideration. Touch the Sky carefully gauged the mood of the Comanche warriors. Their weapons were to hand—was a bloody battle guaranteed the moment Touch the Sky killed Big Tree? So long as there was no loss of honor in it, Touch the Sky wanted to spare his comrades from a fight. If they must die, let it be a tribal decision, not because of his actions. A leader's first obligation was the welfare of his men.

A few of his own people hissed when Touch the Sky dropped the war club to the ground. But others, including Little Horse and Tangle Hair, looked at him with open admiration.

Touch the Sky faced the Comanches. He addressed them in English while a Comanche who spoke that language translated.

"I have fought your best warrior. Now here I stand, a living man. In the name of my tribe, I will accept our ponies back and call that debt settled. You may take this one"—he nodded toward the prone Comanche—"with you.

"Only, know this. I have no authority to speak for my entire tribe or to cancel other debts. Our guards were slain, and their ghosts cry out for bloody revenge! This is not a permanent peace I propose now, only a ceasing of present hostilities. What say you?"

There was a long pause while the Comanches discussed this thorny matter. It was Rain in His Face who finally answered.

"Your terms are accepted, Bear Caller! We saw you fight today, and you are a man to be respected. When our leader once again has sap flowing in him, we will send a word-bringer to announce the time and place to surrender the ponies."

This was well-spoken. Both braves had been careful to save face for the other tribe. Since this was ultimately a matter for his war leader to decide, Touch the Sky looked to Black Elk. This fierce warrior nodded once. Despite his hatred for Touch the Sky, Black Elk knew that the youth had acted and spoken like a straight-arrow Cheyenne.

Touch the Sky also noticed a look of relief pass over Wolf Who Hunts Smiling's face. Obviously, he did not want Big Tree killed. That would cost him his newest ally, Touch the Sky thought bitterly.

Clearly, he told himself, despite his narrow escape today, the trouble was far from over.

Wolf Who Hunts Smiling was worried.

His conspiracy with Medicine Flute had been working well. Slowly, steadily, they had chipped away at Touch the Sky's credibility, weakening his position in the tribe. And now this victory over Big Tree threatened to undo all their careful work.

"Brother," he said to Medicine Flute, "everywhere I turn, the talk is all about how White Man Runs Him brought down a charging pony. We can cast shadows over his medicine. But his skill as a warrior is there for all to see."

Medicine Flute nodded, his heavy-lidded gaze making him appear drowsy. The two braves had slipped away from the trail camp to plot their newest strategy.

"It was impressive," Medicine Flute said. "He is a warrior to reckon with. But did you notice how his face showed his loathing when it came time to kill Big Tree?"

"I have ears for this. We think as one, brother. Neither of us would have hesitated to smash an unconscious enemy's skull, though indeed I would have this Big Tree live. A leader of men cannot harbor a soft place in his heart like a woman."

"What can we do now? For, brother, truly, comets do not streak across the heavens often enough to suit our plans."

"No," Wolf Who Hunts Smiling agreed, "they do not. But as usual, I have an idea. And do not forget. We still do not have our pony herd back. Many things may still happen."

Wolf Who Hunts Smiling slipped a few fingers into his parfleche. They emerged holding a small, brightly polished bloodstone. A hole had been pierced into it and a rawhide thong strung through it.

"White Man Runs Him removed the rigging from his horse before the fight. But he left the hackamore on. He carried it with him when

147

he walked off the battlefield. Now it is on his bay.

"Take this. I will distract Woman Face and his companions while you slip in among the ponies and tie this to his hackamore."

Medicine Flute's heavy-lidded eyes widened with curiosity.

"Why, Panther Clan?"

Wolf Who Hunts Smiling grinned. "You will see, all in good time. Just agree with whatever I say, medicine man."

"Brother," Little Horse said, "now I see that your feeling about riding the white mare was just. Big Tree would have skewered you on that second pass, had your pony not attacked his chestnut."

Touch the Sky nodded. "She saved my life, yet I could not save hers."

"She died hard," Tangle Hair agreed. "But you did not kill her, Cheyenne."

"Sadly," Touch the Sky said, "I feel the victory only means more trouble from Big Tree. He is not one to calmly brook defeat."

"Do you think he will return our ponies?" Little Horse said.

Touch the Sky shook his head. "I cannot read the trail of his thoughts. He has treachery in his eyes. And much depends on his silent partner, Wolf Who Hunts Smiling."

The three braves were filing arrow points in the center of the temporary trail camp. All around them, warriors were at work on their weapons and battle rigs. Still, the Comanche word-bringer had not arrived with news about the return of the ponies.

A cooking fire blazed in the middle of camp. The hindquarters of an antelope were roasting over it on a spit. Touch the Sky saw Wolf Who Hunts Smiling walk close to the fire.

Wolf Who Hunts Smiling's hand flicked out quick as a snake and tossed something bright into the flames. A moment later, gunshots rang out and every brave scrambled for cover.

Medicine Flute worked quickly in the confusion. He crossed to the tethered ponies, picked out Touch the Sky's buffalo-hair bridle, and quickly tied the bloodstone to it. He slipped away again, unobserved.

"Brothers!" Wolf Who Hunts Smiling shouted even as Black Elk began barking orders to form a defensive perimeter. "False alarm! Rest easy! My shot pouch rolled too close to the fire and some primer caps went off."

"Such carelessness, cousin," Black Elk said sternly, "is the mark of a green warrior."

Wolf Who Hunts Smiling nodded, his face contrite. But clearly he had only been waiting to address the entire camp. Now was his chance, while he had their attention.

"Brothers, hear me. Medicine Flute has asked me to be silent about a thing. He is modest and desires no credit. But I would speak it."

"We are not coy maidens in their sewing lodge," Black Elk said impatiently. "Speak this thing or hold your tongue."

"Earlier, we all watched White Man Runs Him—"

"His name is Touch the Sky," Little Horse cut in hotly, "a name he lived up to again today. If any brave deserves the name of traitor, Panther Clan, it is you."

Rage smoldered in Wolf Who Hunts Smiling's eyes. But he only smiled mockingly, a smile that promised trouble to come.

"Earlier we all watched Touch the Sky perform amazing feats. Indeed, his skill seemed almost supernatural. And I say it was. For Medicine Flute placed a powerful magic talisman on his pony's hackamore. He blessed it with his strongest medicine."

"There is no talisman on my bridle," Touch the Sky retorted. "I inspected it before the fight."

"Inspect it now, Woman Fa—Cheyenne! I tell you it is there. I caught Medicine Flute tying it on in secret before the fight."

Touch the Sky spoke quietly to Tangle Hair. This brave crossed toward the ponies.

"And tell us, Panther Clan," Touch the Sky said. "Since when has Medicine Flute begun worrying about my fate?"

"Mock, pretend shaman! He did this magnanimous act because he would protect any Cheyenne. He has no quarrel with you. You were riding into an impossible fight, and he did not wish to see you slaughtered. Also, the return of our ponies rested on the outcome of this battle."

Through all this, Medicine Flute sat unperturbed, playing his eerie music as if none of this concerned him. The rest had formed a circle.

They stared hard at Tangle Hair as he crossed back to the camp circle and held up a smooth bloodstone on a rawhide thong.

"This was indeed tied to your pony's hackamore," he said, confusion clear in his eyes.

Chapter Fourteen

At the first opportunity Wolf Who Hunts Smiling rode out, claiming he was on a scouting mission. But he knew the Comanche word-bringer named Stone Club, who like the Cheyenne spoke some English, would be lurking in the area.

Wolf Who Hunts Smiling made sure he had not been followed from camp. Then he tied a white truce flag to his bridle—the prearranged signal that it was safe for the Comanche to reveal himself.

The meeting took place in a sandy wash, sheltered from the eyes of any Cheyenne scouts or sentries. Wolf Who Hunts Smiling explained his latest plan carefully. When he finished speaking, Stone Club's eyes were bright with appreciative mirth.

"Big Tree will like this," he said, slowly nodding. "He lost face in the encounter with the tall one. This plan, it will gain him a fitting revenge. You are aptly named, Wolf Who Hunts Smiling. I see good days ahead for our two tribes now that you and Big Tree have shared a pipe."

"Men of force and action will do well in this rich land," Wolf Who Hunts Smiling said. "It is there for the taking, as the hair faces understand.

"But my people, led by compromising cowards and white men's dogs, hope to follow the peace road. They must be more like your tribe, who kill the paleface intruders and steal their goods at every opportunity. First we must kill or remove from power these pretend Indians who preach coexistence with hair faces."

"I have ears for this. We Comanche have earned the name of the Red Raiders of the Plains. We have killed more white settlers than any tribe. Especially have we slaughtered these bragging, swaggering Texans, whom we hate above all other white intruders.

"But truly, the paleface numbers are vast, as vast as the very plains they hope to conquer. You speak the straight word, Cheyenne. We red men must bury the hatchet, put our own battles behind us, and turn with a vengeance to the slaughter of these stinking foreigners."

Stone Club added a sly smile as he prepared to ride out. "And of course, while eliminating these whites and the Indians who play the dog for them, perhaps a few Indians will profit handsomely?"

Wolf Who Hunts Smiling matched his grin. "Our thoughts run one way, Red Raider. Perhaps I would have been happy as a Comanche."

Stone Club nodded. "You would make a fine Quohada! You are brazen and crafty and make the he-bear talk with the best. I will take your message to Big Tree. And count upon it, he will approve this plan."

Big Tree had indeed lost face in the encounter with the tall Cheyenne warrior who rode the pure white pony.

True, the Comanche had not been seriously hurt. Nor had the battle been an outright victory for the Cheyenne. After all, Touch the Sky had been knocked to the ground first, and his pony had been killed.

But unknowingly, the Cheyenne had humiliated Big Tree by not killing him. To many of the Comanche braves, the gesture of sparing his life was also a gesture of contempt. It suggested that Big Tree was too worthless to bother killing, as one might leave a coward to wallow in his own disgrace.

Big Tree had sent a word-bringer to announce the time and place for returning the ponies. But in fact, he had no plans to keep his word. Instead, he had intended to herd them fast toward the Blanco Canyon, the nearly impregnable Comanche stronghold in the middle of the burning Staked Plain.

Now, however, he listened with great interest as Stone Club explained the latest plan.

"It is simple," the brave said. "We are to drive

the ponies to the designated spot as you promised. Then, in an apparently surprise move, we are to form a skirmish line and attack. At this point, the Cheyenne called Medicine Flute will ride forward and play his magic flute.

"Wolf Who Hunts Smiling has spread the word among his brothers that his music can frighten off an enemy. At the first notes, our warriors are to shriek, as if in mortal terror, then flee."

Big Tree thought about this. "But we would lose the ponies?"

Stone Club nodded. "We would. But the encounter will be bloodless for us, yet it will finally turn the Cheyennes against this Touch the Sky. This would place Medicine Flute in a special position of power. And we will then profit much more handsomely later."

Big Tree was ironic enough to appreciate all this. For of course, once Medicine Flute rose to power, so would Wolf Who Hunts Smiling. But Big Tree was no fool. This Wolf Who Hunts Smiling, he had no intention of sharing any wealth or power with other leaders. He would use them so long as they were helpful, then kill them. For after all, this was what Big Tree himself would do.

"Still," he said, musing out loud, "according to this plan, the tall shaman would still be alive."

"He would be," Stone Club agreed, watching his leader's weather-seamed face shrewdly. For though Stone Club had spoken conciliatory words to Wolf Who Hunts Smiling, he knew his leader would have his own plans.

Big Tree said, "If we must sacrifice the ponies, we should at least have the satisfaction of killing the tall one and a few more Cheyennes."

The Comanche leader made up his mind. "Tell Wolf Who Hunts Smiling that I agree to his plan. But now have ears, Quohada, for we Comanches will add a surprise of our own."

Touch the Sky knew some serious treachery was afoot.

A Comanche word-bringer had arrived with news from Big Tree. As promised, the Cheyenne pony herd would be returned. The exchange was due to take place in one sleep, on the same wide-open flat near the Pueblo Mountains where the fateful duel had taken place.

But Touch the Sky knew better. Long ago Arrow Keeper had assured him there was no more despicable and untrustworthy tribe in the red nations than the Comanches. Even the Pawnee did not surpass them in cunning and deceit and sheer, bloodthirsty evil. Clearly, trouble was in the wind.

Black Elk, as war leader, was no fool either. He called an informal outdoor council on the night before the exchange was set.

"Brothers, if all goes well we will have our ponies back before the next appearance of the Always Star. I do not think the cricket-eating Comanches are keen for a fight with us. Our fathers and uncles defeated them at Wolf Creek in the bloodiest battle they have ever seen.

"And yet, they are fully capable of some

deceit. Their fighting style has been shaped by long contact with the barbarous Spaniards. More than one of their victims has died in his sleep after being invited into their camp for food and drink. Watch their eyes closely, keep your best weapon to hand, and do not turn your back on them."

"Your words are well-spoken," Chief Gray Thunder said. "What is said of the Apaches is equally true of the Comanches. 'When you can see them, be careful. When you cannot see them, be even more careful.'"

Wolf Who Hunts Smiling rose to speak. "Brothers! Black Elk and our chief have spoken wise words we may pick up and examine. Medicine Flute and I have discussed this thing. He agrees that some danger looms. Therefore, he has strong medicine planned against our enemy."

Touch the Sky, Little Horse, and Tangle Hair all exchanged glances in the flickering light of the campfire. Not all had been completely convinced by the talisman found tied to Touch the Sky's hackamore. But this, added to the miracle of the burning star and his two visions, had many convinced that Medicine Flute was a straight-arrow shaman.

Even now, Medicine Flute sat aloof and drowsy eyed, his leg-bone flute silent in his lap. He had only reluctantly stopped playing, in recognition of the council. His eyes met Touch the Sky's for a moment, mocking him.

"What manner of strong medicine, cousin?" Black Elk said.

"You have been listening to it for many sleeps now. Many in the tribe have foolishly complained of the music produced by his bone flute. And yet, why do you think he made that instrument from the bone of a defeated enemy? The answer is simple. Because the notes it produces are powerful medicine against any enemy."

Black Elk's fierce scowl took on a thoughtful cast. He knew, of course, that his cousin and Medicine Flute had cleverly been playing the fox to discredit Touch the Sky. And Black Elk approved of it because he hated this squaw-stealing dog who would put on the old moccasin by bulling his Honey Eater. But what was Wolf Who Hunts Smiling up to now? This leg-bone flute, truly its music was odd and unnerving. Was there medicine to it? More likely, his cousin was simply counting on the Comanches not to attack.

"This night," Wolf Who Hunts Smiling continued, "Medicine Flute will separate himself and perform a sweat-lodge ceremony. He will pray and make offerings to the High Holy Ones. And then, if trouble takes us by the tail tomorrow, his flute will save us. For played on the battlefield, it will scatter an enemy as surely as shotgun pellets scatter crows."

This claim caused a low hum of conversation around the fire. Touch the Sky rose.

"Brothers! Gray Thunder has reminded me of my promise not to publicly accuse Wolf Who Hunts Smiling of grazing with our enemy. I will respect my chief on that score and hold

GET FOUR BOOKS TOTALLY
FREE—A VALUE BETWEEN
$16 AND $20

PLEASE RUSH
MY FOUR FREE
BOOKS TO ME
RIGHT AWAY!

Leisure Western Book Club
P.O. Box 6613
Edison, NJ 08818-6613

AFFIX
STAMP
HERE

my tongue. I have only this to say.

"Earlier, I saw Wolf Who Hunts Smiling deliberately throw something into the fire. The objects were small and bright, like primer caps. Moments later we were all distracted by what we thought was gunfire. And then, only behold! Suddenly a talisman appears on my horse. Warriors, draw your own conclusions. I say only this. Nothing can destroy a tribe more quickly than treachery from within."

"I agree," Wolf Who Hunts Smiling shot back. "And I say only this. I have never drunk strong water with paleface dogs. I have never deserted my tribe during danger to go fight white men's battles. I did not collaborate with white miners to build a road for the iron horse across our ancient homeland. I have never scattered the buffalo herds with my white man's stink.

"Who is the traitor here? A straight-arrow Cheyenne whose father was killed by blue-bloused devils, or a pretend Cheyenne who arrived among us wearing shoes and offering his hand for us to shake?"

Touch the Sky leveled a murderous stare at his enemy. "Strut and throw your arms about. You are like the white liars who leap on tree stumps to scream their untruths. Only my promise to Gray Thunder forces me to bite back a reply about traitors. I say this again, Panther Clan. The time is fast approaching when I am going to kill you."

Later that night many watched, respectfully curious, as Medicine Flute fashioned a sweat lodge from hides draped over a bent-branch frame. He heated a circle of rocks to a red glow, then poured water on them. Late into the night, while steam billowed from the makeshift lodge, he chanted and prayed and played his disturbing music.

Touch the Sky, in contrast, quietly separated himself from the rest. He found a little copse where pinon trees grew close, forming a little covered shelter. He ensconced himself within. Long into the night, as the noises from camp settled into slumber, he lay wide awake.

For every battle road, Arrow Keeper had once told him, *there is a spirit road.*

Touch the Sky did not chant. He did not make offerings or shake snake teeth in a gourd. He merely lay quietly, stopping all conscious thought and attending, instead, to the language of his senses. Thus, Arrow Keeper had assured him, could the true visionary reach the upward path of the Spirit Way.

When his guiding vision finally arrived, it was neither very dramatic nor very detailed. He simply saw himself, riding alone in front of the rest of his companions. He carried no weapons, performed no amazing riding tricks. In fact, only one detail was out of the ordinary. Instead of being stripped to his clout for battle, as Cheyennes did, he wore the beautiful mountain lion skin Arrow Keeper had once given him.

It was a paltry revelation. So little, in fact, that he wondered if it had truly been a vision.

But he decided to act on faith and assume it was.

Tomorrow, against the most treacherous enemy of the *Shaiyena* people, he would ride unarmed into the teeth of his foes.

Chapter Fifteen

"Brother," Medicine Flute said, a nervous edge to his voice, "a thing troubles me."

He and Wolf Who Hunts Smiling stood a little way off from the rest, rigging their ponies. This was the day that Big Tree had named for the return of the ponies. Throughout camp, a grim sense of purpose could be felt. Braves attended to their weapons and applied their battle paint. They carefully rigged their ponies for possible combat, securing weapons and shields so they would be ready to hand in the heat of battle.

Wolf Who Hunts Smiling frowned impatiently. The normally imperturbable Medicine Flute showed signs of nervous tension now that the confrontation approached.

"Buck," he said, "I am not skilled in divination. Either speak this thing or get on with your preparations."

"These Comanches, they are no braves to fool with. And Big Tree, his cunning would make a fox blush."

Wolf Who Hunts Smiling shrugged. "So? Everyone knows this."

"But, brother, your plan would have me ride out ahead armed only with my flute, since I cannot play it and wield a weapon. What if these marauders have deceit in their sashes? I will be among the first to fall."

"And what of that? You will thus die the glorious death of a warrior. Do you think I will be riding at the rear? Would you rather die in your tipi like some ancient squaw with drool on her chin?"

In fact, Medicine Flute did hope to die of old age in his tipi. But the men of Wolf Who Hunts Smiling's Panther Clan would tolerate no fainthearted braves. They placed great importance on never showing fear in their voices or faces. Either a man was a stout warrior or he was a woman. A young man of the Panther Clan had once fled from a battle. After that, he was forced to wear a dress and wait on the men until, in mortal shame, he fell on his own knife.

"I am not afraid of death," Medicine Flute lied. "But like you, I have great ambition. I wish to taste the fruits of power before I cross over. If I die now, all of our careful scheming comes to naught, a thing of smoke. And, buck, if I die, you lose your best chance for doing the hurt dance on Woman Face."

These words flew straight arrow and struck the sarcasm from Wolf Who Hunts Smiling's manner.

"Well said, brother. Only, do not shed so much brain sweat worrying about Big Tree. True it is, he is a treacherous Comanche. But he, too, thirsts for power as we do. However, you are right, we have no assurance he will not outfox us. Therefore, know this. I will ride beside you, close as your very shadow, and protect you with my life. You know how I fight."

"Like ten men," Medicine Flute said, genuinely reassured. Many considered Wolf Who Hunts Smiling the best warrior in the tribe—though just as many gave the nod to Touch the Sky.

As for Wolf Who Hunts Smiling, he was less worried about Big Tree than he was about his cousin Black Elk. Once Medicine Flute's playing scattered the Comanches, he would again suspect Wolf Who Hunts Smiling of grazing with their enemy. But his joy at seeing Touch the Sky humiliated would make him less eager to cry traitor.

And Wolf Who Hunts Smiling already had his strategy ready. He would remind his cousin that the Comanches, too, were superstitious—witness the roadrunner skins tied to the tails of their ponies for good luck. Perhaps, he would argue to his cousin, the leg-bone flute might actually frighten them. After all, Woman Face had once sent the entire Pawnee tribe running merely by painting a naked white boy and telling him to act insane.

Besides, Black Elk was clearly confused on the question of medicine. He still believed things Wolf Who Hunts Smiling had rejected in his thirst for power. He might well end up believing in the medicine flute—even better for Wolf Who Hunts Smiling's plans.

"If Big Tree does have some tricks in his sash," Wolf Who Hunts Smiling added, "know this. In the heat of battle, it is not uncommon for warriors to accidentally kill their own men."

Medicine Flute watched his companion's wily, furtive face closely. "You mean Touch the Sky?"

"Who else, buck? For I have made up my mind. If the Comanches flee when you start playing your flute, as agreed, White Man Runs Him will lose the last of his credibility. If they outfox us and attack, I will kill him in the confusion. Either way, after this day he will sleep with the worms."

"Brother," Little Horse said, watching Wolf Who Hunts Smiling and Medicine Flute confer, "I am no more of a shaman than Medicine Flute. But I clearly see trouble preparing to rear its ugly head."

"Indeed, brother. It needs no strong medicine to read such sign as they make."

Touch the Sky, Little Horse, and Tangle Hair were making their final preparations. Using claybank paint, they smeared their faces red, yellow, and black, the traditional Cheyenne battle colors. Bow strings had been checked, rifles cleaned, and shields prepared.

"Cheyenne," Tangle Hair said to Touch the Sky, "you are painted, and I see that you plan to wear the fine mountain lion skin you wear for the Sun Dance. But why are you not attending to your weapons?"

"I am wearing my weapons, buck."

Confused, Tangle Hair looked to see if a knife or pistol were tucked behind the skin. "Then you have made them invisible, brother."

But Little Horse, who knew Touch the Sky better than anyone else in the tribe knew him, understood immediately. This had to do with the vision Touch the Sky had sought last night. However, Indians carefully skirted too much direct talk about holy matters. Things of the spirit were private and to be respected.

"Know this much," Little Horse said to Tangle Hair, "and then let it alone. The hand of the Good Supernatural is in this thing. Count upon it, no brave riding out today goes better armed than Touch the Sky."

Understanding glimmered in Tangle Hair's eyes, and he fell respectfully silent. But secretly, Touch the Sky wished he had as much confidence as Little Horse. For even now the words of old Arrow Keeper drifted back from the hinterland of memory:

Be warned. A medicine vision can be either a revelation or a curse. An enemy's bad medicine may place a false vision over our eyes, and we may act upon it, aiding our enemies and destroying those whom we seek to help.

* * *

The Cheyenne warriors rode out in a double column, singing their battle songs.

Black Elk led one column, his cousin Wolf Who Hunts Smiling the other, Medicine Flute close at his side. The day was clear, a bright yellow ball of sun blazing from a sky of deep, bottomless blue except for a few puffy white clouds out over the horizon. In the distance, the Pueblo Mountains pushed their round humps into the soft belly of the sky.

Touch the Sky spotted the dust haze even before they reached the vast, open field where he had recently battled Big Tree. The cry went up throughout the ranks.

"Here come our ponies!"

"See them?"

"There is our herd!"

At least Big Tree planned to show up. It just might be possible, Touch the Sky told himself, that Big Tree would return the herd. Yet, his shaman's sense told him otherwise and never had he known it to steer him wrong.

His powerful little bay, too, sensed some excitement in the wind. Several times Touch the Sky was forced to pull hard on her hackamore to bring her back into line.

"Look here," the Bull Whip trooper named Snake Eater called out to his companions, nodding toward Touch the Sky. "He has dressed in a fine skin, but carries no weapon. Like the Crow warriors who fuss like women over their hair, he cares more about his looks than his manhood."

"Would you care to bridge the gap, Bull Whip," Touch the Sky replied calmly enough, "and see if I have my manhood with me?"

Snake Eater wisely declined this invitation. Now the ground thundered and trembled as the vast herd was driven closer by the skillful Comanches.

Black Elk halted his warriors on one flank of the grassy field.

"Live close to your weapons!" he called out. "Watch their eyes, and do not let them slip behind you. Whatever they say or do, no matter how friendly they may act, do not be foolish enough to let down your guard. These dogs will offer one hand to shake while the other guts you."

The herd thundered closer. Despite the mounting tension, Touch the Sky could not help marveling at the magnificent sight of so many fine ponies.

Then something began to trouble him. By now, the Comanches should have started ringing the herd to slow it. Instead, they were all riding behind the herd, driving it relentlessly on. A moment later a cool tickle moved up the bumps of his spine as he realized that Big Tree meant to overrun them with the charging herd!

"Black Elk!" he shouted. "They mean to trample us!"

And instantly Black Elk, too, saw the plan. Quickly, he formed the narrow columns into one single line stretching across the field.

"Charge the ponies!" he screamed. "Turn

them to the right flank and expose the enemy!"

"Hi-ya, hii-ya!"

Loosing their fierce battle cry, firing their weapons into the air, and waving their streamered lances, the Cheyenne warriors rushed forward. The plan worked perfectly. The line angled so that the ponies veered to the right. And within moments the two tribes were charging each other in a classic plains battle formation.

Medicine Flute's normally heavy-lidded eyes were wide with fright. He started to follow the ponies, but Wolf Who Hunts Smiling caught his bridle.

"You white-livered coward! Put that bone to your lips and play or I will have your guts for garters."

"But Big Tree has decided to attack!"

"His plan failed, fool. Now he will have to keep his word. Ride forward and play or die on the spot!"

Caught between the sap and the bark, Medicine Flute did as ordered. He had played perhaps a dozen notes when a Comanche bullet shattered his flute, driving a jagged piece of it through his cheek.

A heartbeat later an arrow caught Snake Eater in the eye, sending him to the ground writhing in agony. Now the two bands were within easy range of bullets and arrows.

But Touch the Sky felt his mouth dry with fear when he realized most of the Comanche braves were armed with the new repeating rifles of the type used by white buffalo hunters. It would be a slaughter against the Cheyennes armed with single-shot percussion rifles.

"Save a place for me at the scalp dance tonight, brother!" he shouted to Little Horse, even as he jabbed his knees hard into the bay's flanks.

Now the tough little mustang showed her magnificent breeding as she surged ahead of the rest. Touch the Sky bent low over her neck and urged her on. Another Cheyenne flung his arms to the heavens and flew from his pony as a bullet struck him in his lights. But now the Comanche warriors had noticed Touch the Sky in his colorful skin, surging unarmed ahead of the rest.

Repeated flashes of light told Touch the Sky where Big Tree was, his mirror-speckled shield reflecting in the bright sun. Deliberately, Touch the Sky bore down on their best fighter.

Big Tree's two quivers were stuffed with new arrows. He grinned, ignoring the rifle in his scabbard, and reached back to grab a handful of arrows. This was going to be like shooting a prairie chicken.

"He is mine!" he shouted to his men.

The fool rode even closer. Big Tree had launched five arrows before the first one had found his target's range.

Still the tall Cheyenne charged closer.

Big Tree frowned, grabbed another handful of arrows, launched them with lightning rapidity. Pieces of Touch the Sky's kit and rigging flapped loose, his hackamore snapped, several arrows snagged in his doeskin leggings but never touched his flesh. Still he charged, so close now he could count the silver conchos on Big Tree's tall shako hat.

Big Tree's face went numb. He had fired at least 15 arrows!

By now the rest of the Comanches had noticed what was happening and halted their charge, shock and confusion distorting their faces. Little Horse surged closer. His revolving-barrel shotgun blasted, and the Comanche named Stone Club dropped from his pony, his face shredded to raw meat.

Tangle Hair's British trade rifle cracked, and the brave named Gall took a slug flush through the throat.

"Kill him!" Big Tree shouted to his men as Touch the Sky was on the verge of overriding him.

A score of Comanche weapons opened up at almost point-blank range. Bullets and arrows fanned Touch the Sky's locks back off his forehead, hummed like angry hornets around his ears, and shredded the rest of his rope rigging and demolished his kit.

Still, the tall, broad-shouldered Cheyenne rode closer, his face split by a mocking grin.

This finally unstrung the Comanche nerves completely. They did not wait for a command from Big Tree. As one, those who had not already fallen spun their mounts around and fled from this terrible big medicine, from this terrifying Cheyenne shaman.

It took most of the daylight remaining to round up the scattered ponies and group them in the field for the night. Black Elk sent out a small guard to make sure their enemy would not return, but no one really expected them to. Nor was one sign of them spotted.

The mission had ended perfectly. They had regained almost the entire herd, minus the few ponies sacrificed by the Comanches along the way. Just as important, they had killed a half-dozen Comanche braves, evening the score for the Cheyenne herd guards slaughtered when the ponies were taken.

An impromptu scalp dance was indeed held that night. The warriors danced fast and hard around a blazing fire, their knees kicking high while fellow Cheyennes kept time with sticks on a hollow log.

True, two braves had been killed, four others wounded including Medicine Flute. But all agreed that it was a light price to pay for this victory. And even Touch the Sky's enemies admitted he had saved them from disaster against so many repeating rifles.

"Medicine Flute," a brave called out as the would-be shaman sulked by himself at the edge of the circle. "I saw you wearing a piece of bone in your face earlier today. Is this the new fashion of your Spotted Ponies Clan?"

Several braves laughed. But the disgruntled Wolf Who Hunts Smiling was never one to admit defeat.

"You mock, fools! Were you present when this shaman set a star on fire and sent it across the heavens? Do you deny this?"

His words were greeted by silence. For they

contained a hard nugget of truth. Everyone had indeed seen this thing.

Once again Touch the Sky chafed. For he could not reveal the truth without placing Honey Eater in mortal danger.

"This thing today," Wolf Who Hunts Smiling continued. "You all say it was Woman Fa—Touch the Sky's big medicine that saved us. Only, think on this thing. Did he bless this mountain lion skin? Was his magic involved? No! This skin was given to him.

"And truly, how do you even know the mountain lion skin is blessed with strong medicine? Maiyun reveals himself in strange ways. It could well have been Medicine Flute's bone instrument that cast the magic aura about Touch the Sky. Stranger things have happened."

Most ignored him, returning to their dance. But later, as Touch the Sky turned his bay out to graze with the rest of the herd, Wolf Who Hunts Smiling caught him alone.

"Gloat, Woman Face. In the Panther Clan we have a saying. The worm turns slowly, indeed, but it always turns. Best have eyes in your back. I once walked between you and the fire. I have not taken back that promise to kill you."

Touch the Sky met his enemy's furtive, swift-as-minnow eyes.

"You are a murderer, Panther Clan. You have shed the blood of your own, and I no longer consider you a Cheyenne. I will not kill you in cold blood while you sleep, as you would kill me. But count upon it, I will kill you."

Wolf Who Hunts Smiling grinned, clearly enjoying this. "Then we understand each other?"

Touch the Sky nodded, his mouth a grim, determined slit. "We understand each other."

"I will enjoy killing you, shaman. You are a worthy enemy."

"Is it so? As for me, I will not enjoy killing you, for I consider you a pig's afterbirth, not a man."

The grin faded from Wolf Who Hunts Smiling's eyes, and rage twisted his face. Now it was Touch the Sky's turn to grin.

"Look. Even now the woman shows her feelings in her face," he said, borrowing one of Wolf Who Hunts Smiling's favorite taunts.

Still grinning, Touch the Sky walked away to join his fellow warriors in the victory dance.

MANKILLER

Prologue

In the year the white man's winter count called 1840, a Northern Cheyenne infant was the sole survivor of a bluecoat ambush on his band near the North Platte. His Cheyenne name lost forever, he was adopted by white parents in the Wyoming river-bend settlement of Bighorn Falls.

John and Sarah Hanchon named the boy Matthew and raised him as if he were their own. He grew to be a tall, broad-shouldered youth with the even and pleasing looks that had earned the Cheyenne tribe the name of the Beautiful People among their red brothers. There were constant reminders of the fear and mistrust many settlers felt toward an Indian in their midst. But his parents were good to him, as were his young friend Corey Robinson and the former mountain man called Old Knobby. Matthew grew up sensing something was wrong, but nonetheless feeling accepted in his limited world.

Then came his sixteenth year and the tragedy that would leave him an outcast. When the wealthy rancher Hiram Steele caught his daughter Kristen with Matthew in their secret meeting place, Steele ordered one of his wranglers to viciously beat Matthew. He also warned the hapless youth that if he caught them together again, he would kill the Cheyenne. Fearing for Matthew's life, Kristen lied and told him she never wanted to see him again.

Hard upon the heels of this followed more trouble. Seth Carlson, a cavalry officer stationed at nearby Fort Bates, had staked a claim to Kristen. To Matthew's misery Carlson added a threat. If Matthew didn't clear out of Bighorn Falls for good, Carlson would destroy the Hanchon's contract to supply Fort Bates, which was the main reason why their mercantile business was flourishing.

Rejected by the white world, and fearful of hurting his adopted parents by staying, Matthew hardened his heart for whatever lay ahead. Then he left Bighorn Falls forever and fled north to the Powder River country of the Northern Cheyenne. But he quickly discovered that the red man, too, feared and mistrusted him. Captured by braves from Chief Yellow Bear's camp, he was declared a spy for the whites and sentenced to torture and death.

A wily, hotheaded young brave named Wolf

Who Hunts Smiling was on the verge of gutting Matthew when Arrow Keeper interceded. The tribe's medicine man and keeper of the sacred Medicine Arrows, Arrow Keeper had recently been to Medicine Lake, where a great and epic vision was placed over his eyes. This vision prophesied the arrival of a young stranger— the long-lost son of a great Cheyenne chief named Running Antelope. This stranger would someday lead the Cheyenne people in their last great struggle for freedom. But he would also be doomed to suffer many hardships before he could lift high the lance of leadership.

Arrow Keeper discovered the mark of the warrior buried past Matthew's hairline, and that sign convinced him the youth was the same war leader of his medicine dream. But Wolf Who Hunts Smiling was outraged when Arrow Keeper's interference spared the prisoner's life. So was his older cousin, the stern, young war leader Black Elk, who was jealous of the glances exchanged between Matthew and Honey Eater, Chief Yellow Bear's unmarried daughter. Many others, too, were angered when Arrow Keeper announced that the accused spy would not only be spared from execution—he would live with the tribe and train under Black Elk as a warrior!

Arrow Keeper buried Matthew's white name forever in a hole, renaming the tall youth Touch the Sky. In the beginning, his fate seemed hopeless. Hated and scorned, called Woman Face and White Man's Dog, he could not ride bareback, hunt buffalo, or even aim a throwing ax. Adding to his grief, Wolf Who Hunts Smiling walked between Touch the Sky and the campfire—the Cheyenne way of announcing his intention to kill the tall stranger.

Then Chief Yellow Bear's camp fell under attack by a vastly superior Pawnee force. Teaming up with his new friend Little Horse, Touch the Sky managed to use white man's trickery to frighten away the superstitious Pawnees and save his tribe. He was honored in a special council, but such recognition only further hardened his enemies—especially Wolf Who Hunts Smiling and Black Elk—against him.

Thus began his long and bitter struggle for acceptance. He faced Henri Lagace and his murderous whiskey peddlers; Wes Munro and his well-armed land-grabbers; Kiowas and Comanches and Comanchero slave traders; Seth Carlson and his Indian-killing regiment; the crazy-by-thunder renegade Blackfoot Siski-dee; white buffalo hiders and the vindictive Comanche war leader Big Tree. Through all this he developed into a warrior worth five braves.

Arrow Keeper, recognizing Touch the Sky's gift of visions, selected him to be the tribe's next shaman and Keeper of the Arrows. Yet, his Cheyenne enemies cleverly turned appearances against him, planted damaging rumors, and otherwise intrigued to keep many in the tribe suspicious of him.

Forced to marry Black Elk when her father died, Honey Eater still loved only Touch the Sky. Black Elk's jealous wrath could have exploded at any moment, leading him to kill either or both of them. And numerous enemies outside the tribe, red men, soldiers, and hair-face settlers, were eager to lift Touch the Sky's scalp.

Chapter One

"Brothers!" the young brave called Tangle Hair shouted. "Look to the north. Thunder Bonnet is flashing a signal!"

Tangle Hair sat his pony on a grassy rise between the Powder River and the many clan circles of Chief Gray Thunder's camp. Below him a group of young braves sat in the new grass, fashioning arrow shafts from green oak and chipping points out of flintstones. Among them were Touch the Sky, Little Horse, Two Twists, and several of Tangle Hair's troop brothers from the Bow String Soldier Society.

Touch the Sky was by far the tallest and broadest in the shoulders, muscled more like the Apaches to the southwest than a typical slender-limbed Plains warrior of the north country. Like his companions he had recently abandoned his leggings and leather shirt as the warm moons took over. All wore soft doeskin clouts, elkskin moccasins, wide leather bands around their left wrists to protect them from the sharp slap of bow strings.

Touch the Sky and his companions rose and looked toward the serried peaks of the Bighorn Mountains. Day and night a sentry was kept posted there on the high benchland between the mountains and the confluence of the Powder and Little Powder, site of Chief Gray Thunder's summer camp. The sentry always kept a fragment of mirror to flash signals back into the valley on sunny days.

"Tangle Hair, call his message out for us," Touch the Sky said. "From here we cannot see over the tipis."

Others in camp, too, had seen the signals. The word spread through the Indian village like grassfire in a windstorm. Cheyennes frustrated their enemies by keeping many dogs for security; upset by the unusual activity, they were raising a howling, barking clamor. Any message from a sentry was important and meant someone was approaching. But was it friend or foe?

Tangle Hair shaded his eyes with one hand. He squinted into the brassy glow on the horizon, where a late afternoon sun reflected off rock spires and endless veins of mica and quartz and feldspar.

The clamor of excited dogs and ponies and children was too loud to shout above. Touch the Sky watched his friend pull a finger across his forehead, signifying the brim of a hat.

"White men approach," he said to his friends, translating Tangle Hair's sign language.

Touch the Sky's words brought a sense of urgency to the faces of his companions. Their Sioux cousins had spent a miserable winter fighting white soldiers and militiamen in the Black Hills. It was rumored the whiteskins were ready to subdue the Cheyennes and force them to accept a reservation far from this place.

"But these whiteskins come in peace," Touch the Sky said, watching Tangle Hair lift two empty hands toward them. "It is a caravan bringing our talking-paper goods!"

A cheer rose throughout camp as others farther up the bank translated out loud. This was indeed an important event. The cold moons had been hard. Long had the people huddled over the firepits in their tipis, depleting their supplies of meat, flour, tobacco, and sugar. The arrival of this caravan meant the end of much suffering, a chance to let the winter-starved ponies graze and fatten for the hunts to come.

"Look there," Little Horse said, pointing across the vast central clearing toward the circle where the Panther Clan pitched their tipis. As was the custom, each entrance faced east to the rising sun. "Wolf Who Hunts Smiling and Black Elk hurry to rig their horses and ride out. Like bully coyotes snatching the red meat, they want to make first claim to the best goods."

"In this they show many faces," Two Twists said bitterly.

He was the youngest of the group and named after his preference for wearing his hair in two braids instead of one. Under Touch the Sky, he had led the junior warriors in a successful defense against Kiowa and Comanche raiders. Like Little Horse, he was loyal to Touch the Sky, though many in the tribe called the tall brave a spy because he had been raised by whites and still had friends among the settlers and blue-bloused soldiers. To be his friend within the tribe was a risky business.

"They hurry for their share," Two Twists said, "yet they bellowed loudest when Touch the Sky agreed to be a pathfinder for the hair-face miners and their iron horse. They called Touch the Sky a white man's dog. They said Caleb Riley and his crew were thieves stealing the red homeland. They huffed up their chests, played the big Indians, and said they wanted no part of the profits."

"Now look," Little Horse said. "Carrion birds flocking to the kill."

Touch the Sky said nothing, though certainly his friends had truth firmly by the tail. He and Little Horse had risked their lives to earn this annual delivery of goods—goods which Black Elk, Wolf Who Hunts Smiling, and many of their brothers in the highly feared Bull Whip Soldier Society had sworn never to touch. Caleb, younger brother of the cavalry officer Tom Riley, had promised a consignment every year. This profit sharing would continue so long as his company transported their ore on a railroad spur line across Cheyenne hunting grounds to Laramie, where it was shipped back to the St. Louis settlements.

13

"Thunder Bonnet adds more!" Tangle Hair shouted. The clamor had quieted some and he could be heard again. "The caravan will arrive in the time it takes the sun to travel the width of three lodge poles."

Suddenly a holiday mood prevailed throughout camp. Toothless old grandmothers smiled wide, anticipating fine white sugar for their yarrow tea; young women spoke excitedly of new calico and linsey cloth for dresses; even the stern-faced warriors grinned sheepishly at each other, heartened by the prospect of folding knives, moist brown tobacco, and bars of pig lead for moulding new bullets.

Against his will, Touch the Sky let his gaze cut to the finest tipi within the Panther Clan circle, one boasting new hide covers and meat racks out back—Black Elk's. And there, speaking to her aunt, Sharp Nosed Woman, was Honey Eater.

Black Elk had ridden out, and Touch the Sky knew it should be safe to look at her. But long, careful habit made him slow to do so. In matters pertaining to battle, Black Elk's mind was usually clear and strong. But his jealousy turned even a glance from another warrior into an excuse to punish Honey Eater savagely. When Touch the Sky's eyes found her, she was looking his way.

They held each other for a long moment with gazes of mutual need, unaware of anyone or anything else. Their love had become such a hunted, forbidden thing that moments like these were as rare, pleasing, and disturbing to them as stolen caresses. It was the great, unspoken secret of village life. An old grandmother of the Sky Walker Clan had once sung their love to entertain the young girls. Since then, the verses had been sung over and over in the sewing lodge.

But when Touch the Sky spotted one of Black Elk's friends from the Bull Whip's staring at him, he turned away and avoided Honey Eater. Black Elk flew into rages against his squaw at the slightest excuse. It had been an important moment in their love when Honey Eater had told Touch the Sky she considered him her only husband—that she would come to him and lie beside him if he sent for her. But it was a moment important for the offer, not the possibility of doing it—certainly not while Black Elk was alive.

Many had mounted their ponies and ridden out to meet the caravan. The lead horses and mules were visible, skirting around the benchland through widely scattered cotton-woods. The white men conducting the train were a hard, dirty lot—unshaven men with long, lanky hair hanging loose or tied in knots under broad-brimmed hats.

As the pack animals filed into camp, panniers and pack saddles bulging, braves from the soldier societies were forced to keep the excited people back. The Bow Strings patiently sidestepped their ponies and nudged the people back; the Bull Whips, in contrast, resorted to their whips, making them hiss and crack and even raising a few welts on those who moved too slow.

"H'ar now! Git the hell back, you red niggers!" the lead bull-whacker shouted in English.

"Move your flea-bit blanket asses, yuh heathen sonsabitches!"

Touch the Sky stepped close to him, one hand resting on the beaded sheath of his knife. "Next time you ride into a Cheyenne camp," he said in perfect English, "hold one palm up in peace, or kiss your sitter good-bye. Now leave the supplies and make tracks out of here. And if you insult my tribe one more time, I'll feed your guts to the dogs."

The bull-whacker stared, measuring not only the brave's considerable stature, but also the fierce, barely restrained hatred pulsing to be unleashed in quick and violent action.

Some in the tribe—encouraged by the constant talk of Wolf Who Hunts Smiling, Swift Canoe, and others—suspected Touch the Sky's English greeting was a mark of fawning, another proof he played the dog for whites. But this notion was quickly dispelled when the bull-whacker's eyes widened for a moment in fear.

Then he caged his eyes, much as the Indians themselves were doing.

"Whatever you say, John," he said, employing the name frontier whites always used in direct address to an Indian. "I'm more 'n happy to get shut of this load and clear out. I ain't one for spilling chin music with Injuns."

He shouted brief commands and soon the entire delivery of crates, bags, and kegs was heaped in the central clearing. The Cheyenne soldiers kept the people back while River of Winds—who was highly respected for his honesty—made a quick initial inspection.

The bull-whackers had turned the pack animals back toward the mountains with loud cracks of their own long whips. Abruptly, River of Winds called out.

"Hold!" Touch the Sky's shouted command in English halted the whiteskins.

River of Winds had just examined a huge slab of bacon, peeling back the layer of cheesecloth covering it. He looked from Chief Gray Thunder to both of the soldier chiefs, Spotted Tail of the Bow Strings and Lone Bear of the Bull Whips.

"Look here! Someone has played the fox."

River of Winds peeled the outer slab back. Packed under the cheesecloth were several large, flat stones.

"And look here," he said to Touch the Sky, pointing at a big hunk of salt pork. "Never before has the meat had these odd blue symbols on it. What do they mean?"

Touch the Sky peered closer and read the words stamped on the meat: *Condemned For Troop Use*.

"And here," River of Winds said, "look at the blankets. Somehow they are different."

Suddenly the camp was filled with indignant outcries. An old woman who recognized the shiny surface of shoddy-and-glue blankets stepped forward with a gourd full of water. She poured it on one of the blankets, then easily pulled it apart.

"This," she said bitterly, "is what happens to them in the first rain. We were given wagonloads of these after all the chiefs signed the talking papers at the soldiertown called Fort Laramie."

The bull-whackers spoke no Cheyenne. But clearly things were turning ugly. They bunched tighter together as angry braves began to form a dangerous wall around them.

"H'ar now!" the leader said. He looked at Touch the Sky and pulled a sheaf of papers out of his sash. "You talk good English, John. Read 'er, too?"

Touch the Sky nodded. The other thrust the papers toward him.

"That's mighty providential, then. 'Cuz iffen you glom over that paper, you'll see for certain that we ain't got squat to do with this here consignment 'cept to deliver it. We done that. I'm a freighter, not a supplier. Who you want to chew it fine with is whoever owns the Frontier Supply Company in the Kansas Territory."

At this point Black Elk stepped forward from a knot of warriors. His face was stern with anger. The effect was made even more fearsome by the leathery hunk where one ear had been severed by a bluecoat saber. Black Elk had killed the soldier, then sewn the ear back onto his skull with buckskin thread after the battle.

"These whiteskins tried to cheat us," he told Touch the Sky angrily. "No more secret councils with them in the hair-face tongue as you are doing now. Tell them to produce our goods, or we Bull Whip troopers will exact the value from their hides."

When Black Elk cracked his whip and several of his troop brothers followed suit, Touch the Sky felt a familiar trap closing on him again. Everyone was staring at him, waiting for him to prove his loyalty to the Cheyenne people once and for all. Yet this disgusting freighter with lice in his beard had a legitimate point: There was certainly no proof they were behind the deliberate fraud.

"Father," he said, turning directly to Gray Thunder, "this place hears what I say! I, too, am enraged by this cruel crime. And I would speak with two tongues if I told you the lives of these dogs matter to me. No doubt they have shot more than one red man in his sleep. And no doubt they knew the supplies were worthless.

"But, Father, we have no proof that these hair faces robbed us. Indeed, if we punish them, the crime will then be treated as smoke behind us, and the true culprits will go unpunished to steal from red men again. I am for wading in a bit slower and seeing how deep we are in. We must try to get the goods that are owed to us."

Gray Thunder was a vigorous warrior with some 40 winters behind him. He was popular with his people, a strong believer in voicing the will of the tribe rather than trying to dictate it. He joined old Arrow Keeper and several of the headmen in nodding at the fairness and good sense of Touch the Sky's words.

"Fathers! Brothers! These are familiar and dangerous words!" Wolf Who Hunts Smiling said. "Do you remember how this one, this Touch the Sky, praised his paleface friend, Caleb Riley? 'Let the hair faces build a path for their iron horse across our hunting grounds,' he cried. 'They are friends to the red man,' this one insisted. 'They will make us rich.'

"But this day we see how our white friends treat us! The yellow beard, Caleb Riley, is behind this treachery. And now this pretend Cheyenne, whom I now openly call White Man Runs Him, once again coats the bitter truth with honey. He grew up wearing white man's shoes, and truly, he still walks in them despite his Indian moccasins."

By now the bull-whackers were too scared to go for their weapons—a move that would surely kill them, surrounded as they were. Showing this fear was their second mistake, especially in front of Black Elk.

"Truly my cousin speaks the straight word," Black Elk said. "These shivering cowards will die, and I will kill the first."

His obsidian blade had not quite cleared its sheath when Gray Thunder spoke up with unaccustomed sharpness.

"Black Elk, you are our war leader, and I never smoked the common pipe with a better one. But this is not a battle matter. Nor is this which you propose a battle—it is outright murder. Touch the Sky spoke straight arrow. For all we know, these white fools are no more guilty than the horses and mules that carried this worthless load. I say the whites will ride out unharmed."

"What if they are guilty?" Wolf Who Hunts Smiling said, backing his older cousin.

But it was old Arrow Keeper who spoke up. His voice was cracked and sere with age, even more with recent illness. But his words still resonated with great authority.

"What of that, buck? Many crimes go unde-
tected, do they not? For instance, some in
this tribe have attempted to kill a fellow
Cheyenne, spilling the blood of our own and
thus staining the sacred Medicine Arrows with
bloody dishonor. Indeed," Arrow Keeper said,
staring shrewdly at Wolf Who Hunts Smiling,
"some in this tribe, in their brutal quest for
power, may have shed the blood of our own
by huddling with our enemies. Yet they prate
about playing the big Indian and speaking of
Cheyenne honor."

Touch the Sky was sure he saw blood rush into
Wolf Who Hunts Smiling's face. Clearly Arrow
Keeper was hinting about Wolf Who Hunts Smiling's suspected collaboration with the Comanche
renegade, Big Tree—a crime Touch the Sky alone
had sure knowledge of. He had sworn, in front of
council, to kill Wolf Who Hunts Smiling for the
tribal blood he had shed.

But the hotheaded, wily Wolf Who Hunts
Smiling was never at a loss for words.

"And perhaps some others in this tribe, Grandfather," he said, stressing the last word with
great meaning, "have grown tangle brained and
thunderstruck in their frosted years, mistaking
shadows for enemies. Perhaps it is time for
younger bulls who see better to lead the herd."

An awkward silence followed this exchange of
remarks. But Gray Thunder's stern resolve never
wavered. Reluctant, but loath to rebel against
a peace chief he respected, Black Elk stepped
back and slipped his knife into the sheath.

"Very well. Let the white dogs flee with their

tails between their legs," he said. He joined his younger cousin in staring hard at Touch the Sky. "Once again this one has defended the people who raised him. He speaks of holding back now, of burying the hatchet in the interest of securing our goods.

"But only wait. Snow will blow into our tipis. The white men will be warm and fat, and we Cheyennes will be doing the hurt dance. This pretend Cheyenne will do nothing for us except help the whiteskins take our land and destroy our way of life!"

"I have had a vision placed over my eyes," Arrow Keeper said later that day. "It was sent by Maiyun, the Day Maker."

This abrupt announcement startled Touch the Sky. The two friends sat crosslegged on a pile of buffalo robes near the firepit of Arrow Keeper's tipi. It was still cool in the evenings, and a sagewood fire sent fragrant clouds curling out the tipi's smokehole.

"A vision, Father?"

"Yes. That is why I called you over. I will speak more about it in a few moments. It is true, is it not, that you plan to ride out after sunrise? You and Little Horse?"

Touch the Sky nodded, not at all surprised that Arrow Keeper knew this even before he told him. It was necessary to lean even closer to hear his old friend. In the dancing firelight, Touch the Sky noticed how deeply etched were the age lines crisscrossing the old shaman's face. His breathing was hard, often labored. Now and then the old man coughed into a piece of sack-cloth. Touch the Sky noticed bright red flecks of blood speckling the cloth.

"You are riding to the mining site to visit Caleb Riley?"

Touch the Sky nodded. "He is no thief, Father. Like his brother, Tom, he speaks only one way to the red man. But he may know something useful about this theft of our goods."

"He is a good man," Arrow Keeper said. "But there are many, like Black Elk and Wolf Who Hunts Smiling, who preach that no whites can be decent. And failing to understand that there are as many white men as there are blades of grass on the plains, these young Cheyenne hotheads are for exterminating all whites. They would find it easier to drink the Powder dry."

Arrow Keeper paused while a spasm of hard coughing racked his body. He fell quiet and stared long into the fire. Touch the Sky waited patiently, knowing the old shaman would eventually speak words of great importance to his destiny.

"Soon, stout buck, you and Little Horse will be up against it again. The battle will be hard. You will ride a great distance and find yourself in unfamiliar lands. An old enemy from your past is back—and he means to kill you."

Touch the Sky's mouth was a grim, determined slit. Arrow Keeper had spoken as if in a trance, and the words made Touch the Sky's palms throb.

"An old enemy, Father? Who?"

Still staring into the fire, his rheumy old eyes

aglow from the flames, Arrow Keeper shook his head.

"As always, there was much to my vision which the Powerful One did not mean for me to understand. But things are the way they are, and this much I can tell you."

Arrow Keeper looked at Touch the Sky, his eyes intense with urgency. When he spoke, he said words that did not seem to emanate from him, but from some higher power. Touch the Sky felt his nape tingle.

"Beware the man with an eagle's grip," Arrow Keeper said in the trance voice, "and be prepared to die before you are dead!"

These words baffled Touch the Sky and left him numb with confusion. When Arrow Keeper fell into a deep silence, unable to say more, Touch the Sky, long familiar with the mysterious old medicine man's ways, once again tasted the familiar, coppery taste of fear.

Chapter Two

In 1860 the vast Kansas Territory was a turmoiled region on the brink of statehood. Like other areas on the American frontier, it attracted many profiteering adventurers inspired by the acquisitive spirit of the times—those following the popular adage that the sun traveled west, and so did opportunity.

One growing source of windfall profits was the vast region known as the Indian Territory—huge tracts of land set aside by Congress as reservations for the Five Civilized Tribes forcibly relocated by the Removal Bill of 1830: the Seminoles, Cherokees, Chickasaws, Choctaws, and Creeks. Each tribe was promised regular payments of trade goods from the U. S. Government. Now certain white men, and their corrupt Indian lackeys, were making a fortune by routinely cheating the tribes.

For years Hiram Steele owned a successful mustang ranch near the Wyoming Territory settlement of Bighorn Falls—successful because he was ruthless and believed in destroying competition by whatever means it took.

But he had recently gone into the much more profitable enterprise of supplying contract goods to various Indian tribes. He had so far landed contracts—private and government—to supply tribes both on and off reservations: the still wild Cheyennes and Arapahos up north as well as the "dust scatterers" or "praying Indians" at the Great Bend Cherokee Reservation, presently his major source of lucrative contracts for services and goods.

In fact, Great Bend was so important to his growing empire that Steele had sold his ranch in Wyoming, pulled up stakes, and moved with his daughter Kristen to the small but thriving river town located on the western boundary of the Cherokee reservation, which bore the same name as the town. A few friendly meetings with the reservation agent, a professional bureaucrat from Virginia named Ephraim Long, had quickly evolved into a partnership that was making both men rich.

At the same time that Touch the Sky and Arrow Keeper were holding private council in the upcountry of the Powder, Hiram Steele was entertaining guests at his new home in Great Bend. They sat around a cloth-covered puncheon table, smoking cigars and sipping aged Scotch: Hiram Steele, Indian Agent Ephraim Long, and the Cherokee Chief called Red Jacket.

"Gentlemen," Steele said, carefully picking a speck of tobacco from his lip, "before we get down to cases, just a brief word of caution. The citizens of Great Bend were more than grateful when I donated the funds to employ selected Cherokees as a private police force for the reservation. But this brave you picked to head them, this—"

"His name is Mankiller," Long said. "An amazing tracker and woodsman."

"Among other things," Steele said dryly. "I'm concerned that you and the chief here aren't keeping a tight enough rein on him."

Red Jacket seemed to find this idea amusing, but he was polite and restrained his mirth to the silent abdomen laugh Indians employed to show restraint around whites.

"No one puts reins on a crazy grizzly," Red Jacket said, but the other two ignored him as usual.

"I hear rumors in town," Steele said. "Talk about a violent Cherokee constable, about Indians turning up dead. Don't forget, we started this police force to protect our interests, not to jeopardize them."

"Valid point," Long said. "But it was you who said you wanted a man as mean and hard as the job itself."

"I can't deny that. I also believe that money should be put to work making more money, which is the real point of this meeting. This side deal I recently concluded with the Far West Mining Company up north proved quite profitable. Panned out damn tidy, matter of fact. I supplied numerous trade items to some tribe of Northern Cheyennes. I was able to cut my expenses considerably by selecting the goods with thrift. Now I think it's time to put those profits to work generating more."

Steele's eyes had clouded with anger when he mentioned the Cheyennes. Ephraim Long noticed this and filed the fact away for later use. Now he grinned slightly at Steele's allusion to cutting expenses. The agent was a tall, slender man with muttonchop whiskers. He was a fastidious man and now wore a gray duster to protect his dark twill suit. He carried no weapon openly, but tucked into his right boot was a two-shot ladies muff pistol—so-called because wealthy women in London carried them in their muffs when passing through unsavory sections of the city.

"The way I see it," Long said, "those who teach the red man to plow and pray deserve some reward for their difficult labors. Just what have you got in mind, Hiram?"

Steele settled back in his chair and crossed his ankles. He was in his forties, with flint-gray eyes and a seamed face too stern to call handsome. The man was true to his name—hard and unbending, even his smile was rigid.

"Well now, I think maybe it's about time that you and Red Jacket thought about petitioning the Indian Bureau for a vocational school on the reservation. I hear that the Indian lovers in Congress like to fund vocational schools. They teach the younger ones something besides hunting and stealing. Someplace where the boys could learn how to tend a furnace or mend saddles, the girls how to sew and cook and what not. Whaddya say, Chief? That sound jake to you?"

Red Jacket helped himself to a little more whiskey from a glass carboy on the table. He was thoroughly civilized, as were many in his Cherokee tribe. He could read and write English, and he dressed in white man's clothing and called himself a Christian. Some of his people, however, called him a cracker-and-molasses chief: an Indian leader in name only who licked the white men's hands for crumbs and put himself before his tribe. His name derived from a pompous penchant for wearing red wool jackets tailored in the style of British military tunics.

"I am always ready to do what I can for our young people," he said piously. "True it is, the great white chief named Jefferson confused us by speaking two ways at once. First he sent us hoes and plows, telling us to cease being hunters. Then they found gold on our land, and the Great White Council praised the hunting further west, urging us to move here.

"And now, we are here. More than four thousand of us died during the journey. But have we rebelled and joined the heathen warriors of the Plains tribes as some Sacs and Foxes did? No! Only look. We are the sole tribe with a recorded language, the only reservation with its own newspaper. We wish to be like our white brothers, not to kill them. I am for this school. I—"

"That's real nice, Chief," Steele said impatiently, cutting the loquacious Indian short. Once he started drinking, Red Jacket loved to hear himself talk. "You're a true credit to your tribe. Here, have another cigar. Take a few for later, too. That's it. Don't be bashful."

Red Jacket smiled wide and slipped several of the fine smokes into his pocket.

"This school," Steele said, addressing Long again, "would of course have to be funded. There would be materials. You'll need a new building, and money will have to be appropriated for teachers' salaries."

Long nodded. He and Steele had teamed up before on these contract deals, and they were both leaving much unsaid. The distance between here and Washington, and the general indifference toward Indians, made frontier fraud easy. The materials they would bill to the U. S. Government would be vastly different from whatever cheap trash was actually purchased for the benefit of the Cherokees. The government would be charged for a new school building when, in fact, both men knew they would simply use one of several abandoned buildings of cottonwood logs and mud already standing on the reservation. As for the monies that would be requested to pay teachers, Steele had ideas in that direction, too.

"Kristen!" he shouted, turning his head toward the stairwell behind him.

A young woman's voice answered hesitantly from above: "Yes, Pa?"

"C'mon down here for a minute."

Ephraim Long sat up straighter in his chair and combed his hair with his fingers. "And just how is your daughter doing, Hiram? She adjusting all right to the move from Wyoming?"

Steele shrugged one beefy shoulder. "Ah, you know how it is with women. Always moping and sulking. She's just like her ma was, God rest her soul. Kristen's only problem is too much time on her hands. She needs something useful to occupy her."

"Idle hands are the devil's playmates," Long said, a faint smile tugging at his lips. He was beginning to understand the drift things were taking, and he approved.

There were light footsteps on the stairs, a faint rustle of skirts and whiff of honeysuckle perfume. Then Kristen appeared in the doorway and paused there. She was a tall, slender girl of about 19 or 20 with almond-shaped eyes of bottomless blue and wheat-colored hair swept back under an amethyst comb. She made a point of avoiding Long's hawk-eyed stare, which she could almost feel probing her like greedy fingers.

Long stood up, followed by a slightly unsteady Red Jacket.

"Miss Steele." Long bowed low over the table. "And how are you this evening?"

"Fair to middling," she replied indifferently. Her father frowned at the cool tone.

"I wondered," Long said, his eyes still aggressively pursuing hers, "if you ever received the invitation I sent? The invitation to dine with me? Once each month I host a little soiree for some of our civic leaders. Your father has a standing invitation. But of course you're an adult now, and I thought you should receive your own invitation."

"My very own? It makes me feel like such a big girl."

Her sarcasm made Hiram double his fists in anger. He opened his mouth to speak, but Long beat him to it.

"I ask only because I never received your reply."

"Oh?" she said vaguely. "I could've sworn I posted it."

"Well?"

"Well what, Mr. Long?"

"Will you be attending?"

"I think not."

"May I ask why?"

Kristen's eyes ran from her father's. But she spoke up with surprising frankness. "Why? Because I don't enjoy eating fancy food purchased with money meant to feed starving Indians. While you and your civic leader friends stuff your faces at the soiree, I know of Cherokees who are hungry—especially since your bully policemen beat them up for the crime of hunting meat."

Her accusing stare met Red Jacket's surprised face. The chief flushed slightly and hastily pulled the cigar from his lips.

Steele had gotten his rage under control. He winked briefly at Long.

"Well now, daughter! All this here compassion you feel for the red man is downright noble. You sound just like those Quakers who write letters to *Harper's Magazine.* But are you ready to prove these noble feelings in someway besides sneaking around behind my back?"

Kristen's eyes narrowed in suspicion. She knew he was talking about the Cheyenne youth Touch the Sky, whom her father had driven off several years ago when he had caught Kristen and the boy meeting secretly. "What do you mean?"

"I mean that Chief Red Jacket and Ephraim here are looking to start a school on the reservation. How'd you like to be one of the teachers?"

For a moment Kristen's eyes had gone bright at this prospect. But the sly smirk on her father's face warned her.

"I'd love the chance, assuming there really will be a school. But I've noticed how things seem to get forgotten about around here once they're funded."

"Maybe you notice too much," Steele said, sudden anger spiking his tone. "Maybe you have too damn much time on your hands to worry about the goddamn pagan redskin—"

"Ah-hmm," Long said, casting a quick eye toward Chief Red Jacket.

Steele seemed to recollect himself. Then he changed his tack. A paternal smile eased onto his face.

"Well, Ephraim here is right, I suppose. Girl your age is a woman, especially out here. Either you'll take up a useful skill and make your living or you'll get married. Can't stay in the nest forever." The threat marking his tone was unmistakable.

"Marrying the right man out here," Long said, "could open up a whole new life. A man smart enough to avail himself of the ample opportunities. A man rich enough to give you the best things life has to offer."

"A man like you perhaps, Mr. Long?"

Long only smiled and flicked an ash off his duster. "Yes, Miss Steele. A man like me."

"If and when I do get married, Mr. Long, I hope it is to a man who makes a clear distinction between an opportunity and outright theft. There seem to be plenty of men"—here she glanced at her father, too—"who can't tell the difference. Now, if you gentlemen will excuse me, I'm rather tired and would like to rest."

By federal law it was illegal for white men to sell alcohol on Indian reservations. This did not prevent the proliferation of grog shops that infested the borders of the Indian Territory, bootlegging 40-rod whiskey to the Indians for their annuity blankets, flour, and pork.

Pawnee Creek formed the western border of the Great Bend Cherokee Reservation. It separated the reservation from the white settlement. Early in spring, swollen with snow melt and mountain runoff, the big creek was actually a small river.

Two Cherokees named Tassels and Dragging Canoe had slipped across the river after noon roll call on the reservation. They took several pairs of new beaded moccasins and an oilskin full of smoked fish with them. They visited the grog shop of a former mountain man named

Jediah Jones and swapped their goods for a few glasses of watered-down liquor. As the setting sun began to rim the western horizon in a copper glow, the two friends headed back toward their cabins on the reservation.

They had just swum Pawnee Creek, and were still climbing the grassy bank, when a sudden, sharp *whack* brought them up short. Both Indians recognized the dreaded sound: a boot being struck by a rawhide quirt. It was followed almost immediately by a voice as deep as a thunderclap.

"Why, see here! Two fish that got thrown up on the bank."

Tassels and Dragging Canoe stared up toward the crest of the bank. There stood Mankiller with one of his deputies on either flank. The sight half sobered both of them.

Again Mankiller whacked his boot with a quirt. He was a mountain of a man, thick limbed and barrel chested. Twin braids fell from under the distinctive broad-brimmed hat of the Cherokee tribal policemen: the hat turned up on the right side, the brim held to the crown by a small hook and eye. This allowed a rifle to be aimed from horseback even at a gallop.

His most striking feature, however, was his huge, powerful hands. Each finger was as thick as a picket pin, each knuckle like a big stone. They were powerful, menacing, dangerous hands—hands capable of choking a bull.

"These fish know the law," Mankiller said sadly to his deputies. "They know what happens to red men who get caught leaving the reservation."

"No," Tassels said, starting to back down toward the water. "No!"

But Mankiller's deputies moved with amazing skill and speed, leaping down the bank with ropes coiled in each hand. When the two lawbreakers started struggling too hard, Mankiller slid the Remington out of his sash and fired it once overhead. Now the two prisoners submitted quietly.

Casually Mankiller thumbed the spent cap out of the pistol and recharged the empty chamber. Below, his deputies trussed each victim similarly: both legs tied tight together at the ankles, left arm trussed tight to their sides. Only their right arms were left free.

"Toss them," Mankiller ordered.

One at a time, the deputies lifted the vigorously protesting men and carried them out into the swirling water, dropping them in. Desperately, heads bobbing up and down like corks, the one-armed swimmers struggled to make it back to shore. They choked and sputtered, sent up a wild, splashing spray. Quickly their breath began rasping in their chests.

Tassels made it to shore first.

"This fish is no good," Mankiller said. "Too small. Toss him back in."

Tassels barely had breath left to protest when the deputies picked him up and carried him out into the current. This scene was repeated several times with both men until they were limp with exhaustion. One of the deputies untied them and left them gasping in the grass.

Mankiller rode a big 16-hand bay. He returned

to his mount and squatted to untie the hobble. As always, he made a point of avoiding the right side, the Indian side, when he mounted, going around instead to the left side as white men did. He had just stepped up into the stirrup when the defiant words were shouted behind him.

"You are a bullying pig who licks the boots of white men!" Tassels said. "You and Red Jacket, two turncoats who help the white men destroy us! You have no honor, and I despise you."

Mankiller dropped his reins, slipped his feet from the stirrups and dismounted. Tassels had crawled to the top of the bank. He held a small rock in his right hand.

Mankiller grinned. "This fish is feisty! Perhaps I'll have to tie him back up, then ride to his cabin. He has a fine little wife waiting there for him. Perhaps I will lift her skirt and top her, show her what it's like with a real man."

Mankiller threw his head back and laughed. Tassels snarled in rage, staggered closer, and threw the rock.

It was a lucky toss and hit Mankiller square in the forehead, skewing his hat. But if he felt the fist-size rock hit him, he didn't show it— except that the mocking smile bled from his face, replaced by a gray, silent wrath.

Mankiller closed the distance between himself and Tassels, encircled the man's neck with his powerful hands. Mankiller's grip was so huge it cut off both the jugular and the trachea, stopping blood and air simultaneously. He squeezed one time, hard, and there was an audible snap like green wood breaking. Tassels tried to scream, but nothing came out except a gurgling froth of spittle.

Mankiller squeezed even harder, and Tassel's flailing feet left the ground. The Cherokee policemen held him up until he went slack, then threw his dead body to the ground and stared at Dragging Canoe.

"He attacked a Cherokee policeman. I killed him in self-defense. You got any complaint?"

Dragging Canoe, still too weak to rise from the grass, only stared at his dead companion. Tassels's neck had turned an ugly black and blue, swollen to twice its normal size.

Mankiller carefully straightened his hat. Then he returned to his horse, mounted, and rode out as if the dead man behind him was none of his business.

Chapter Three

"Brother," Little Horse said, "a thing troubles me." He and Touch the Sky had ridden out early, just as an old grandmother of the Crooked Lance Clan was singing the song to the new sun rising. Pockets of mist still floated over the Powder, and from the wooded thickets, orioles and thrushes sent up their warbling melodies.

Their legging sashes were stuffed with pemmican and dried plums, their foxskin quivers bristled with new arrows. Little Horse's four-barrel revolver protruded from the boot tied to his rope rigging; a percussion-action Sharps filled Touch the Sky's. Their ponies were battle rigged: lances, throwing axes, new oak bows—all were tied where they would be ready to hand if an attack came suddenly.

"Speak this thing which troubles you, buck."

"It is Wolf Who Hunts Smiling."

Touch the Sky frowned. "Truly, he is enough trouble for ten braves. But what of him?"

"He has always been mean and bloodthirsty. From the moment you were captured still wearing white man's clothing, Wolf Who Hunts Smiling has been eager to kill you. You have other dangerous enemies, the jealous Black Elk leading the pack. But, brother, Black Elk is at least loyal to his tribe. As you have learned the bitter way, Wolf Who Hunts Smiling not only lusts after power; he has no honor. Such men are dangerous. Now we are again riding out, what treachery will he stir up against you?"

Touch the Sky nodded. "You speak straight arrow, buck. He no longer has any honor, though once he did. He could have killed me after I pretended to summon a grizzly and saved him from the Pawnees. Instead, he lowered his rifle. And there was a time when he would not play the turncoat against his own tribe.

"But that time is smoke behind us. Now I know that he plotted with the Comanche Big Tree to kill our herd guards and steal our ponies. He has cleaned his parfleche of loyalty and stuffed it instead with ambition."

"And you," Little Horse said, "are blocking his path to glory. He knows he must either kill you or fail in his plans. I only hope this new trouble with our contract goods does not work in his favor. Many in the tribe are bitter and disappointed at being cheated, and he is clever at stoking their rage. And now he has this supposed shaman Medicine Flute to assist him in his treachery by claiming supernatural guidance. This further confuses the people."

Touch the Sky fell silent, letting his pony set her own pace across a loose shale slope. Caleb Riley's Far West Mining Company was a full sleep's ride from the Powder River camp. The mine itself was not located on Cheyenne hunting grounds, only the railroad spur line that hauled the ore to Laramie. Touch the Sky had served as pathfinder for the railroad crew, going up against the insane, murderous Sis-ki-dee—the Blackfoot renegade also known as the Contrary Warrior.

Recalling Sis-ki-dee's smallpox-scarred face, raggedly cropped short hair, and crazy-by-thunder eyes could still send a cold prickle down Touch the Sky's spine. But even more menacing were Arrow Keeper's recent words about this new trouble: *Be prepared to die before you are dead.* What could such apparent strong-mushroom talk possibly mean?

Sister Sun tracked higher across the hazy blue sky as the two young Cheyenne braves rode north toward the foothills of the Sans Arcs Mountains and Caleb Riley's mine. Although the Cheyenne tribe was currently at war with neither red men nor white, they kept a keen eye out for riders. Several times they paused to water their ponies in small streams and rills.

The battle will be hard, Arrow Keeper had warned him. *You will ride a great distance and find yourself in unfamiliar lands.* Arrow Keeper— his first and best friend in the tribe, a venerable old warrior and medicine man whose vision a long time ago at Medicine Lake had saved Touch the Sky's life. That vision foretold much suffering, but also much glory along Touch the Sky's turbulent path. Touch the Sky himself had finally experienced that same epic vision—and with that vision came his final determination to find his place once and for all as a Cheyenne.

Guiltily, Touch the Sky surfaced from these ruminations and woke to his surroundings. They were riding through a series of jagged cutbanks, the country rolling more now. They left the plains of the river bottom. How many times had he advised the young warriors to stop thinking so much and attend instead to the language of the senses? Fortunately, he could see that Little Horse was being vigilant for both of them.

For a moment Touch the Sky reached to feel the set of badger claws on the medicine pouch dangling from his clout. Arrow Keeper had given them to him, claiming it was the battle totem of Chief Running Antelope—Touch the Sky's dead father.

But there was no luxury now for such useless reflection. The trail suddenly narrowed and the two friends were forced to fall into single file. Touch the Sky tried to quell the activity of his thoughts, tried to observe things more with the hidden shaman's eye Arrow Keeper had taught him to open and see with.

Nonetheless, Arrow Keeper's warning from his latest medicine dream kept a claim on his awareness, nagging him like a sharp regret.

An old enemy from your past is back, and this time he means to kill you.

42

*   *   *

"It's got a damn bad smell to it," Caleb Riley said when Touch the Sky had finished speaking.

Caleb, Touch the Sky, Little Horse, and a burly man in twill coveralls named Liam McKinney stood around a wagon loaded with crushed rock. The two Cheyennes had made a simple meat camp in the foothills of the Sans Arcs the night before, riding in early the following day. Now morning sunlight illuminated the vast, dark scar of the mine, located farther up the mountainside above the mining camp.

"You sure," Liam said, "it wasn't just some stuff that got damaged or went bad during the hauling?"

Liam McKinney had a merry grin and plenty of laugh lines in a tough face. He had been the gang boss for the rail crew when the spur line was built. Caleb had kept him on to supervise the constant repair work to the rail line required by the rigorous mountain route, where spring melts, rock slides, and sabotage by Indians were common.

"Hell," Caleb said, answering for Touch the Sky, "hard slogging don't explain rocks in the bacon and blankets made of shoddy. It wasn't no damage, it was outright thievery."

Caleb was young and sported a shaggy blond beard. He was a big-framed man wearing buckskin trousers and shirt, with elkskin moccasins instead of boots. Nor was his preference for moccasins his only Indian trait. Touch the Sky recalled how impressed the Cheyenne tribe had been when they learned this white man hated spurs and bridled his horse with a headstall only, refusing to shove a bit into its mouth.

"Any problem with last year's consignment?" Caleb said.

Touch the Sky shook his head. "Everything was delivered, and it was good quality."

"Well, the thing of it is," Caleb said slowly, puzzling it out, "we hired on a new business manager in Register Cliffs. Slick young feller, said he could start saving us money faster 'n a finger snap. One of the things he did, he put your supply contract up for bid. Told me he found a lower bidder to supply your tribe."

Caleb turned toward an unpainted clapboard office at the edge of the tent city formed by the campsite.

"I got the letter from him filed away someplace. Hold on a bit, I'll be right back."

While Caleb went to hunt for the letter, Touch the Sky translated the little he had learned so far for Little Horse, who spoke no English. All around them the camp came to life as miners emerged from their tents, yawning and scratching. They lined up outside the huge mess tent. Some stared curiously—some with open hostility—toward the new arrivals.

"Hey, shorty!" one of them called over to Little Horse. "That's a right purdy braid you got there. Maybe I'll cut it off for a soo-vee-neer!"

"You go ahead and try, pilgrim," Touch the Sky called back affably in English. "The white man's hell ain't half full."

The miner stared in surprise at the young buck's good English. But the lump of burn tissue on Touch the Sky's chest, the network of bullet, arrow-point, and knife scars, the lean, tall, hard body, the grim and determined slit of his mouth—the miner took all this in and decided to take a sudden interest in staring at his own boots.

The door of the clapboard shack slapped open and Caleb stepped back outside, reading a letter.

"Here it is. Listen to this:"

"As for that other matter we discussed, I have good news. I have located a supplier in the Kansas Territory, the Frontier Supply Company, who has agreed to take on the contract to supply the Northern Cheyenne tribe located at the juncture of the Powder and Little Powder. This company has plenty of experience, being the sole supplier to the huge Cherokee reservation at Great Bend. They have assured me they will match the quality of the current supplier's goods while charging us one thousand dollars less."

Caleb looked up. "Tarnal hell! It's my fault. I never should've let him switch. They say you shouldn't pick up a happy baby. Your tribe was doin' fine with the last supplier."

"You didn't switch the goods," Touch the Sky assured his friend. "You've been plenty fair to us. Sounds to me like the source of the trouble is this Frontier Supply Company down in Great Bend. You got any names to go with it?"

Caleb scanned the letter. When he spoke the

familiar name, Touch the Sky felt cold blood rush into his face.

"Here you go. The man who signed the contract is named Steele. Hiram Steele."

An old enemy from your past is back, and this time he means to kill you.

Hiram Steele—hearing the name had opened a flood gate and sent memories tumbling through Touch the Sky's mind like storm-tossed driftwood. Memories of the quiet little copse where he used to meet Kristen Steele; memories of the ruthless hired hand, Boone Wilson, who had savagely beaten him at Steele's command; memories of his adopted parents' fear and suffering when Steele tried to drive them out of the mustang business, just as he had driven them out of the mercantile business.

Touch the Sky and Little Horse talked it over long and carefully during the ride back to camp. They agreed that a visit to the Great Bend Reservation was unavoidable. But they also agreed that, things being the way they were, it was best to try to avoid a regular council of the headmen. A routine council, with the tribe this angry over the shoddy goods, might be taken over by Touch the Sky's enemies.

The best plan, they agreed, was to ask old Arrow Keeper to take an extraordinary step. He must approach Chief Gray Thunder privately and ask him to secretly convene the Star Chamber.

The Star Chamber was the Cheyenne court of last resort. Made up of six headmen whose names were known only to Gray Thunder, the Star Chamber held extraordinary power and could override even votes of the Council of Forty. But because it was so powerful, any good Cheyenne chief was reluctant to abuse his authority by convening the Star Chamber.

Arrow Keeper listened carefully to his young apprentice. When Touch the Sky finished presenting his case, the old shaman nodded thoughtfully.

"I am loath to call on the Star Chamber. But I agree with you and Little Horse. This matter cannot go to council. Not now. Your enemies would hobble you. They would demand an attack on Caleb Riley and his miners.

"By indirection we will find our direction," he said quietly. "However, do not expect the Star Chamber to easily approve such a secret mission. I will do what I can. But if they say no, then it is hopeless."

While they waited to learn their fate, Touch the Sky and Little Horse went about their usual business. They mounted guard for the far-flung pony herds, drew camp sentry duty at night, and served as guards when the women and girls went out on the open plains to dig wild turnips, onions, and yarrow roots.

One day Touch the Sky rode into camp toward midday, having just been relieved on herd guard. He turned his pony loose in the rope corral. As he crossed to his tipi, he spotted the youth named Two Twists waiting near his entrance flap.

"Are you waiting for me, little brother?"

Two Twists assumed a look of exaggerated

innocence. "Waiting, Touch the Sky? Of course not. I was only strolling past. Only, now that you are here, I wonder a thing. Do you know a little pine-sheltered hollow just south of camp? Down the river a double stone's throw?"

Puzzled, Touch the Sky nodded. "I know it. What of it?"

Two Twists glanced across the clearing, toward the largest tipi in the Panther Clan circle.

"It is a very pleasant place to rest and meditate, is it not? And did you also know that Black Elk has ridden out on a scouting mission? That he will not return until sunset?"

With that, Two Twists suddenly added, "Well, I must go. I think I will walk over and talk to Honey Eater. Perhaps she might decide to take a walk."

Touch the Sky felt his blood suddenly humming when he realized what his loyal young friend was up to. As Two Twists started across the central clearing, Touch the Sky circled behind his tipi and angled down the long, sloping bank of the river. He stepped behind a willow brake and followed the current as it wound its way through hawthorn thickets and huge, narrow-leaved cottonwoods.

He reached the little sheltered place and slipped inside. The pines grew so thick they formed natural walls, and falling needles made a soft and springy bed underfoot. The wind gusted, soughing in the treetops with a rustling murmur.

Despite his usual warrior's vigilance, this quiet

place lulled him. He didn't hear Honey Eater approach. Suddenly, she was simply there beside him, her hand cool and light on the hard muscle of his shoulder.

"Is it really you this time?" she said, her voice a caress to his soul. "And not another dream tormenting me?"

She left her hand on his shoulder, dropped down to sit beside him. She had just braided her hair with petals of fresh white columbine, and the clean fragrance filled his nostrils. Touch the Sky buried his face in her hair, drew his lips to her nape, and delicately kissed the soft skin until he felt her shudder beneath him.

"If it is a dream," he murmured in reply, "I am having it, too."

For a long moment their eyes met and held, the shadow patterns on their faces changing as the pine boughs overhead swayed in the wind.

"You will soon be riding out again?" she said.

"Who told you this thing?"

"No one told me. No one had to. Lately the larks have quit singing. And I listened to the jays chatter about the great sadness to come."

Once again he was powerfully aware of not only her great beauty, but also her extraordinary perceptions and feelings. Honey Eater boasted of no shaman's skills. Yet long before the leaves turned their white sides up, Honey Eater knew a storm was coming.

"I may ride out," he said, "or I may not. I will know soon. But even if I go, the stone will still be there."

She leaned closer into him, both of them happy

with this rare intimacy. They both knew what stone he meant: the piece of marble he had placed on the ground in front of his tipi. That stone symbolized his love for her. Once, during vicious torture at the hands of the whiskey trader Henri Lagace, Touch the Sky had defied his tormentors by shouting out to Honey Eater, 'Do you know that I have placed a stone in front of my tipi? When that stone melts so, too, will my love for you.'

"I visit the stone when you are gone," she said. "Although sometimes doing so is dangerous."

She didn't need to elaborate. Black Elk had not found that stone yet, but he knew it was there and he had already punished her brutally for visiting it.

"You risk far too much to love me," he said.

"I would risk everything."

Those last words lingered in the air like a scent. Now each of them was thinking about the same thing: a promise Honey Eater had made when Touch the Sky rode out to fight the white buffalo hiders. Though the two of them had not performed the squaw-taking ceremony, in spirit they were already husband and wife. And Honey Eater had finally decided she would be his wife in body, too, whenever he sent for her. So far the great risk to her had held him back. But now they were alone.

He felt his heart stomping against his ribs and her breath moist and warm on his eyelids. Their eyes met again, his bright with powerful desire, hers turning to liquid under the burn of his stare.

One rawhide string held Honey Eater's soft doeskin dress closed in front. Without willing it, Touch the Sky raised one hand and untied the thong. The soft flaps fell back, revealing the high and hard swells of her breasts. A soft moan of surrender escaped her lips as he lowered his mouth over one plum-colored nipple and gently kissed it stiff.

Fire blazed to life in his loins, and the need was on him to merge his flesh with this woman he loved. He pressed her back into the soft mat of pine needles, feeling her body yield and mold to his.

Abruptly, so close they both started, an owl hooted. Only they both knew it was no owl. Two Twists was warning them that danger approached!

Quickly, his breathing still clumsy with desire, Touch the Sky closed Honey Eater's dress. Then he rose and slid through the shifting shadows to the edge of the hollow. Cautiously he peered out, glanced both ways along the river bank. Then he saw several old grandmothers approaching from camp, reed baskets over their arms as they gathered rushes for weaving.

His disappointment was keen. They might soon wander into the hollow. He could not endanger Honey Eater any longer. He slipped back and said low in her ear, "Somebody is coming. You stay here as if you were merely resting and enjoying the quiet. Good-bye, sweet Honey Eater. Think of me."

"How will I think of anything else?"

Already he was stealing toward the opposite

side of the pine hollow, planning to double around back into camp.

"Touch the Sky?" she said and he turned around. "Be careful, and come back to me." She crossed her wrists over her heart: Cheyenne sign-talk for love.

He crossed his, too, then slipped out of the thicket. He returned to camp, unobserved, and lifted the entrance flap of his tipi.

His breath caught in his throat: a figure was standing there in the grainy shadows of the interior.

"The Star Chamber has met," Arrow Keeper said. "You and Little Horse will ride to the Cherokee reservation to defeat this hair-face thief called Hiram Steele."

Chapter Four

For this mission, saving time was not as crucial as conserving strength. Therefore, Touch the Sky and Little Horse did not push their ponies hard on the ride south and east toward Great Bend. Remounts would be too cumbersome, yet neither brave was eager to show up riding exhausted ponies among potential enemies in a strange land. And more than one man without remounts had died after his only horse foundered on the plains.

Instead, they let their spirited ponies set their own pace, grazing them often in the lush buffalo grass and resting them frequently. Nor did the two braves neglect to build their own strength. Game was plentiful as they moved onto new ranges. They spotted plenty of elk and antelope, prairie chickens and rabbits, even a small herd of buffalo. Tribal sanction would not permit the killing of buffalo except during the annual buffalo hunt. But everything else was fair game, and the two youths made every camp a meat camp. The river growth supplied blackberries, elderberries, and chokecherries.

In fact, the long journey was so easy that Touch the Sky sometimes had to remind himself they were riding into great danger. Mostly the terrain was typical plains country, flat or gently rolling, wooded bluffs and tableland near the rivers and major streams. Lush new grass grew knee high and often they rode through vast meadows of gaily blooming flowers: white columbine, blue morning glories, and yellow buttercups.

Despite such natural beauty and bounty, the image of Hiram Steele's cold, flint-gray eyes seldom deserted Touch the Sky. And a work crew stringing the white men's talking wire, or the occasional patrol of blue-bloused pony soldiers, kept him and Little Horse carefully scanning the horizons.

Nor was nature always friendly. Several times they were caught out in the open under sudden downpours that almost instantly turned the ground to mud. Other times, violent windstorms kicked up out of nowhere, threatening to choke them in thick, debris-strewn dust.

Caleb had sat down with Touch the Sky and carefully traced the location of Great Bend on a good army map. The two Cheyennes knew the town itself—which they must carefully avoid, especially since they would be considered renegades far from their legal homeland—was located on a wooded bluff beside Pawnee Creek. This big creek, actually a small river at this time of year, was also the western border of the Cherokee reservation.

Finally, weary but wary, the two Cheyennes crested a long slope and spotted a bluff rising in the distance. The high false fronts of a few frame buildings and a lone white church steeple rose up against the gray sky.

"Great Bend," Touch the Sky said. "It must be. We cannot see Pawnee Creek from here, but all that land beyond is the Cherokee nation."

"From where I sit now, brother," Little Horse said, "it looks like most of the land hair faces give to the red man. Empty and useless, good neither for hunting or the gardens that palefaces are so keen to see us hoe with the women."

Touch the Sky nodded. "We get the land they do not want. Until they discover the yellow rocks on it. Then it is time to get a chief drunk on strong water so the red men can be moved farther west. These Cherokees have been driven even farther from their ancient lands than our tribe was."

Having little contact with them, the two Cheyenne braves knew only a little about this proud tribe from east of the river called Great Waters. They had been hunters and farmers back east, and though they had taken on many of the white man's ways, they had also fought some fierce battles against them and were said to be no warriors to fool with. Touch the Sky hoped that warrior tradition still lived in these people. If

Arrow Keeper's vision was true, a hard fight lay ahead.

"We will skirt the town by riding through the trees behind the bluff," Touch the Sky said, pointing. "Then we will ford Pawnee Creek and ride onto the reservation. First we must search for a good, safe camp."

Little Horse nodded. His eyes met his friend's. The sturdy little brave grinned.

"Brother, we are up against it again! I fought Hiram Steele beside you in Bighorn Falls when we saved your white clan's ranch. We beat him then, buck! What Cheyennes have done, Cheyennes will do."

But as they pointed their buffalo-hair bridles north toward the shelter of the trees, Touch the Sky admitted to himself that he felt far less confident than his friend's bold words. They had not one ally in this entire land, yet no doubt more than enough enemies. If whites spotted them, most likely they'd be shot on sight. Nor did he know if the Cherokees would be any less hostile toward Cheyenne interlopers.

Besides, he had learned to pay attention to the newly awakened sixth sense that Arrow Keeper had taught him to use. And that sixth sense told him bad trouble was extremely close at hand.

The two young Cheyenne warriors angled north and rode single file through a forest of sycamore and oak, dense with deadfalls and undergrowth. They emerged on the bank of what must be Pawnee Creek, well upstream from the settlement of Great Bend.

The water flowed near to the top of the banks, the current churning foam where trapped branches had formed a sawyer out in midstream. But the bottom was solid and the well-rested ponies waded in gamely, swimming the rest of the way with little difficulty. They climbed out on the opposite bank and set first foot on the Cherokee reservation.

"Brother," Little Horse said, "things do not look any better from here. Look there, how the grass has already been overgrazed. See how barren this land is of trees except here by the water. I am no farmer as these Cherokees are said to be. But I have been told that farmers like to plant their crops in soil good enough to support trees, especially nut trees for these grow where the best soil is."

Touch the Sky nodded, looking carefully all about them. His uneasy feeling had increased despite the apparent emptiness.

"Speaking of trees, before we ride farther let us climb one and see what we can see."

The sun blazed behind them, casting elongated shadows to the east. They shinnied up the bole of a huge cottonwood tree. From its uppermost branches they got a good view of the new Cherokee homeland, and it was discouraging to their plans.

Getting about unobserved would be a nearly impossible task. Most of the visible land was barren or given over to cultivation or the grazing of livestock. Small herds of sheep and cows were clumped here and there, alternating with small fields or kitchen gardens surrounded by fences.

Tidy cabins of cottonwood logs chinked with mud were scattered here and there. They spotted a figure with twin braids protruding from under a floppy-brimmed hat, moving patiently up and down behind a mule and harrow.

"Buck," Little Horse called over from a nearby limb, "it is going to be the Wendigo's own work, moving about without being spotted. There is no cover! Where will we make a camp?"

"Straight words, *Shaiyena*. As for moving about, we must operate as we did when we fought Hiram Steele's men before."

"You mean, move about by night?"

Touch the Sky nodded. Cheyennes did not normally like to leave the safety of their firepits after dark. But he and Little Horse had learned to make a virtue of necessity.

"As for a camp," Touch the Sky said, "clearly our only hope is Pawnee Creek. We must find a secluded spot from which to operate. And where else could we water our ponies safely? I think we should ride north, farther from town."

Little Horse approved this plan. Just before he climbed down, Touch the Sky felt another uneasy prickling at his nape. Again he glanced carefully around them, spotting nothing to cause alarm.

They slipped the hobbles off their ponies' forelegs and bore slowly north again, watching for opportune spots. Several times they encountered a promising copse or hollow. But when Touch the Sky searched for signs of animals, he found few. This hinted that men had recently passed through these areas, so they rode on.

Sister Sun was now a dull orange ball just above the horizon. Still they had found no spot safe enough to trust. Worse yet, the trees and ground cover began to thin out as they moved farther north. Discouraged, they turned their ponies and retraced their steps.

It was too quiet. They heard only the steady rhythm of cicadas and the harsh calls of grebes and red-tailed hawks circling overhead.

They were forced to pass dangerously close to the white settlement. Only a cypress brake and dense thickets protected them. They heard occasional noises from town: the rattling of trace chains, a shout of greeting. Both Cheyennes rode quietly, letting their ponies walk. They watched for any sign of danger: birds suddenly taking off from the bank or their ponies abruptly pricking their ears forward.

The sun still shone, but the shadows were deepening. They reached a dog-leg bend in the river. Touch the Sky bent low to avoid an overhanging branch; when he sat back up again, fear suddenly stuck a lance point in him.

A giant bear of an Indian sat his saddle directly ahead of him—a huge Cherokee with a broadbrimmed hat turned up on the right side. A Spencer carbine was balanced across his saddletree.

"Fly like the wind, brother!" he said to his friend, suddenly pulling hard on his hackamore and turning his calico mustang around.

But now Touch the Sky saw they had ridden into a death trap. Four more heavily armed

Cherokees sat their mounts across the trail behind them! They wore butternut-colored hats exactly like the other one's.

The creek flowed by to their left, but they would be shot before they reached the halfway point. Beyond it a fairly steep bank gave way to the settlement—hardly good cover. They were trapped despite their combined vigilance. Whoever these Cherokees were, they were no novices at silent movement.

"Brother," Little Horse said quietly, "do we draw and fight?"

"Perhaps we will have to," Touch the Sky said grimly. "But hold off a moment."

He reined his pony back around to face the lone figure ahead, clearly the leader. He knew many Cherokees spoke good English. So he spoke in that language.

"We have come in peace. We are Northern Cheyennes from the Powder River country. We have no quarrel with our Cherokee brothers."

The big Cherokee's face registered momentary surprise at the stranger's good command of English. He replied in a voice so deep it seemed to vibrate Touch the Sky's skin.

"Brothers? Did you suck my mother's dug? Oh, but we have a quarrel, Cheyenne. You say you come in peace. But only look at your pony's rigging! That is a battle rig or I will eat my hat. By what right do you sneak onto our land ready for battle?"

"Ready for battle is not a battle," Touch the Sky said. "On the frontier, only a fool would not be ready."

He knew this was another kind of trap. For Touch the Sky and Little Horse could have no way of knowing who these Cherokees were, whether they served white masters like Hiram Steele or their own people. It was not yet safe to state the true purpose of this visit.

"You speak of owning the land, like the whiteskins do," Touch the Sky bluffed. "We know nothing of any Indian land. We are merely trying to skirt the white settlement. We are traveling south to visit our Southern Cheyenne kin."

The big Cherokee seemed to consider this reply. After all, it was quite possible. There were indeed Cheyennes camped to the south of this place. But Mankiller really didn't care who they were or what their purpose was in being here. It was all one to him—the main thing was to have a little fun.

Touch the Sky watched the big Cherokee whack his boot with his quirt. Even from this distance, Touch the Sky easily saw the big hands, each finger like a thick rope.

"I am called Mankiller," the Cherokee said. "I am Chief of the Cherokee Tribal Police. But our justice is not bound by the white man's law-ways. I am the sheriff, the judge, and the jury. And I find both of you guilty."

"Guilty of what?"

"Guilty of trespassing with the intention of committing some mischief."

"Trespassing! That is white man's peyote talk. How can Indians trespass? We are only pass-ing by."

"Good," Mankiller said. He signaled to his men. "After such a long ride, perhaps it is time for a cool swim."

Little Horse looked at Touch the Sky, waiting for the signal. But Touch the Sky shook his head. Only if they were clearly about to be killed would he signal for resistance against such odds. These braves had the cold, flat gaze of experienced killers.

One at a time, they were each dragged roughly from their ponies. The weapons trained on them made resistance useless. Mankiller's deputies bound their legs tightly together with rawhide cords and strapped one arm to their side, leaving just one free. Touch the Sky understood why when two of the deputies hoisted him like a sack of grain and splashed into the water with him.

He felt himself being swung, heaved. Then he hit the ice-cold water. Unable to kick, he swam desperately with one arm, barely keeping his chin out of the water. Another splash nearby told him Little Horse, too, had been thrown in.

"Look at the odd fishes!" a Cherokee warrior taunted. "Are they trout with braids?"

"No, they are Cheyenne warrior fish!"

"They swam all the way down from the north country just to call us their brothers!"

"They have no quarrel with us. They only want to swim and play."

Touch the Sky neared the bank slowly, but it was impossible to swim straight with only one arm. He was immediately seized and thrown back out into midstream. Little Horse received similar treatment.

Already Touch the Sky's swimming arm was exhausted from the hard, constant motion of staying above surface in the brisk-moving current. Once, twice, again he went under, water rushing down his throat and choking him. He made it close to shore once again, coughing and gasping, and again he was flung back.

Over and over he and Little Horse made it close to shore only to be tossed back in. Now his arm was so weak it felt heavy as a stone club, and he was swallowing more and more water. The merciless taunts continued although by now he heard little in his desperate struggle to stay alive.

Another mouthful of water choked him until he almost blacked out. He went under and barely managed to break surface. Again he reached shore, so exhausted his heart was stomping his ribs and his breathing came in short, ragged gasps. And now Touch the Sky finally realized he was only a few heartbeats away from death.

His foot struck bottom. Hands grasped him, ready to heave him out one more time. Only this time, he knew, would be the last. He could swim no more. Clearly Little Horse, too, was utterly exhausted.

As Touch the Sky was lifted and swung, he began chanting his death song. But before his captors could heave him to his death, a high-pitched scream rose from the bank above them—a young woman's scream.

"Stop it!" the new arrival demanded. "Oh, please dear God, stop it!"

The expected toss never came. His head hanging upside down, water running out of his lungs, Touch the Sky looked up toward the top of the bank.

It took him a long moment to understand what he was seeing. The tall, pretty, horrified blonde standing with one fist squeezed to her mouth in fright was his first love, Kristen Steele!

Chapter Five

There was a long, surprised silence after Kristen's outburst. All the Indians, including the half-drowned Cheyennes, stared at the pretty girl. Her sunbonnet was tilted back to reveal an oval face with skin as fair and flawless as moonstone. The modest blue cotton dress could not completely hide full, high breasts and the long sweep of her hips. Her presence near the creek was explained by the wicker basket hooked over her left arm, bright with golden daffodils and scarlet verbena.

Mankiller's sudden laugh broke the stillness. It was loud as a clap of thunder.

"What? The daughter of Hiram Steele begging for Indians? I could understand this pity if we were kicking a dog. Everyone knows that paleface girls like to hug and kiss pups. But does the little sun-haired one know that these Cheyennes eat dogs? Indeed, I hear they boil their favorite puppies until they float in the pot. Then, their eyes streaming tears, they praise the animals' virtues while chewing their eyeballs."

Kristen, realizing the danger to Touch the Sky and Little Horse, had quickly hidden her shock at recognizing them.

"I suppose that's why you're drowning them? Because the Cheyenne people eat dogs?" she said indignantly.

Mankiller threw back his head and laughed again, whacking his boot with his quirt.

"Stomp your foot, Sun Hair," he teased her. "Then you look like a fiery little warrior!"

Kristen looked as if she did indeed want to stomp her foot. Instead, she only said coldly, "I thought you were supposed to be a lawman, not a bully. These two have done nothing."

Something in her tone made Mankiller suspicious. He lost his mocking smile, staring hard at her.

"You are quick to champion strangers. And how are you so sure they have done nothing? Any man is guilty if you ask him the right question. Or do you perhaps know them well enough to bespeak their honesty?"

"Of course not. But whatever they might've done," she said hastily, "surely they don't deserve to die?"

"Die? But Golden Top, I am not killing them.

Only bathing the trail dust off our Cheyenne guests. A bit of fun."

Kristen frowned. "Yes. A bit of fun like you had with Tassels."

The amused glint left Mankiller's eyes. "Already the whites have heard about Tassels? It is an Indian matter. He attacked me."

Clearly Kristen had more she wanted to say on that score. But she bit back any reply. Instead, she only said, "Will you let these two go now?"

Touch the Sky and Little Horse were sprawled on the grassy bank, sides still heaving. Mankiller stared at them. "The sun-haired girl with her nose in the air amuses me. I like her haughty manner. You two drowned rats may go. But witnesses hear me when I say I am ordering you off the Cherokee reservation permanently. If I or any of my men see you here again, we will kill you. Do you understand?"

Both Cheyennes had sat up by now. Touch the Sky nodded once.

"Good," Mankiller told them. "Now ride. You may follow the creek until out of sight of the town. But keep riding, and you must avoid the reservation."

Touch the Sky rose unsteadily, his body exhausted from the ordeal. He joined Little Horse in a hard struggle up the bank. The Cherokees had not touched their weapons or gear. But all five policemen held rifles and pistols on them, making sure they didn't make any sudden moves.

They swung onto their ponies, chucked them up the bank. Kristen had turned as if to return to town. With her back to the Cherokees below, she said in a voice meant just for Touch the Sky:

"Sneak into town after dark, but be careful! I live in the white two-story house at the end of Congress Street. Watch for a light in the back upstairs window—that's my room."

She dared say no more, but Touch the Sky heard her. Holding his face impassive, revealing nothing, he pointed his bridle downstream and rode south of Great Bend, the Cherokee policemen silently watching until the two Cheyennes disappeared in the thickets.

A policeman named Creek Hater looked at Mankiller. "Those two mean trouble. We will see them again."

Mankiller nodded. A little grin twitched at his lips.

"I know we will. That is why I let them go, not for her. I am curious about their purpose in coming here. We will kill them, all in good time. But first let us enjoy a little sport with them."

At first the two friends did as instructed. They stuck close to Pawnee Creek until the settlement of Great Bend was out of sight. But as soon as it was dark, Touch the Sky halted them. He had already explained the brief message from Kristen, whom Little Horse had recognized immediately as the beauty from Bighorn Falls.

"Uncle Moon is hiding among the clouds tonight," Touch the Sky said. "We should ride back to Great Bend now while light is scarce."

Little Horse agreed. "When we get close, we

can tether our ponies back at the creek and sneak in on foot."

"The town will be dark. Still, we will be up against it if we are spotted sneaking about at night. We will be shot on sight."

"Nor can we be sure," Little Horse said, "where this stone-faced Mankiller is lurking. Brother, I looked deep into the crazy eyes of the Blackfoot named Sis-ki-dee. And I glimpsed the mad light in the eyes of Big Tree, the Comanche Terror. But this Cherokee is colder than either of them.

"I say it now, and this place hears me. Of all the dangers we will face on this mission, he will surely be the worst. His eyes tell me he lives up to his name, and I fear he takes great pleasure in what he does best."

They turned their ponies and made good time despite the dark night. The water whispered and chuckled to their right; occasionally a lone coyote raised a solitary howl from the vast plains to their left. They chewed on pemmican and dried plums, feeling the air grow cooler and cooler against their bare skin.

Touch the Sky was even more silent than usual. Seeing Kristen Steele so suddenly had jarred him to the core of his soul. Old feelings that he had thought were long dead surfaced from the burial ground of painful memories. Feelings which troubled and confused him— especially with the recent touch of Honey Eater's tender flesh still burning his skin.

Soon the lights of Great Bend winked into view. They found a good patch of graze near the water and tethered their ponies with long strips of rawhide. After a brief debate, they decided to take no weapons except their knives. Despite the moonless night, they took the precaution of smearing their bodies and faces with mud from the creek. Knowing some dogs would be on guard, they determined the wind direction so they could approach into it.

Great Bend fit the pattern of many settlements on the American frontier. A tightly grouped cluster of houses and businesses was bisected once by a main central street and crossed in the opposite direction by several side streets. There was no gradual change from town to surroundings. The buildings simply stopped and the prairie grass took over.

This practical layout made the settlement easy to approach. The two Cheyennes took advantage of hillocks and swales, moving within a stone's throw of the nearest building.

"Wait here a little," Touch the Sky whispered. "I can read the signs that name the streets. Once I find Congress Street, I will come back for you. I do not like the thought of us sneaking around inside their town until we know exactly where to go."

This made sense and Little Horse nodded. Touch the Sky listened for a long time before he moved out. He could hear piano notes tinkling from a saloon, and it surprised him that he easily recognized the tune from his days among the whites: "Little Brown Jug." Now and then a voice called out or a horse whickered. Otherwise, all seemed quiet.

The Cheyenne rose, sprinted to the back of the building, and hugged the frame wall as he followed the shadows around to the street it faced on. A quick glance both ways told Touch the Sky that all the buildings on this street were businesses. He stayed in the apron of shadows and moved to the first side street. Luck was with him. A crudely painted shingle nailed to a corner building identified this collection of deep wagon ruts as Congress Street.

Touch the Sky ducked back just in time—a trio of riders came down the main street, hoofclops echoing off the high false fronts. They passed an open doorway, and the light within washed over them. They were wranglers, judging from their sharp-roweled spurs, woolly chaps, and bright bandannas.

The Cheyenne glanced both ways down Congress Street and spotted one two-story house. It sat all the way at the far end of the street, surrounded by a big yard but no fence. Touch the Sky made a quick map in his mind, then sneaked back to get Little Horse.

Touch the Sky leading, the two braves avoided the streets altogether. They moved in a wide berth around the town, approaching from the open vastness to the rear of the Steele residence.

Even as they crept near, a lantern flared to life in the upstairs window. A pale, slanting shaft of light stabbed down into the backyard like a bony finger. Touch the Sky saw Kristen's figure move into the window, searching the darkness below.

"Wait there," he said to Little Horse, pointing to a little storage shed behind the house. "If I am spotted I will run like a thieving coyote, and you had best do the same. This is no place to get caught in a fight. If we must flee, we will meet back at the ponies."

Little Horse nodded. Touch the Sky glided forward, silent as a shadow. When he was close to the house he groped for a pebble and flung it up against the window.

He heard it open. Then Kristen whispered, "Is that you, Matthew?"

His old name struck his ear with an odd, unfamiliar sound. "It's me," he whispered back.

"If you're careful, I think you can climb up the lightning rod. But do be careful please! My pa is downstairs in his study, and he's got ears like a cat."

Touch the Sky's moccasins made little noise, yet gripped well, as he clung to the metal pole and walked his way up the side of the house.

Just shy of the window casement, a shingle broke under Touch the Sky's foot. The board cracked loudly and clattered against the house as it fell. To make matters worse, Touch the Sky lost his footing and banged one knee loudly against the house.

"Kristen!" Steele's voice shouted from downstairs. "What the hell you doing up there?"

Kristen turned white as new snow and whirled from the window. "Nothing, Pa! I just dropped something."

His heart pounding in his throat, Touch the Sky finished his hazardous climb. Moments later he stood beside Kristen in a small but tidy room. A bed with an eiderdown quilt, an oak highboy, a washstand, an armoire on clawed feet, and a single ladderback chair made up the room's furnishings. Some of the flowers Kristen had gathered earlier had been placed in a pottery vase atop the highboy.

They stepped back away from the window. The lantern's light revealed a wild and magnificent spectacle to the girl's eyes. Clearly the half-naked man standing before her, his body smeared with musty-smelling mud, was a savage. His hair hung in a confusion of tangled black locks, and some of his many scars were visible even through the layer of mud. And the stains on the beaded sheath of his knife—surely they were old bloodstains! And yet, his piercing black eyes were bright with intelligence. His high cheeks and hawk nose lent his face a handsome nobility and strength.

"Is it really you, Matthew?" she said. "Are you really standing here next to me?"

Arrow Keeper had buried Touch the Sky's white name forever. But now it sounded right again on her lips, as if the intervening years had suddenly been erased.

"It's really me, right enough. But I wouldn't be standing here if you hadn't saved my bacon earlier. I thank you, lady."

"Matthew, I'm so happy to see you I could just burst! But what are you doing here? Don't you understand? My father hates you with a passion that frightens me. He's the brooding type. And he's been brooding ever since you and Little

Horse whipped him at Bighorn Falls. If he finds out you're here, he'll move heaven and earth to kill you."

"He'll find out soon enough. Your father is why I'm here."

Briefly, he explained about the load of bogus contract goods delivered to the Cheyennes—worthless goods traced back to Hiram Steele's Frontier Supply Company.

Kristen's eyes blazed with anger by the time Touch the Sky finished speaking. "I've heard my father boasting about how much profit he made from a delivery to the Northern Cheyennes. Knowing him, I suspected shady dealings. But I never dreamed it was your tribe."

"The loss of the goods is bad enough. My people need those things and looked forward to them all winter. But I'm the one who talked the tribe into trusting Caleb Riley in the first place. It leaves both of us smelling mighty bad to the tribe."

"Oh, Matthew, it's awful! I hate my father. If I had money of my own, somewhere to go, I'd be long gone by now. I've even considered—well, considered a loveless marriage just to get away from him. But, Matthew, what can you possibly do?"

"My tribe is powerless to fight your father in the courts. No jury in the country would convict a white man for fraud against Indians who haven't signed a recent government treaty. But the Cherokees can fight him because he's robbing them, too."

"Of course he is," she said bitterly. "But you

can't fight him, Matthew, he—"

"I whipped him before and I'll do it again."

"Matthew, no! Don't you see? You met Mankiller and his police today. Who do you think pays their wages? My father."

"I didn't ride all this way to talk it over."

"That's it? You're determined to fight?"

He nodded.

"Nothing will change your mind?"

"Nothing."

She studied his face closely, debating something. Then, abruptly, she turned and crossed to the highboy. She took a folded sheet of paper from the top drawer.

"Well, if you're mule mind is made up," she said, "take this. It's a letter my father wrote to Ephraim Long. He's the agent for the Great Bend Reservation. I found it recently. You can see where father spilled ink on it, which is why he never sent it. Probably wrote it over—he's obsessed with neatness. I don't know what you can do with it, if anything."

Touch the Sky unfolded the note and read it quickly.

"It might come in handy," he said, folding the note again and tucking it carefully into his parfleche. "I'm surprised he put this in writing. Maybe he thought better of it and never sent it. Anyway, thanks. Now I need one more favor from you—not that you haven't done enough already."

"What"

"A name. The name of one good Cherokee brave who might be willing to fight what your father and Mankiller are doing."

She shook her head. "It's too dangerous. Nobody—"

"Listen, lady. There's always somebody willing to fight. Always one person willing to stand up if he gets half the chance. Just give me one name."

"Well, there is someone who I've heard my father and Long call a troublemaker. One who doesn't like Chief Red Jacket. His name is Jack Morningstar. He's a skilled tradesman, a cooper. He makes barrels and kegs for my father's company. My father employs him because he does good work cheap. But believe me, there's no love lost between them."

"How would I find him?"

"His cabin is located at a place called Sundown Ridge, not far from where you had your run-in with Mankiller. Just due east from there. Two rain barrels out front."

"Good."

A thump from downstairs made Kristen start.

"I had better go," Touch the Sky said. "Little Horse is waiting."

"Matthew?"

"Hmm?"

Suddenly they were both aware of how close together they were standing. Her honeysuckle perfume teased his nostrils, and he watched a vein pulse in her soft white throat.

"Do you remember when my father ordered Boone Wilson to beat you up?"

"How could I forget?"

"Well, do you also remember when you asked

me—in front of my father and Wilson—if I wanted to see you again?"

His pained silence was answer enough.

"Matthew, I lied when I said no. Don't you see? I was so scared for you. I was afraid that if I told the truth it would get you killed right there."

Despite all the years and battles and suffering since then, a huge weight of doubt was lifted from his chest. A smile divided his face.

"Then it's prob'ly a good thing you lied. That lie helped send me packing. And they would have killed me if I had stayed."

"And they'll kill you now if you aren't careful."

Another noise came from downstairs, as if to emphasize Kristen's warning. For a moment she stepped up on her toes to kiss him lightly. "If you're determined to fight, I'm going to do what I can to help you. There's a shed in the backyard. Some bricks are piled by the door. If I have a message for you, I'll put it under the bricks."

He nodded. "Thanks. I mean it. But don't cross your pa."

She turned down the wick and he wriggled back out the window. He was halfway down the lightning rod when he heard her whisper. his name into the darkness.

"Matthew? Don't you cross him either. Please be careful!"

Chapter Six

Touch the Sky and Little Horse knew it was useless to search for a campsite that night. So once again they followed Pawnee Creek south at a good pace, leaving Great Bend well behind.

They found a spot sheltered by willows and made a simple cold camp for the rest of the night. They put down a canvas groundsheet Little Horse had won from a Lakota in a pony race, then unrolled their buffalo robes. After watering their ponies and picketing them in good graze, they stretched out under a star-shot sky. Touch the Sky reported his conversation with Kristen.

"The girl with sunlight trapped in her hair," Little Horse said when his friend had finished. "The girl you once held in your blanket for love talk. And now you have climbed into her lodge—and perhaps will again?"

"Why do you play the coy maiden, buck? Speak straight arrow and tell me the thing you mean."

"I mean only that she is very beautiful. That when she looks at you, the sun shines in her eyes, too. You must be careful. I have seen how you look at her."

Little Horse stopped there. He was too good of a friend to embarrass Touch the Sky by saying Honey Eater's name. But Little Horse had a deep affection for her, as did most in the tribe. He trusted his friend, yet his brotherly concern for Honey Eater made him protective; and after all, this pretty golden-haired girl was a paleface. If she lured Touch the Sky back into her world, Little Horse would lose a blood brother.

The next day they began searching early for good shelter. At one point, skirting a thick deadfall of brambles, Touch the Sky felt his shaman sense tingle at the back of his neck. He took a closer look at the seemingly impenetrable deadfall. A tunnel had been burrowed through it, the result, perhaps, of large animals.

He bade little Horse wait while he explored the tunnel. After a few feet, the tunnel opened up into a clear corridor that permitted him to stand. Enough light filtered through to show him the dark cave entrance ahead, leading back under the steep bank.

He poked his head in carefully. But if any wild animals had sheltered here, they were long gone. There was no animal smell lingering. The cave formed a dry shelter about the size of a tipi. He returned to Little Horse and explained his find.

"Look," his friend said, walking well to one side of the deadfall. He pointed toward an opening in the trees. It was hard to spot at a quick glance. "We can tether our ponies there by day and graze them out away from the creek after dark. It will be risky, but this is a fool's mission anyway—the only kind we seem to favor."

They stored their gear in the cave, dug a firepit, and moved the ponies into the hidden clearing. Little Horse killed a fat rabbit, then spitted it with the same arrow that had killed it. They cooked it over the firepit, then enjoyed their first hot meal in two sleeps.

"What next, brother?" Little Horse said, licking grease from his fingers.

"We can do nothing by ourselves. This is not just a Cheyenne battle, but a Cherokee battle, too. We have to help these red men find their fighting fettle."

"How?"

"Jack Morningstar," Touch the Sky said. "He is our only chance. After dark, we will pay him a visit."

The two Cheyennes took turns sleeping for the rest of that day, one remaining on guard outside the hidden cave. After dark they rigged their well-rested ponies. Then, fording the creek, they entered the Cherokee reservation.

A full moon and a starry sky made night riding easy, but also exposed them. They moved by carefully predetermined bounds, always picking an object dead ahead to aim for so they would not wander astray. They avoided ridges that might give them away, sticking to the swales and ground cover.

Once in a while one of them would dismount and place his fingers lightly to the ground, feeling for the vibrations of riders. Even so, they made good time. Soon they had reached the long, narrow spine that Touch the Sky guessed must have been Sunset Ridge.

Moonlight backlit the ridge, limning a small cabin with a light blazing in one oil-paper-covered window.

"Two rain barrels out front," Touch the Sky said, pointing. "Jack Morningstar."

They hobbled their ponies foreleg to rear. Then they climbed the rest of the way up the ridge. Several barrels and kegs, in various stages of completion, littered the cooper's yard. Nearby was a pond fed by a quiet rill. They stopped well back from the dwelling.

"Hello, the cabin!" Touch the Sky called out in English. "Is this Jack Morningstar's place?"

After a long silence, punctuated by the throaty croaking of bullfrogs near the pond, a man said suspiciously, "I don't recognize your voice. Step into the light."

The two Cheyennes did as instructed.

"What the hell? You Sioux?"

"Cheyenne."

"I'll be—"

A squat, solid man wearing machine-made trousers and a flannel shirt stepped into the doorway. He wore his hair in long twin braids.

81

He held an ax loosely in his left hand.

"An English-speaking Cheyenne who knows my name. Should I be scared or curious?"

"I'll explain everything," Touch the Sky said. "But can we step out of this light first? The last thing we need is to be spotted by Mankiller again."

A sympathetic look passed over Morningstar's deadpan face. He set the ax aside. "So you've met the noble lawman of the reservation. Well, stranger, any enemy of Mankiller's is welcome here. Come in."

The inside of the one-room cabin was as spartan as the exterior: a shakedown bed in the back corner, a rammed-earth floor, a crude deal table with kegs scattered about for seats. Crossed sticks on the back wall formed shelves for a few pottery dishes.

Little Horse stared at the coal-oil lantern, marveling that such a small flame could give off so much light—and how could this cloudy water inside it actually burn like wood?

Morningstar looked at their clouts, the tufts of enemy scalps tied to their sashes, the hunted-animal gleam in their eyes.

"You two ain't no praying Indians," he said with conviction. "You lost or just drunk?"

Touch the Sky told him their names and explained about the fraud by Hiram Steele that had sent them on this long journey southeast. He added that the only way for the Cheyennes to achieve justice would be to expose Steel's similar fraud against the Cherokee Nation—official wards of the U.S. Government.

"Steele's daughter gave me your name," Touch the Sky said. "She told me you might help us. Will you?"

Jack Morningstar was silent for a long time. He stared at his knuckles, scarred from hard work.

"Kristen Steele sent you? You're telling me she knows what you came here to do?"

Touch the Sky nodded. "She's watched me whip Steele before. I swear it on my medicine bundle."

"Kristen Steele," Morningstar said, "is one fine girl. When my wife was dying of the smallpox, Kristen stuck with her to the end. Held her hand, talked to her, prayed with her. Prayed with her, when that stinking Ephraim Long wouldn't even send for the Methodist minister—this, even though the government gave him money for medicines that Hiram Steele never supplied. All we got for smallpox and consumption is Epsom salts and quinine!

"I like that girl. But her father? Hiram Steele is a piece of shit, just like his partner Long. I know I take his money, but a man has to live. I hate that bastard. When the paleskins drove us off our farms back east, as soon as the troops marched us off at bayonet point, white thieves descended on our property like jackals. Took everything. Thieves just like Steele and Long."

Touch the Sky said, "Then you'll help us?"

Morningstar shook his head. "I talk tough, but it ain't that easy, Touch the Sky. I take it you've already locked horns with that ugly son of a bitch Mankiller?"

Touch the Sky nodded. "Granted, he's a mean one, and dangerous as a badger in a barrel. But he's only a man, and he bleeds like the rest."

"The hell he's only a man! He's the devil himself, and I'm damn near convinced no mortal man will ever put him under. He's above the law because he is the law. He just recently killed a man in cold blood for sneaking off the reservation to get drunk. Crushed his neck like a bird egg. He's got a police force of twenty of the meanest Indians west of the Mississippi. Steele and Long can go right on stealing our goods. Hell, they can order us lowly Injuns to piss in a cup and drink it if they want to because they got Mankiller to enforce the orders and keep the complainers scared spitless. Especially now that Long has brought back tithing."

"What's that?"

"Tithing? It's supposed to be illegal now. But who's to stop him? The Long Knives did it back east before they took our land. You pick one Indian out of every ten, make him responsible for any problems with the other nine. A man gets so scared of punishment, he starts to spy on his friends, to report them to the bosses."

Little Horse was anxious to know what was happening. Touch the Sky translated the gist of the conversation so far. Then he switched back to English.

"Seems to me," he said slowly to Morningstar, "like you're really saying that some Cherokees might fight Steele and Long if they stop seeing Mankiller as a little tin god. That they need to see how he and his policemen are not above the law, that they can be punished, too."

"All that's a mighty tall order, Cheyenne. But sure, if that ever happened, Steele and Long would have to call it quits. A rattler ain't shit without its fangs."

"All right then," Touch the Sky said. "We'll start with one of Mankiller's favorite deputies. The meanest one he's got."

"That would be Creek Hater. He'd flay his own mother for a cheap cigar."

"Good. Tell us where to find him."

Just after sunrise the next morning, the Cherokee policeman named Creek Hater packed his drinking jewelry into his saddlebags. That was what Mankiller called them—iron knuckles made from horseshoe nails. All of the Cherokee policemen carried them, but none used them as frequently or eagerly as did Creek Hater.

Creek Hater was patrolling his favorite area, the huge tract of forest along the southern boundary of the reservation. By reservation law—strictly enforced by Ephraim Long and the police—hunting was forbidden. It was the Indian Bureau's intention to discourage the red man's dependence on hunting, to increase his reliance on farming and skilled trades.

But Creek Hater didn't care about the intentions of white fools. All he cared was that this stretch of forest offered good hunting. And though firearms were illegal and scarce on the reservation, bows and arrows were not. With luck he would catch a hunter and have himself a little fun while also earning his pay.

He let his sorrel set its own pace through the trees while he searched left and right for signs of movement. He was detouring around a patch of bog when he spotted movement dead ahead, on the far side of a small clearing.

His horse was trained to stop when the reins touched the ground. Creek Hater threw them down, then quietly slid off his mount. He took his carbine from its boot and removed a coil of rope from his saddle horn. Then he moved silently from tree to tree, working his way around the edge of the clearing.

He spotted movement again, then grinned as he recognized the skinny frame of the youth named Oliver Lame Deer. The boy was still in his teens, and Creek Hater had already caught two of his brothers hunting small game around here.

Creek Hater moved silently for a big man. Oliver had his back to him and was down on one knee behind a tree to aim at a rabbit. Creek Hater waited until the youth had released his arrow and skewered the rabbit. When he stood to retrieve the kill, Creek Hater spoke up.

"Drop the bow and stand real still."

Oliver started, looked quickly back over his shoulder, and turned pale when he recognized the highly feared lawman. Only a few minutes later, the frightened youth was tied tight to the same tree he had hidden behind. Creek Hater ambled over to the dead rabbit, picked it up, and pushed the bloody arrow through. He snapped the shaft so it couldn't be used again. Then he tied the rabbit to his belt. Would be damn good eating later in a stew.

"My family could use that meat," Oliver said. "You're gonna thump on me anyway. Why not least give me the rabbit? Our rations was way short this time, and we ran out of pork in a month."

Creek Hater smiled and walked back to his horse. As he returned, he donned his drinking jewelry. "Bullshit. Your drunken old man traded all the best stuff for grog."

"He tried, sure. But the pork was so putrid this time they wouldn't take it!"

"It's against the law to trade allotment goods. Liquor is illegal, too."

The youth stared back defiantly. "A-huh. That don't stop the policemen from drinking good white man's whiskey."

Creek Hater doubled his iron-reinforced fist and drew it back for a short, hard punch to the ribs. But it never connected—a heartbeat later a menacing voice called out behind him in English:

"Hit him even once, Cherokee, and you cross over today."

Instantly, Creek Hater regretted having returned his carbine to the horse. He turned slowly, expecting a white man. Instead, he confronted the same two Cheyennes the tribal police had almost drowned. The little one held a nasty-looking four-barreled shotgun on him, the tall one a percussion-action Sharps rifle.

"You know I'm a policeman. Kill me and you're in a world of hurt."

"You're a bullying pig," Touch the Sky replied. "A coward who licks the white men's boots and lords it over unarmed Indians. You probably will need killing eventually, but it's going to be your own people who do it, not me. For now, we have other plans for you."

Little Horse cut Oliver Lame Deer loose. The same ropes were now used to secure Creek Hater.

"Stay," Touch the Sky told Oliver, making it an order so Creek Hater wouldn't punish him later. "I want you to see this. And then I want you to spread the word. The red men are united in this battle, all tribes are one. From now on it's open season on Hiram Steele, Ephraim Long, and these criminals who call themselves policemen."

Creek Hater wore his black hair long and loose, proud of his hair as were many Indian men. Touch the Sky moved closer and suddenly grabbed it, wrapping it several times around his wrist and jerking it back hard.

A moment later his knife was in his hand. Creek Hater stared in wide-eyed disbelief.

"No!" Creek Hater shouted. "No!"

His sneering disbelief gave way to cold panic as he realized this crazy Cheyenne fool meant to scalp him!

Chapter Seven

But Touch the Sky did not exactly scalp the brutal policeman.

He and Little Horse had talked it over carefully before they jumped him. It didn't matter how badly hated Mankiller and his brutal deputies were—not if the rest of the Cherokees saw the Cheyenne action as going too far, as interference by outsiders. Most tribes valued intense loyalty to the group as basic to survival in war and other hardships. The proud Cherokees were no exception.

But also like many other tribes, their men took great pride in their long, thick, shiny hair. Most Indians interpreted a mutilation of the hair as a grave insult to the victim's courage and manhood. So the two Cheyennes chose a more effective strategy—they humiliated Creek Hater's character as an individual, not as a Cherokee.

While Little Horse put his knife to work shredding the highly prized campaign hat, badge of the Cherokee police, Touch the Sky chopped Creek Hater's hair. He sawed it off in ragged handfuls, leaving Creek Hater's head looking like a plucked prairie chicken.

The moccasin telegraph was quick on every reservation. Within 48 hours, everyone knew the story about how the bully Creek Hater got his feathers clipped. When Hiram Steele heard the story—first through Ephraim Long, then directly from the sheepish Creek Hater—he had double cause for alarm. For this was not just a serious threat to his control of the reservation. It also meant that his most dangerous enemy in the world was out to defeat him again.

So Steele called an emergency meeting, at his house, with Long and Mankiller. Kristen was impressed into reluctant service as cook and servant. While the reservation Cherokees nearby subsisted on a foul concoction of flour and tripe, Kristen served the three men a dinner of venison steak, beans with bacon, biscuits and butter, apple pudding, and coffee.

But Hiram Steele was irritable and distracted and hardly touched the delicious food.

"I'm telling you right now," Steele said emphatically, looking at Mankiller, "you made a serious mistake when you didn't kill those two."

Mankiller, busy devouring his third mound of pudding, paid no attention to the white man whose money paid his salary. The spoon looked tiny in his huge bear paw.

"A serious mistake," Steele repeated. "Why did you do it?"

Kristen hovered near the table, refilling coffee cups from a blue enamelled pot. Mankiller watched her turn white as bleached bones at her father's question. The wily Cherokee had left her name out when he told her father what happened at Pawnee Creek.

"Any more pudding?" he said quietly to Kristen, and she nodded a bit too quickly, taking his empty bowl and hurrying into the kitchen. Mankiller grinned, enjoying himself.

"I don't get it, Hiram," Long said. "You damn near had kittens the last time you mentioned the Cheyenne. Now you're getting all steamed up over a pair of brazen renegades. Simmer down. If they're foolish enough to hang around here, Mankiller will give them a comeuppance they'll never forget."

Mankiller devoured three biscuits in as many bites, then wiped his fingers on the lace tablecloth. Steele was too distracted to notice.

"Mankiller isn't the issue," Steele said. "It's these goddamn Cheyennes! I'm telling you, I know who they are. The description Mankiller gave fits them like a glove. These ain't just a pair of blanket Indians turned maverick. I can't be sure why they're this far south. But you can write it on your pillowcase—we're up against it now!"

"Hiram, be reasonable, man. There's only two of them."

Steele shook his head violently. "No. No. Don't even think that way. These two can't be counted like other Injuns."

91

Kristen returned with Mankiller's pudding. "That's the last of it," she told him apologetically.

"'Preciate it. Got any pie or cake?"

She looked startled. "Some blueberry pie, I think."

"That'll do. Some milk'd be real nice, too." He wiped out the pudding in two bites. Kristen returned to the kitchen. Hiram finally seemed to notice that something odd was going on between Mankiller and his daughter. This was one damned uppity Indian, ordering a white girl around like that. But even Steele, who brooked insolence from few men, had no desire to confront Mankiller.

"The thing of it is," Steele said slowly, thinking out loud, "they don't just happen to be here. Not these two. It's damned important to stop them, and pronto."

Kristen returned with a big hunk of pie and a cup of milk for Mankiller. Steele watched her, his eyes squinting shrewdly shut. For the first time he wondered where his daughter was when the Cheyennes had been caught by Mankiller. But before he could ask, Long spoke up.

"On second thought, you may be right, Hiram. Maybe these renegade bucks are up to something besides the usual hell-raising and thieving. This thing with humiliating Creek Hater—it was done deliberately to cast aspersion on the reservation police, to foment the rest to rebellion against my authority."

"Now you've caught the gait! That's what I'm telling you. You and Mankiller have to make it a priority to catch them before this snowballs into something we can't handle."

"Well," Long said, scratching thoughtfully at one of his mutton chops, "if these Cheyenne intruders enjoy playing Robin Hood so much, let's give them another opportunity."

"What do you mean?"

"I've got a plan." Long started to speak, but Steele's eyes cut to the end of the table. Kristen was clearing away serving dishes. Her eyes met her father's.

Steele lifted his hand, stopping Long. Then he looked at his daughter. "That can wait," he told her. "You got something to do up in your room?"

She nodded. Long rose hastily as she left.

"Delicious dinner, Miss Steele," he told her, bowing slightly. "A man could get spoiled by that kind of cooking."

"Not if he gave half a thought to those who aren't eating," she retorted.

Mankiller sat right where he was, picking his front teeth with a thumbnail.

"Pie's a little stale," he told her, belching loudly. He grinned at her confusion and even wider as Hiram Steele again looked at them, befuddled but suspicious.

When the girl was gone, Hiram looked at Long. "All right," he said. "Let's hear this plan of yours."

It was all Kristen could do to keep from collapsing from nervous fear while Mankiller teased her. Her father sensed something. She could tell. Somehow the crafty Cherokee had guessed that she knew the Cheyennes and that her father knew she knew them and didn't like the fact.

As she escaped upstairs to her room, her legs trembled as if she'd just run a long way uphill.

If her father ever found out that she had begged for the Cheyennes' lives, his anger would be too great to tell. Never would she forget his cold, stone-eyed rage and hatred when he had caught Matthew and her together back when they were only sixteen. Her father had already struck her and thrown her to the floor and threatened to disown her as punishment for brief meetings since then. Kristen did not doubt that he was even capable of killing her if he ever found out she was in touch with Matthew again.

And certainly he must be suspicious now. He would be watching her, sticking to her as close as ugly on a buzzard. But she couldn't simply sit back and let her father kill Matthew. And Mankiller—she was beginning to suspect that he only let the Cheyennes go for the sheer pleasure of toying with them again before he killed them. He was insane and brutal, yet crafty as an old fox.

Once in her room, she closed and locked the door. Then she crossed to the cast-iron heating vent near her bed. There was a huge fireplace in the dining room below, and this grate opening in the floor let heat from below into her room. It also, she had already noticed, permitted her to eavesdrop on conversations below.

She lowered herself to the floor and slowly,

inch by inch, opened the vent. Now and then it screeched like a rusty hinge, and she cringed. But eventually it was wide open, and she could easily hear Long's and her father's voices and Mankiller's occasional grunts.

As she listened, slowly comprehending their plan, her nostrils flared in indignant anger. It was a veritable deathtrap they were plotting! Cold-blooded murder, pure and simple. She had to do something.

She thought about her arrangement with Matthew to leave messages under a brick near the shed door. Kristen couldn't be sure how often he checked that spot—nor that he would check in time, should she leave a warning there. But it was the only chance she had to help him and Little Horse.

But how to get the message there? Leaving the house by the front door was out of the question because she would have to pass her father.

She glanced at the window. Could she climb down the lightning rod without breaking her neck? And what if she couldn't climb back up? But she decided she had to try.

Kristen hastily changed into her leather riding pants and a pair of boots, then tied her hair in a ponytail. Next she wrote a quick note to Matthew, folded it, and tucked it into her blouse. Heart pounding loudly in her ears, she crossed to the window and slid it open.

It seemed a long way to the ground, and the dark maw of the night held numerous dangers. But Matthew's life was on the line, and besides, her father and Long were simply wrong. Too many were suffering so that they could live high on the hog. Somebody had to fight them.

Taking a deep breath for courage, feeling very little like a brave hero, the frightened girl lifted one leg over the sill.

"Father, I am frightened for Touch the Sky," Honey Eater said. "For three sleeps in a row now I have dreamed of crows."

Her words startled Arrow Keeper. It was late into the night, and though it was only mildly cool, the ailing shaman had a hot fire blazing in his firepit to warm his old bones. The orange flames emphasized the deep furrow between his eyebrows, the network of seams on his weathered face. Honey Eater's face, in contrast, was taut and flawless, though pinched with worry.

"You, too, little daughter?" he replied. "I, too, have dreamed of death omens. However, when one has as many winters behind him as I, this thing is not unusual."

His smile was meant to comfort her. But Honey Eater was beyond comfort tonight. It was always hard for her when Touch the Sky rode out to face unknown dangers. Black Elk was riding herd guard, but his followers were everywhere. She had sneaked to Arrow Keeper's tipi at great risk.

"Father, you know how Black Elk, Wolf Who Hunts Smiling, and the rest plot against Touch the Sky. Despite everything he has done for his tribe, all his suffering, the blood he has shed, his enemies cleverly keep the pall of doubt over Touch the Sky. Now, with many upset over these worthless goods, they are speaking against him again. And this time, I sense they are close to serious treachery."

Something in her tone, and the urgent look she cast him, alerted Arrow Keeper. "What do you mean, little one? Speak the straight word and shame the Wendigo."

"Father, recently I heard Wolf Who Hunts Smiling tell Black Elk that the only obstacle to banishing Touch the Sky forever is you. I am afraid for him and you."

Arrow Keeper reached one scrawny arm out from under his blanket and patted the girl's shoulder.

"Little Honey Eater, I would speak bent words if I told you your fear is only a thing of smoke. As for Wolf Who Hunts Smiling, his treachery knows no bounds. You are right to fear him. But he will not kill me—my time to cross over is near at hand. And know this. Maiyun, the Good Supernatural, has His own battle plan. No mortal warrior can interfere with that plan."

Honey Eater took a little comfort from these words. "I hope so, Father. As much as I fear Touch the Sky's tribal enemies, I also fear he faces great danger from a powerful enemy without. One who stalks him right now."

Again Arrow Keeper's eyes narrowed thoughtfully as he studied this remarkable girl. Long had he suspected that she, too, possessed a bit of the shaman's hidden eye.

"Daughter, what have you seen?" he asked.

"It sounds foolish, I know, but I have dreamed

of a huge man whose face is all in shadow. Only—"

"Only what, Honey Eater?"

"Only, instead of hands, this big man has eagle's talons. Huge eagle's talons."

A chill moved up Arrow Keeper's spine. It was the same image from his own medicine dream.

Something in his face alerted her. "What is it?" she demanded. "What do you know?"

He shook his head evasively. "Only this," he said. "Maiyun has His own battle plan."

Mankiller moved slowly along the bank of Pawnee Creek, following it south out of Great Bend.

He let his big 16-hand bay set its own pace in the generous light of a full moon. The good dinner he had enjoyed earlier at Hiram Steele's place still lay warm in his belly. The Cherokee sat slumped far forward in the saddle, leaning low first to the left side, then the right. He had eyes like a cat and could read sign in the moonlight.

He encountered fresh horse droppings. Mankiller dismounted and broke them apart to see if they were made by white men's or Indian ponies.

Indian ponies. . . .

His deputies grained their horses and fed them rough forage, so the police horses were ruled out. And though it was allowed, very few Cherokees on the reservation even owned ponies. Those who did seldom rode in this direction.

Mankiller stood up again and adjusted his

broad-brimmed hat. The trap they were setting for the two Cheyennes might work. In case it didn't, Mankiller planned on eventually smoking this pair of foxes out of their den.

He avoided the Indian side when he mounted, swinging up from the left. Then he chucked up his horse and resumed his slow journey, bringing death steadily closer for the two Cheyennes.

Chapter Eight

Fortunately for the Cheyennes, Touch the Sky visited the secret hiding place only hours after Kristen left the note for him.

Kristen's light had been on, and once he even saw her standing in the window. But he knew that he would seriously endanger her if he sneaked up into her room too often. He hadn't really expected any word from her this soon. But after he read her cryptic note, he realized the war was on. Steele knew he was here, and the rabid Indian hater planned to get sweet revenge for that humiliating defeat in Bighorn Falls.

"Clearly," Little Horse said when Touch the Sky had returned to their cavern camp and translated the note, "our little sport with Creek Hater worried the hair-face chiefs. This punishment the note mentions—clearly it is meant to show the folly of challenging Long and Mankiller."

Touch the Sky nodded. "Not only that. It is also meant to flush us out of cover."

Little Horse grinned, recognizing the mischievous glint in his friend's eyes. "Well, brother? Will it flush us out?"

Touch the Sky nodded. "It will. It will also flush out a surprise. Now listen, Cheyenne, for I have a plan."

On the day after Ephraim Long and Hiram Steele hatched their latest plot, a brief notice was posted throughout the Cherokee reservation. It was also published in the weekly reservation newspaper.

A NOTICE TO ALL MEMBERS OF THE CHEROKEE NATION: RESPECT FOR THE LAW OF THE LAND IS ESSENTIAL TO GOOD GOVERNMENT. REPEATED VIOLATIONS OF RESERVATION LAWS AND OPEN ACTS OF DISRESPECT TOWARD RESERVATION POLICE HAVE NECESSITATED THE FOLLOWING PROCLAMATION: ON MONDAY, MAY 12, AT NOON, AN HABITUAL VIOLATOR OF RESERVATION LAW WILL BE PUBLICLY WHIPPED AT THE CEREMONIAL SQUARE ADJACENT TO AGENT LONG'S RESIDENCE. SUCH PUBLIC DISCIPLINARY MEASURES WILL CONTINUE UNTIL LAW AND ORDER PREVAIL ON THE RESERVATION.

Knowing morbid curiosity would draw more Indians, Long deliberately omitted naming the habitual violator or his supposed crimes. The desire to know who the unfortunate victim was would fetch the Cherokees, he thought. With luck, it would also lure the Cheyennes.

One day before the public whipping was scheduled, the youth named Oliver Lame Deer went out spear-fishing as usual.

The ban against hunting was strictly enforced, but fishing was still permitted and widely practiced. The Cherokees had been famous spear-fishers back east of the river called Great Waters. Those who survived the deadly forced migration known as the Cherokee Trail of Tears brought their skills to the West.

Oliver had a favorite spot on Pawnee Creek where bass and bluegill and trout were plentiful. Not only did his skill supplement his large family's meager diet, but some of the catch would be smoked on wooden drying racks and swapped for badly needed trade items.

Like many others on the reservation, Oliver had been heartened by these mysterious Cheyennes who sheared Creek Hater's hair. Now a few of the leaders on the reservation—skilled tradesmen like Jack Morningstar—were firing up the people. Still, Mankiller and his deputies were no Indians to trifle with.

Oliver thought all of these things as he lay patiently on his stomach, staring down the steep bank into the swift-moving current of Pawnee Creek. His three-tined spear was balanced in his right hand. Something flashed in the water below. He drew his arm back and tried to throw, but the spear wouldn't move!

More confused than frightened, he looked back to see what had caught it. His eyes went big when they met Mankiller's. The huge policeman gripped his spear.

"You're under arrest," he said.

"For what, Mankiller? Fishing is not illegal!"

"No. But stealing corn from the reservation garden is."

Oliver blinked. "What? I haven't been around the gardens since I drew hoeing detail. What are you—"

Mankiller lay the wooden spear against his knee and snapped it as easily as a dry twig. He threw both pieces into the water.

"I said you stole corn from the reservation garden. I caught you in the act. Me and Creek Hater."

Now Oliver understood. It didn't matter that the Cheyenne had ordered him to stay when Creek Hater was humiliated. Because he had witnessed Creek Hater's hair being razed, he had been selected for the public beating.

"I won't beg," he said. "It's not fair and you know it. But I ain't begging. You've whipped me and my brothers plenty just because we ain't impressed when you play the big Indian."

Mankiller whacked his boot with his quirt. The hand holding the rawhide quirt seemed as big as a pannier. "I whipped you plenty, and I

103

plan on whipping you plenty more. I don't play nothing, tadpole. I am a big Indian."

Several miles east of the settlement of Great Bend, a huge, grassy meadow formed a tree-bordered park on the reservation. This was the central gathering place for religious ceremonies. It was also the site of the official residence of the Cherokee Agent, Ephraim Long, whose large fieldstone house stood on one flank of the meadow.

Indians were gathering in scattered groups, milling near a huge oak tree that stood by itself in the grass. There were children, elders, and young women with bear grease in their hair and babies in backboards. The policemen, conspicuous in their hook-and-eye hats, controlled the people and kept them from getting too close to the tree.

Many cast hateful glances at the mounted policemen, but few said anything. Names of complainers ended up on lists and their allotment goods could mysteriously disappear. Still, several grinned or stifled laughs when they spotted Creek Hater wearing an old slouch hat to disguise his new haircut.

The most conspicuous guest was the stern-jawed Hiram Steele. He stood by himself, proudly remote from the Indians around him. Oliver Lame Tree stood near the tree, his eyes fearful but defiant. It had not been necessary to tie him up. Mankiller had put Uncle Sam's watch and chain on the prisoner: a six-foot chain and an iron ball weighing 25 pounds. The chain was attached to the youth's skinny ankle by an iron band.

Ephraim Long came out of his house and crossed the meadow to address the crowd, speaking from a hastily erected wooden platform. The policemen maintained silence while Long deplored the lack of law and order on the reservation. He also warned the Cherokee people about the dangers of outside agitators from uncivilized tribes, pagans who would interfere with tribal unity and authority. At one point he stared directly at the cooper, Jack Morningstar, a known malcontent. Morningstar matched his stare.

While Long delivered his spiel, Mankiller repeatedly cast his glance toward the thick stand of trees behind them, then toward a long spine of rocks that nearly split the meadow.

If trouble came, Mankiller told himself, it would come from those trees. But Mankiller, too, had a little surprise in store.

He glanced toward the rocky spine and grinned with pleasant anticipation. Whoever emerged from those trees must pass the spine.

Long finally wound up his speech and nodded at Mankiller. The police chief dismounted and took a knotted-thong whip from his saddlebag. He cracked it a few times as he crossed toward the tree.

He squared off, planted his feet, and cracked the whip again for good measure. The crowd went as silent as a burial forest. Mankiller raised one arm and drew it back.

"Hi-ya! Hi-ya!"

It wasn't clear where the Cheyenne war cry came from. But there could be no mistaking the buckskin-clad warrior bearing down on them! Clearly, from the warrior's lance and headdress and his pinto mustang, this was one of the Cheyennes currently plaguing them. Mankiller laughed in open delight, waiting until the attacker came abreast of the rock spine.

Then Mankiller drew the Remington pistol from his sash and fired an offhand shot.

This was the prearranged signal to the six Cherokee policemen who had been held in reserve, hiding behind the rock spine. As one they rose and drew a bead on the Cheyenne, carefully avoiding the valuable pony.

Their rifles cracked, the Cheyenne flew from the saddle and landed sprawling in the dirt. The frightened mount turned and bolted for the trees again. The police had dismounted when Mankiller did. Now they raised a triumphant shout and raced on foot toward the fallen Cheyenne. Long and Steel trailed them at a run.

Mankiller's face creased in an ear-to-ear smile. The plan had worked beautifully! He was still clearing a hole in the bystanders when the first angry shouts went up from his men.

Mankiller literally threw several people aside, then stared down at the Cheyenne in the grass. They had been foxed again. The victim was merely a buckskin suit filled with grass, complete with a crude headdress and lance!

Rage sent hot blood into Mankiller's face. But the foxes weren't finished quite yet. Steele raised an angry shout of warning.

He pointed back toward the clearing. The police horses were all gathered there, hobbled. But one of the Cheyennes had sneaked out from the opposite tree line and slipped their hobbles while the crowd was distracted. Now the Cheyenne fired his shotgun, and the horses scattered at the resounding blast.

"Goddamn it!" Steele screamed at the top of his lungs. "Catch those bastards! Chase 'em!"

But few in the crowd seemed at all inclined to capture these brave and reckless Cheyenne intruders. As for the policemen, they were too busy trying to chase down their horses.

Chapter Nine

"I told you," Hiram Steele said, fuming. "Didn't I by God tell you those two meant trouble? What they dished up yesterday was just a taste."

Steele was so distracted and angry that he had neglected to touch his Scotch. Mankiller kept a steady eye on Steele's full glass from his side of the table. Ephraim Long cocked his head in curiosity and watched his business partner closely.

"I don't get it, Hiram. Those Cheyennes are giving you a fit. You said you ran into them before. All right. But why are you taking ignorant aboriginals so damn personally? What's this bad blood between you and them?"

Steele's eyes cut away evasively. He wasn't about to confess that his own daughter had once been sweet on a full-blood Cheyenne—

hell, might still be. That she had hung on him and kissed him and God knew what else. His glance went to the kitchen, where Kristen was rustling up a quick supper for this hastily arranged meeting. Again the suspicion cankered deep inside him. Had she warned those two Cheyennes about the trap? By God, if she had. . . .

"The details ain't important," he replied. "Just mark my words. Those two spell real bad trouble, the worst kind."

Long picked at some lint on his coat sleeve. "Well, that little dog-and-pony show they put on yesterday was trouble enough for me, all right. I heard a few of the Cherokees cheer when the deputies had to chase their horses down. This kind of thing is dangerous. I've worked hard to teach these savages some discipline, to put the fear of God in them. These damn upstart Cheyennes could get us caught in the middle of a nasty rebellion."

"Now you're reading the sign! That's what I been trying to tell you. We got to blow out their lamps and quick. When it comes down to busting caps, the red men will all side together against the white man every time."

Steele's eyes cut to Mankiller. The huge Cherokee was still staring at his employer's full glass.

"You gonna drink that?" Mankiller said.

Startled, Steele knuckled the glass across the table to Mankiller. "Kristen! Bring the liquor in."

Long rose gallantly when the pretty girl

109

entered, skirts rustling, and set the cut-glass carboy on the table.

Steele watched her closely, suspicion again narrowing his eyes. She paled under the stare. She met Mankiller's eyes and the Cherokee winked intimately. The girl flushed and hurried back into the kitchen. Steele's anger at this brazen savage's behavior toward a white woman gave way again to nagging doubt. What did he have on her?

"Anyway," Steele said, looking at Long and Mankiller, "it's so important to stop these Cheyennes that I'm putting up good color. To be exact, one thousand in double-eagle gold pieces to the man who kills them and brings me proof."

Mankiller suddenly lost the bored glaze over his eyes. "One thousand for both of them?"

"For both of them. You won't get one without the other, believe me."

"The reservation Indians don't have firearms," Long said. "But I'll spread the word among the whites I know."

Mankiller polished off his Scotch, stood up, and clapped his broad-brimmed hat on his head.

"Don't bother," he said. "That money is mine."

The Cherokee skilled tradesmen had their own lodge on the reservation—a large, one-room cabin with crude plank tables and backless benches. On the night after the bold Cheyenne raid, Jack Morningstar wandered down to visit with some of his lodge brothers. The talk, naturally, centered on the mysterious Cheyenne strangers.

"Who the hell are they?" said a burly, middle-aged blacksmith who called himself Captain Bill.

"Who cares?" said a cobbler from the Virginia River Clan. "They're making life hard for the whiteskins who steal from us. They're welcome here."

Morningstar had still not mentioned to the rest his visit from the Cheyennes. Now he glanced quickly around to make sure none of Mankiller's men was present.

"They're fighting for us," he said. "That's more'n I can say for us."

Several heads turned to stare at him. Morningstar was not one to speak in riddles.

"What do you mean?" Captain Bill said.

Morningstar shrugged his shoulders. "Look at it. Ain't their reservation. Ain't their battle. But they're fighting it anyway."

"Hell," the cobbler said. His name was Otto and, like Morningstar, he wore white men's machine-made clothing. "My father and my uncle both died fighting the Creeks. I got their war shields, and they're plenty scarred up."

"I've seen them," Captain Bill said. "Your clan was all warriors back in the Ohio River country. So was mine. My grandfather died defending his grist mill when the Long Knives came to take it. My grandma fell at his side."

"Any of us can make brags on our ancestors," Morningstar said casually. "Point is, them Cheyennes're fighting for us now, and all we're doing is sitting on our duffs talking about past bravery."

"So what can we do?" the cobbler demanded.

Morningstar shrugged as if all this were merely a speculative game, not a real plan of action. "We've got some horses in the common corral. We got axes, bows and arrows, and knives. We could, say, draw straws. See who rides with the Cheyennes."

"Rides with 'em? Rides where?"

"Well, for instance," Morningstar said, "Steele's got a new shipment coming in day after tomorrow. It'll be going to his warehouse on Exposition Street in town."

"That's where he stores the shoddy goods," Captain Bill said.

Morningstar nodded. "Sure. He stockpiles them there. But what if a raiding party met the freighters north of town and destroyed all that crap?"

A long silence followed this suggestion. Resentment against Steele, Long, and Mankiller ran deep—even among these skilled tradesmen, who were better off than most on the reservation. But years of hopeless suffering had dulled their fighting instincts.

"Even if I didn't think it's a foolish plan," Otto said, "how in the hell would we get wind of it to those Cheyennes?"

Morningstar held his face impassive, not revealing his elation. Clearly his lodge brothers were more willing to fight than he had believed. Watching those young Cheyennes yesterday had inspired them. All it needed was one spark—the fighting Cheyennes from the north country—to perhaps set this hotbed of misery ablaze. He had agreed to meet the Cheyennes again this evening. Now he could surprise them with some potentially encouraging news.

"Don't worry about that," he replied. "They ain't far away."

Less than 48 hours after the discussion in the tradesmen's lodge, five riders forded Pawnee Creek well north of the settlement of Great Bend: Touch the Sky, Little Horse, Jack Morningstar, Captain Bill, and Otto.

Only the two Cheyennes were equipped with firearms. The Cherokees each had powerful osage bows and a few axes lashed to their mounts. The Cherokees' horses were far from prime horseflesh: swayback draft animals liberated from the small common corral.

"You see like an eagle. Drop behind and watch our back trail, brother," Touch the Sky told Little Horse. "Make sure Mankiller or his deputies have not cut sign on us or spotted us leaving."

With Jack Morningstar pointing out the way, this unlikely war party followed the deep-seamed freight road that bore north toward the storage docks at Fort Hays. The teamsters hauling Steele's goods were due to reach Great Bend late this morning. Touch the Sky intended, however, to intercept them well outside of town.

"They're sure as hell gonna have armed guards," Morningstar said. "At least two. And the teamsters will be armed, prob'ly with scatterguns. But they won't be expecting trouble. Most of the Indian flare ups are west of here."

Touch the Sky nodded. "Don't forget, no blood-letting if we can avoid it. We've got no quarrels with these freighters. It's the cargo we want to attack."

Several miles farther north, Little Horse caught up to the rest. "All clear," he reported. "No one is trailing us yet."

The five Indians rode in a loose skirmish line, the sound of hoofclops and bit rings from the Cherokee mounts the only noise. To their right, the morning sun tracked higher, looking like a dull yellow ball; to their left the plains rolled on, unbroken brown, until lost in the haze on the far horizon. Now and then one of the Cherokees would catch a companion's eye and grin self-consciously. Despite their tribe's warrior legacy, these Cherokees had seen little combat.

"Brothers!" said the sharp-eyed Little Horse, pointing north. "Look there!"

Straight ahead, little dust puffs rose above the horizon.

Touch the Sky felt a familiar humming in his blood. The battle was close upon them! He pointed to a long ridge on their left.

"All right! Cherokees, you know the plan! Take cover behind the crest of that ridge. Have your fire arrows ready. Little Horse and I will do the rest. When your last arrow is spent, return to the point where we forded the Pawnee."

He and Little Horse angled their ponies off to the right and chucked them up to a canter, keeping first a line of cedars, then a low bluff between them and the approaching pack train. Touch the Sky was following the advice of old

Chief Yellow Bear, who had spoken to him from the Land of Ghosts during his Medicine Lake vision quest. *When all seems lost, become your enemy.*

Touch the Sky's plan was simple and based on one of the bluecoat's favorite battle strategies: the pincers movement. It was up to him and Little Horse to nudge that supply train closer to the ridge. Once the wooden wagons were easy targets, the Cherokees would get a chance to demonstrate their marksmanship.

They cleared the bluff, the supply train now easily visible on their left flank. There were a half-dozen mule-team wagons and, as Jack Morningstar had predicted, an armed guard riding in front, another in the rear. Both men carried Henry rifles, noted for accuracy at long distances.

"Charge them!" Touch the Sky said in Cheyenne to Little Horse. "We will count coup on the guards. Do not ride in a straight line or they will lead us and shoot plumb. We have got to get them nervous enough to swerve well right."

"Hi-ya!" Little Horse shouted. "Hi-ya, hii-ya!"

They dug their knees into their ponies' flanks and surged forward. The two friends split wide, Touch the Sky angling toward the front guard, Little Horse the rear. They crouched low over their well-trained ponies' necks, making small targets. They also ran in a carefully practiced zigzagging charge, frustrating the guards with the long rifles.

Touch the Sky felt his calico mustang straining beneath him, the damp foam against his skin, and the wind streaming in his loose black locks. He bore down on his man, divots of dirt flying behind his pony's hoofs. He could see the drivers hastily snatching up their weapons, the armed guards squaring off to meet the attack.

He surged closer, his man fired, and a bullet whirred past Touch the Sky's ear. The guard hastily began recharging his piece. Shouting a triumphant war cry, Touch the Sky cracked his lance down hard on the hindquarters of the other man's horse. For good measure, and to heighten the panic, he drew his Sharps from its boot and snapped off a round over the head of the lead driver. The mules and horses in the remuda were bucking, jack-knifing, and crow-hopping, threatening to break loose from the string.

Now he and Little Horse faded back a bit and faked another charge. As they had hoped, the wagons veered right, but the lead teamster did not order them into a circular defense. They had decided to wage a running battle and race for Great Bend before the rest of the wild Indians showed up for a possible massacre.

The rest came off exactly as planned.

The three Cherokees had only one battle assignment: to pepper those freight wagons with fire arrows. And they performed magnificently. Before the nervous whites knew what had hit them, dozens of flaming arrows had hit their wooden wagons.

Now the two Cheyennes went into action again. Each time a teamster tried to put out a fire, Touch the Sky or Little Horse sent a bullet or deadly, flint-tipped arrow within inches of them. This was risky, forcing them to skyline themselves to aim—the armed guards returned dangerous fire.

But soon, the mission was a fiery, smoke-belching success. None of the teamsters had been injured. But four of the six wagons were burning beyond control, and the other two were substantially damaged.

Well after Hiram Steele and Ephraim Long had fallen asleep that night, both men were startled awake by the sound of shattering glass. Both nerve-frazzled men also found a note wrapped around the rock that broke their windows.

Make good on your legal obligations to the red man, or the harassment campaign continues!

Chapter Ten

Mankiller led his big, 16-hand bay slowly along Pawnee Creek, scouring the earth for the slightest sign of the two Cheyennes.

He knew they must have a base camp near here. That daring raid yesterday finally proved that. True, none of the teamsters had gotten a close look at the Indians who actually fired arrows on them from behind the ridge. But they had recognized the two boldest bucks as Northern Cheyennes.

And if they had a camp near here, Pawnee Creek was the most likely spot. No other place offered enough shelter or water for ponies. Besides, what little sign he had managed to cut so far had been found near the creek.

One thousand dollars in double-eagle gold pieces. Mankiller could almost feel the weight of

Hiram Steele's bounty money in his saddlebags. With such a stake, a man could set himself up as one hell of a big Indian. Lord it around like Steele and Long, smoke big cigars, wear fancy coats as Chief Red Jacket did.

He felt his huge palms itching as he thought about the sheer pleasure of feeling those Cheyenne necks snap like reeds in his powerful grip. Nobody made a fool of Mankiller and lived to brag on it to his children.

Suddenly the bay lifted its head high, pricked its ears forward. Mankiller stared ahead toward a sharp bend in the creek. The trees and thickets grew dense all along here.

The bay snorted. Mankiller slowly, silently slid to the ground. They were close; he sensed it now. Relying on an old Indian trick, he pinched the bay's nostrils to keep it from whinnying. Then he slid the Remington from his sash and moved slowly forward.

"By now," Little Horse said, "both Long and Steele have received the talking paper you made for them and wrapped around the rocks. They understand our terms."

Touch the Sky nodded. The afternoon was late and the two friends sat in the dense cover just outside the entrance to their cave. Their ponies were hobbled out of sight behind the cave. After dark they would water them, then tether them in the open grass to graze.

"About Long, I know nothing," Touch the Sky said. "What manner of man he is, what kind of fighting fettle he has. As for Steele, expect more hard fighting, although he will pay others to do it for him. He knows our terms, yes. But knowing is not accepting."

While he spoke, Touch the Sky felt a strange prickling of his skin—his shaman sense warning him that something was amiss. He glanced carefully around. Nearby, a badger burrowed a tunnel in the grassy bank of the creek. A stone's throw to his left, a rabbit nibbled at tender new shoots. Overhead, a jay chattered madly. Seeing all this made him relax a bit.

"From what you have told me," Little Horse said, "it sounds clear that Long is the important one. He is the big chief on the reservation. If we can turn his liver white with fear, perhaps he will stop doing business with Steele."

The prickling sensation was back, goose-bumping Touch the Sky's skin. He glanced around. The badger still worked furiously at its tunnel; the rabbit still nibbled at shoots; the jay still chattered overhead.

"Perhaps," he finally answered. "But Steele is not one for giving others a voice in the decision."

All this talk made Touch the Sky recall the letter Kristen had given him—the incriminating letter Steele had written to Long, but never delivered. It was tucked into his parfleche. He had read it so many times he had it memorized. Could he ever put it to good use against the arrogant, Indian-hating Steele? That could happen if—

Suddenly, the badger scurried away to cover. The rabbit dashed off deep into the trees. The jay flew off from its branch.

Fear iced Touch the Sky's veins as he realized that some danger was closing in on them—a danger that he also sensed it was best to avoid.

"Brother," he said urgently to Little Horse, "let us catch up our ponies and ride out of here for a time."

Little Horse cocked his head in curiosity, about to ask why. Then he saw the fear in this young shaman's face, and he understood that the hand of the supernatural was in this thing.

A few heartbeats later, the two Cheyenne braves had disappeared in the thick growth surrounding them.

"I'm tellin' you the straight," Steele said. "It's gone too far. You read the note. That buck means to whack the cork on us! Either you do like I tell you, or we're soon out of business. We can't back off now. We got to corral these Cheyennes while the gate's still open."

Ephraim Long seemed unconvinced. "I'm not so sure, Hiram. What if this whole damn thing curdles on us? You heard those teamsters describe the attack. There were other Indians hiding behind the ridge. What if they were reservation Indians?"

"That's the point, damn it. Give an Injun an inch, he wants the whole rope. You get icy boots, and these savages will end up pissing on your grave."

Long still looked reluctant. "If the newspapers back east were ever to—"

"To hell with the goddamn Indian lovers and

cowardly Quakers!" Steele exploded. "These godless savages didn't even know about the wheel until the white man showed 'em! You do what I told you, or it's coming down to the nut cuttin'!"

Finally Long nodded. "All right. You're not one to panic over nothing. I'll put the word out today."

Steele nodded. "That's the gait. Remember, make it clear you're punishing only those few Cherokees who cheered loudest when the Cheyenne renegades disrupted the whipping. You—"

The stairwell door opened and Kristen entered. Steele quickly shut up. Long rose and gallantly bowed. Kristen ignored him.

"Well," Hiram said with the false joviality that always made Kristen shudder, "here's the very girl! Ephraim was just telling me that he has written out his funding request for that new reservation school we talked about. He's submitting your name for the girls' teacher."

"How nice. And I'll bet that, since you'll have so many accounts with the school anyway, my salary could just be paid directly to you?"

Steele poured a little more enamel into his smile. "That would be sensible, wouldn't it? I pay the bills around here."

His smile made her nervous. Kristen knew he was suspicious of her. If he found out she was in touch with Matthew Hanchon—The thought sent a shiver up her spine.

When she was gone, Long looked at Steele. Something had been bothering him since that rock crashed through his window.

"Hiram? This Cheyenne buck you say wrote the notes. How in the hell does he come to know English well enough to write it down?"

Steele waved the question off impatiently.

"Hell, does it matter? You can learn a dog to walk on its hind legs, too, but it's still a dog. All you need to keep in mind about this Injun is that he needs killing and needs it bad."

On the day following the meeting between Steele and Long, Steele got his way. Several Cherokees were publicly whipped by Mankiller and his deputies.

Touch the Sky and Little Horse learned of the beatings that same day from an angry Jack Morningstar. Once again Touch the Sky decided on retaliation with lightning speed.

"Perhaps you were right after all, brother," he told Little Horse. "Perhaps we should take the fight to Long, too, not just Steele. I think we should visit his lodge this very night."

The Cheyennes already knew, from talks with Morningstar and others, that Long lived alone in his big two-story home, where an old Indian woman cooked and cleaned for him during the day. Since the trouble with the Cheyennes had begun, a Cherokee policeman stayed on guard in the yard throughout the night.

Touch the Sky and Little Horse rode out well after dark. It was a moonless, overcast night, and safe movement was easy. They picketed their ponies well back from the house.

The stone building rose up before them,

looming, still, and dark. Armed only with their knives, they crept close to the house, moving with gusts of wind to cover their noise.

"Brother!" Little Horse whispered, touching his arm. "There is the guard."

Both Cheyennes knelt behind a clump of elderberry bushes at one side of the house. They watched the policeman slowly walk around the house, his carbine at sling arms.

"We can avoid him. But I would feel better," Touch the Sky whispered back, "if he were not wandering about."

Little Horse took his meaning. Again the guard circled the house. Little Horse, famous in his clan for his ability to mimic animals, whimpered like a frightened young puppy.

The guard stopped and stared over toward the bushes. Cherokees were famous for liking dogs. Little Horse whimpered again. The guard walked closer.

He poked behind the bush. Touch the Sky rose behind him and whacked him in the temple with the solid bone handle of his knife. The guard folded to the ground as if he'd been pole-axed. They took his carbine and ammunition, then tied his ankles and wrists with rawhide whangs.

Locks on doors were practically unheard of on the frontier. At the front door the two Cheyennes found the latch string out. They slipped inside the big house and found themselves in a dark, silent room with a big grandfather clock ticking loudly from one corner.

"Brother," Little Horse whispered nervously,

"what is that noise like a heart beating?"

"The white man's time-counter. It will not hurt you."

They moved quickly throughout the entire ground floor, making sure Long was not downstairs.

"Follow me, brother," Touch the Sky whispered, angling toward a staircase near the front door. "He must be upstairs."

Touch the Sky had ascended perhaps five or six steps when he heard a nervous call behind him.

"Brother! What is this? Come back down here!"

Curious, he returned to the bottom of the steps.

"Brother," Little Horse said, "what are you doing? What is this thing?"

Touch the Sky was confused. Little Horse was pointing at the risers of the stairway. Then, all of a moment, he remembered a curious bit of information his friend Old Knobby had told him. Most Plains Indians could not climb steps or ladders, never having even seen them! But this was not the time for Little Horse's first lesson, he decided.

"Just wait here, brother," he said. "Another guard may show up, or Long might come in. I will look around upstairs."

Quietly, wincing every time a stair creaked, Touch the Sky went up to the top floor. The hallway was dark, but a straight seam of light, under one door, told him where Long must be. He slipped forward, moccasins silent on the bare wood floor, and gripped the latch.

The door mewed when he opened it, and Long looked up at him from a writing desk, where he sat making entries in a ledger.

The agent turned several shades paler in the light of a coal-oil lamp. The wild Indian crossing toward him gripped a nasty-looking knife and looked hell-bent on using it.

Touch the Sky saw he was unarmed and stopped.

"Who in the hell are you?" Long said.

"No friend of yours, Long. Nor of Hiram Steele's either."

"Your English is good."

"Good enough to tell you to your face that you're a thief, Agent Long."

"You're talking to a white man, John."

Touch the Sky's muscles danced as his right hand tightened on the knife. "Call me John again, hair face, and I'll be talking to a dead white man."

Long moved all at once, lifting his right foot and slipping the two-shot muff gun out in an eyeblink.

"All right, John. Drop the knife. Then turn and walk back downstairs slowly. We're going to see what you did to that guard out there. If he's dead, you just killed a ward of the U. S. Government, John."

Long held the lamp high behind Touch the Sky, throwing a shimmering pool of light down the stairs as they descended. Touch the Sky spoke loudly in English so Little Horse would hear two voices and know they were coming.

"What are you going to do with me?"

Long's laugh was high-pitched and loud. Power surged in his fingertips. He'd captured a real, by God wild Injun!

"Don't feel so frisky now, do you? Thought you were going to lead all of my Indians back to the blanket, didn't you? Well—*oomph!*"

Long went down hard when Little Horse smashed a ladder-back chair over his head, splintering it. Touch the Sky checked his neck pulse: still strong. The man was out, but not seriously hurt.

"Good thing, brother, you cannot climb stairs!" Touch the Sky ran back upstairs and sat for a moment at the writing desk. Before the two braves slipped out of the house again, Touch the Sky had pinned a note to the unconscious agent's vest.

Either clear out or start living up to your legal obligations as a Cherokee agent. Otherwise, you're a dead man.

Chapter Eleven

"Hiram, it's easy for you to stick to your guns," Ephraim Long said. "It's no skin off your ass if I'm scalped. Before you go issuing so damn many hard orders to others, ask yourself if you'd be willing to carry them out. That savage could have killed me instead of just knocking me out."

Steele was so agitated he had risen from the table and now paced the room, staring at Long. The agent had a nasty, egg-size swelling near the top of one of his muttonchops, where the chair had struck him.

"Long, have you been grazin' loco weed? No skin off my ass? Do you know how much freight I lost in that attack? True, it was inexpensive goods. But you don't have to swallow the loss and pay them riled-up freighters to replace ruined wagons.

"And do you know how much I lost in Wyoming fighting those two renegades? Not to mention what I—we—stand to lose if you get snow in your boots now."

"Wyoming," Long grumbled. "Seems to me you're always licking old wounds instead of looking to avoid new ones. I say we negotiate with these two and see if—"

"Negotiate? In a pig's ass!" Steele exploded. "I want those criminal sons of bitches dead."

"That's just how you're gunna get 'em," Mankiller said quietly, adding a fifth spoonful of sugar to his cup of coffee. His finger was too thick to slip through the china handle, so he was forced to pick the cup up like a bowl. "I've damn near located their camp."

"Good. I'll have the gold in your hands before their bodies turn cold," Steele promised him.

"What you two work out privately is your business," Long said. "But I'm going my own way. Nothing personal, Hiram. But something tells me that tall Cheyenne buck meant exactly what he told me."

"How 'bout you, Chief?" Steele said to Red Jacket. "You throwin' in with me or Agent Long here?"

As if to emphasize his point, Steele pushed a platter of fresh-baked currant scones toward the Cherokee leader, who grinned and helped himself to another, dunking it in his coffee.

"We Cherokees have a saying. 'Only a fool sells his best mule,'" Red Jacket said. "I have no mules for sale."

Steele nodded enthusiastically. The wily

chief's meaning was clear. Steele looked at Mankiller.

"How 'bout you, Sheriff? Whose colors you flying?"

Mankiller sucked his cup dry in one long sip. He lifted a corner of the tablecloth and wiped his mouth. "I'm flying the color of gold," he finally replied.

Steele looked at Long, his eyes bright with triumph.

"Everybody's cards are on the table, pard. Do I deal you in or out?"

Long looked confused, like a man just waking up from a long drunk. He glanced at Chief Red Jacket and Mankiller.

"Now hold on here a minute, you two. I'm the agent. How can you two talk about siding with Hiram?"

"'Cuz he's got gold," Mankiller said promptly. "And you ain't. That's how."

"It's a private treaty," Red Jacket added. "You only handle government treaties."

Coffee always put Red Jacket in a loquacious mood. Now he swelled up importantly.

"We Cherokees were proud hunters and farmers back in our ancient homeland. We always liked the Americans. It was the crafty British and Spanish who incited us to war against your people. But I have always admired the whiteskins. True, they exposed my people to smallpox, tuberculosis, syphilis, and measles—"

"That's a real nice speech, Chief," Steele said impatiently. He was still staring at Long. "How 'bout it, Ephraim? You mounting on the left side with us or on the Indian side?"

Long saw it all spelled out, clear as a blood spoor in new snow. Steele was telling him to do what he wished, but he'd best be prepared to die the first time he crossed him. Having Red Jacket on his side meant little. But Mankiller was feeding at Steele's trough, too. That meant plenty.

"Can we strike a deal?" Long said. "You and I will continue with most of our present business arrangements. But I will also appease the Indians somewhat. I want to lift the ban on hunting and scrap the tithing system—that kind of thing."

"Hell," Steele said, "I don't care about that. You got a deal. Just don't go hog wild and promise any changes with the allotment goods. That arrangement stays the same. Beside—"

Steele glanced toward the door to the stairwell. This time Kristen had been sent out of the house on errands while the men talked business. Steele was convinced now that she was eavesdroping somehow, that she was in touch somehow with Matthew Hanchon. And now he was hatching a new plan—one using his daughter as a lure to trap the Cheyenne.

"Besides," Steele said, "I got a gut hunch we'll soon be eliminating the major source of our trouble."

Honey Eater's dream was repeated three nights in a row, which gave it the force of a vision.

She saw herself kneeling in front of Touch the

Sky's tipi. She was holding their special stone, the piece of marble on which he had sworn his eternal love. Tears streamed from her eyes, and she knew she was crying because Touch the Sky had ridden off to face unknown dangers, perhaps never to return.

Always, as the dream started, the entrance flap of his tipi was closed tight. But then, glancing up through her tears, she spotted a sight that made her heart leap into her throat. The flap was up now, and inside was Touch the Sky with a sun-haired whiteskin woman in his arms!

Each time Honey Eater would cry out, and each time the pretty whiteskin would stare outside at her with mocking eyes. But then came the worst omen of all. The sound of rapid hoofclops approached behind her, there was a wild nickering, and then Honey Eater would whirl to face a huge, wild-eyed black stallion, its skeleton rider grinning at her from a death's skull.

As always, Honey Eater started awake, drenched in her own sweat. She sat up in the heaped buffalo robes. Her breathing was rapid and shallow. It was dark in the tipi, the fire in the pit having burned down to mere glowing embers. She realized Black Elk was not beside her, and her first reaction was relief. She could be alone with her thoughts.

Then she heard it. Faint, like the noise heard when one was half asleep: the murmur of men's voices out behind the tipi.

Now she recalled. She had dropped off to sleep early, after preparing Black Elk's evening meal.

132

He, as usual, had wandered off to spend most of his night in the camp clearing, betting on pony races and wrestling matches. He must have returned with some of his friends. The meat racks out behind Black Elk's tipi were a favorite meeting place when trouble was afoot.

Moving quietly, Honey Eater rose and crossed to the back of the tipi. There was a spot where she could roll the hide cover partway up one of the lodge poles and peer outside. She did so now, reminding herself that Black Elk would surely bob her nose if he ever caught her.

"Cousin," Wolf Who Hunts Smiling said, "faint hearts never led a tribe to victory. This Touch the Sky, whom I call White Man Runs Him, again he has ridden out with Little Horse. And once again they have done so without benefit of a council meeting.

"When will you finally read the sign? He has beguiled Arrow Keeper, Chief Gray Thunder, and now even the Star Chamber. Because of him our tribe has gone easy on the paleface intruders. We have even accepted a peace price to let Caleb Riley's miners run all over our hunting grounds. Who knows what treachery White Man Runs Him is up to with hair faces even now?

"It is time for new, younger leaders to force-fully rescue our tribe from this downward path of licking white men's boots."

Wolf Who Hunts Smiling had always been a fiery, effective speaker. Though Black Elk was older, and their battle chief, he nodded once to acknowledge the truth of these words.

"Besides," Swift Canoe added slyly, knowing Black Elk's jealous wrath, "this tall pretend Cheyenne seeks to put on the old moccasin with our married women. Even a man's wife is not safe around him."

A small fire blazed in a circle of stones, outlining their features in a cerise glow. Black Elk's sewn-on ear looked like a flap of tanned leather.

"These things you say ring true enough," Black Elk said. "I trained him. He is a good warrior—as good as any I have seen, and perhaps even the best. But he is not straight-arrow Cheyenne to the quick of him. In his heart he still wears white man's shoes. He carries the white stink for life. He preaches cooperation with those who would exterminate the red man."

"Besides this," said Medicine Flute, a sleepy-eyed, slender brave who claimed to have the gift of visions, "he cleverly sets himself up as a shaman. In this ruse he is assisted by Arrow Keeper, who dotes on him in his frosted years."

"Arrow Keeper," Wolf Who Hunts Smiling said, his furtive eyes constantly in motion, "is tottering on his funeral scaffold. He, at least, will soon be gone. Then White Man Runs Him will have lost his best ally."

"And then," Medicine Flute said, "the tribe will be without a shaman. This is intolerable. It will come down to a choice. Touch the Sky or me."

"There is great anger now over these worthless trade goods," Swift Canoe said. "If it came to a choice now, the headmen would vote for you."

"At any rate," Wolf Who Hunts Smiling said, "the choice will soon be forced upon them. And when it is, White Man Runs Him will not be able to hide behind the Star Chamber. The time rapidly approaches when his guts will string our new bows."

Chapter Twelve

There were five of them squeezed into the cavern.

Touch the Sky, Little Horse, Jack Morningstar, and the burly blacksmith named Captain Bill sat around a new fire in the pit. The cobbler, Otto, sat in the tunnel entrance keeping watch. The Cherokees had again borrowed horses from the work corral. Now they were picketed out of sight with the Cheyenne ponies.

With a 1,000-dollar bounty on the Cheyennes' scalps, all agreed it was safer to take the meeting to them. Little Horse filled his favorite clay pipe with a mixture of tobacco and red willow bark. He knew about the white man's matches; nonetheless, he was thrilled when Captain Bill let him use one to light the pipe. It made the rounds, the fragrant, sweet smell of the bark filling the cave. The Cherokees enjoyed the smoke, but glanced away self-consciously when the two Cheyennes nodded to the four directions of the wind before taking their first puff.

Soon, voices were raised in lively argument.

"I tell you, things are looking better," Captain Bill said. Elation tinged his voice. "The ban on hunting has been lifted. Now we can eat fresh meat without going to jail."

"Bow-and-arrow hunting," Jack Morningstar said. "It's still illegal to own a firearm."

"Well, shit. My osage bow will push an arrow clean through a buff and drop it out on the other side. What? You expect sweet cream and pie, too?"

"This is what makes me mad," Morningstar said. "The white man takes every damn thing we got. Then he gives us some little thing back, and there's always some yack like you to call him generous for it. My old man owned a rifle, and his old man before him. And they didn't bow down to no white man to get 'em."

"It's not just hunting," Otto said from the cave entrance. He couldn't see the others, but he could hear them. "Don't forget that. Long says he's going to drop the tithing system, too. No more making one man suffer for the crimes of ten."

"Ahuh," Morningstar said. "You just wait. Mankiller will still have his spies and informers planted."

Despite the vigorous debate ensuing, a strong bond of camaraderie linked these five. They were fighting back, and already there were encouraging signs. Touch the Sky and Little Horse deliberately held back, letting the Cherokees work this out. In one sense it was every red man's battle, and they were all in it as one. But this was the Cherokee homeland now, and they would have to live with the consequences of whatever decisions they reached in this fight.

"And don't forget," Morningstar said, "Long ain't said word one about our allotments. That flour we been getting, with the weevils in it. The Mexican-grade coffee that tastes like a cup of warm gun oil. Where's the church we was supposed to get? Money was sent from back east for lumber and nails. I ain't seen no building go up."

Touch the Sky translated for Little Horse. This was the crucial point, so far as helping their own tribe up in the Powder Country. Not until the Cherokees set a legal precedent against Steele could Caleb Riley and the Cheyennes also try to seek justice through the hair-face courts. Secretly, Touch the Sky hoped Steele would back down before it came to that. Making good on his promises would benefit both tribes. It would also spare undue suffering for Kristen.

"I'm not forgetting all that," Captain Bill said. "And I ain't never forgetting your wife and all the rest who died because Long and Steele stole the money sent for medicine."

A long silence greeted this remark. Morningstar finished his cigarette and flicked it down into the firepit.

"The thing of it is," he said, "Long has

promised that things're gonna get better. Good. Touch the Sky and Little Horse put the fear of God in the greedy bastard! He's a coward at heart, and I think we can keep him on the straight and narrow just by refusing to take shit from him.

"Steele—I don't know how to call it with him. I'd wager he's no coward in a fight, but he's practical about money. I think he might fold if we make the stakes too expensive. But Mankiller? I can tell you right now. He don't have any boss, neither Steele nor Long and sure's hell not Red Jacket. He makes his own law. It's a hard truth, but we'll have to take him and his police on in battle before it's over."

"Friend, you're a few bricks short of a load," Otto said from the tunnel. "How do we do that without rifles? Bows ain't got the range against carbines. The only weapons're all kept located at police headquarters."

"There're other rifles on the reservation," Touch the Sky said quietly. They all looked at him. It was the first he had spoken in some time.

"Long's house," he said. "He's got a little armory in a room downstairs. I saw it. Fifteen, maybe twenty army-issue carbines, locked in racks."

Morningstar nodded. "Sure. That makes sense. Long wouldn't know what to do with 'em. But the white leaders in Washington would insist on having them there. Well, Long has tripled the guard since Little Horse busted his head open for him. So let's talk about how we plan to get those weapons."

*   *   *

Mankiller moved with stealthy precision in the gathering darkness, a smile tugging his lips apart.

The two Cheyennes were crafty at covering their sign. But not so the Cherokees. And now he had finally found the hidden camp. He crouched behind a fallen log, peering out at the dim figure in the entrance of the tunnel. Otto, he finally decided.

Mankiller knew from the sign he'd read that there were too many to attack now. As badly as his fingers itched to count that gold, he couldn't squander the opportunity to kill those Cheyennes. They were too wily and battle savvy to kill easily in a classic assault.

They would have to be captured another way, according to the ancient laws of the hunt. As for the turncoat Cherokees siding with them—their identities would all be known before the moon above had retired from the sky.

Mankiller slid the Remington from his sash and settled in for a long wait.

"I beg your pardon?" Kristen said.

Hiram Steele said, "Beg all you want, girl. Just do what I said."

"Just like that? You just throw open my door and tell me to pack up everything I own because I'm moving back east?"

"That's the long and the short of it. Your Aunt Thelma can have a go at civilizing you. I give it up for a bad job. You leave on the Tuesday stage out of Nekoma."

"That's insane. You're insane!"

"Don't you take that high-hat tone with me, missy! You act so surprised. Hell, I told you before I ain't running no school for genteel society ladies. You got to pull your own freight. I tried to help you get a career, but you just mean mouthed the idea about teaching at the reservation school.

"You had a chance to marry Seth Carlson, but no, you had to play the big muckety-muck and look down your nose at him because he was a soldier."

"Not because he was a soldier. Because of the kind of soldier he was. A mean-spirited, Indian-hating bully."

Hiram snorted. "Huh! That's rich! You're a good one to talk about Indian haters. What the hell you expect a soldier to do with redskins? Wine 'em and dine 'em? Maybe it galled Carlson like it galled me to know you were kissing Matthew Hanchon, and him a Cheyenne. You can't get much lower than to forsake your own Christian race for heathens that run naked."

"Oh, yes, you can," she said. "Lots lower. You and Ephraim Long proved that."

For a moment, rage mottled his face purple. He doubled both fists until the knuckles turned white. Kristen shrank back from him, sure he would hit her.

But he got control of himself as he thought of something else. A smug smile settled on his face. His calm voice, when he spoke now, was more chilling to her than his enraged shouting.

141

"Go downstairs," he told her. "I left something for you on the dining room table. A little surprise."

She hesitated, not liking his manner.

"Go ahead," he urged her. "Go see what it is. You'll understand things better."

A cold sense of doom accompanied her down the steps. She reached the bottom, opened the door, and glanced into the dining room with her heart thumping hard.

At first she saw nothing on the table. Then she saw what he must mean, but for a moment she didn't understand. Why was there a broken shingle at the place where she usually sat? What could it possibly—A broken shingle!

Cold blood surged into her face, and she whirled to confront her grinning father. He stood a few steps above her.

"Recognize it?" he said softly.

"I don't know what you—" She faltered, her voice failing her.

"I found that in the yard," he said. "Right under your window. Funny thing. And it didn't just fall off. You can see where the nail was bent when somebody put weight on it."

"I don't understand. I—"

"You had that pagan bastard in your bedroom!" he said, his voice heavy with urgent disgust.

She was dizzy, the floor swayed under her like the deck of a storm-tossed ship. "No! I—"

"That loud thump I heard the other night, when you said you dropped something." His face twisted in disgust as he looked at her.

"That was your bed breaking, wasn't it, when that savage topped you?"

Despite the obvious accusation, the enormity of this charge made it impossible to comprehend his meaning. When she finally realized what he was suggesting, anger rose up out of her like a tight bubble escaping. Her only impulse now was to lash back in kind.

"The bed breaking? But, Pa, he's an animal, remember? He took me on the floor."

He slapped her so hard that the sound reverberated all the way up the stairwell.

"You whore," he said gruffly. "A daughter of mine, rutting with wild savages. The only thing keeps me from telling the world and shaming you is that it would shame me even more. But, by God, I will get you out from under my roof. You—"

But stifling a sob, she rushed past him and returned to her room. The door banged shut, and Steele could hear her giving vent to her tears in earnest.

Despite his deep mistrust of his daughter, Steele knew damn well Kristen hadn't done the thing he'd accused her of. Just as he didn't really plan to send her packing next Tuesday. He had no intention of hiring a cook and maid when he had one living there already. And soon he could collect a teacher's salary in her name and reinvest that money to make more.

No, the ruse with sending her back to Thelma's was a gamble. He was sure that she would somehow get word to Hanchon, just as sure that Hanchon would try to see her before she left. Steele had already hired a man to watch the house by night, to follow Kristen anytime she left the house. He planned to give his daughter plenty of freedom of movement between now and Tuesday. Enough rope to hang herself— and Matthew Hanchon.

Chapter Thirteen

There was only one reasonably strong, fast horse in the common corral. And a raid on Long's house would require fast mounts since it was located in open terrain. So it was decided that only three would assault the armory: Touch the Sky, Little Horse, and Jack Morningstar.

They chose the day the white man's winter-count called Monday—a day, according to Morningstar, that Ephraim Long always spent in the hair-face settlement of Great Bend. The three friends agreed the armed guards would be less vigilant with Long absent. For this same reason they decided on a broad-daylight strike, when it would be least expected.

Morningstar had little experience with fire-arms, but he was a fair hand with a bow. For this raid he would carry the Spencer carbine taken from the Cherokee guard at Long's house. But he also fashioned a new bow. Touch the Sky and Little Horse exchanged long, silent looks of approval when the Cherokee carved the battle totems of his clan into the bow. He gratefully accepted several of the Cheyennes' light, flint-tipped arrows and slid them into his tow quiver.

From the crossed-stick shelves at the back of his cabin, the Cherokee took a chamois drawstring pouch. He stuffed it into his hip pocket, instead of tying it to his belt. But both Cheyennes realized it was the personal medicine carried into combat by every Cherokee warrior. No one ever saw it but the warrior or the enemy who vanquished him.

"My father's," he said self-consciously, seeing them watch him. "Ain't been off that shelf in a long time."

For these two battle-scarred Cheyennes, who faced combat or the threat of combat constantly, they were riding out on an all-too-familiar mission. For them, fighting esprit and gallant actions had become a common virtue of survival. For the Cherokee, however, this was a belated rite of passage, a test of his courage and warrior skill—a test he had not passed as had his comrades. Touch the Sky and Little Horse knew this, and they felt the extra measure of respect warriors feel for men who, though frightened and inexperienced, faced the fight bravely.

They rode boldly out from Morningstar's cabin, not worrying about who saw them in the blazing noon sun. They rode three abreast, the two Cheyennes on sturdy mustangs. Morningstar rode a dark cream with black mane and tail—slightly swayback, but strong and sure-footed and quick for short bursts.

All three mounts were battle rigged. Lances, axes, all their weapons secured with ropes where they would be quick to hand. Touch the Sky rode with the butt plate of his heavy Sharps resting against his thigh, the muzzle pointing straight up. He scanned the land all around them, alert for any movement. They spotted a few Cherokees working in the fields or walking along the dirt roads. Some of them waved to this menacing trio of riders. Most, however, stared in astonishment before running off to tell somebody the news.

But they encountered none of Mankiller's deputies. They already knew there were three guards protecting the house. As they topped a long rise, the central clearing rose into view below. Long's house sat on the far side of the big, open meadow.

"There," Touch the Sky said. "See them? Two in the front, one in the back."

"How should we take the fight to them, brother?" Little Horse said, gazing around them. From here to the house there was not enough cover to hide a rabbit.

"Straight and fast," Touch the Sky said, his mouth a grim, determined slit. "Let these fat policemen meet the pony warriors from the Powder Country. Morningstar! Watch us and do as we do—unless you see us get killed," he added, a reckless grin suddenly splitting his face, and his surprised comrades both laughed out loud at his humor.

Touch the Sky raised his rifle high overhead and unleashed the shrill, yipping Cheyenne war cry: "Hi-ya, hii-ya!"

All three Indians urged their mounts to a gallop. As they rode they fanned out in a skirmish line. When their ponies approached the maximum effective range of the Cherokee carbines, Touch the Sky and Little Horse went into the classic Cheyenne riding position for battle. They slid far forward and down on the ponies' necks, reducing the target for their enemies. Morningstar emulated them, though less agilely.

The two Cherokees in the front yard had been playing checkers, the board on the grass between them. They seemed unsure, at first, that they were indeed being attacked. Then one of them shouted to their companion out back, and he joined them in front of the house.

The guards decided to rely on the open country as the best defense. All three Cherokees went into the prone position, digging an elbow into the ground and locking their weapons into their shoulders. They opened fire in earnest when the attackers were perhaps 300 yards out.

Cheyennes never wasted ammunition to make noise, as the Comanches and Kiowas liked to do. So Little Horse was saving his shotgun for close range. Now, aiming from under his horse's neck, he strung an arrow from a fistful in his right hand.

One deputy rose to change his position, and

three arrows raced toward him in as many eyeblinks. The first two zipped wide. The third thumped into the deputy's chest so hard it pushed pink lung tissue in a stream out his back.

Touch the Sky drew a bead on the middle deputy and fired, the big Sharps kicking into his shoulder socket. The shot missed. He dropped the rifle into its boot and urged his mustang forward even as he drew his ax from the rigging. His Cherokee target was desperately thumbing cartridges into the loading gate when Touch the Sky threw the ax. It twirled in midair, sliced into his enemy's head, and opened his skull to expose bloody curds of brain matter.

The third deputy hit Morningstar's horse in its vitals, dropping it stone dead. Jack hit the ground hard, lost his carbine, rolled several times, then came up on his feet with an arrow strung in his bow. His string sang out and the arrow caught the remaining deputy in the left eye. He lay in the grass, screaming piteously, his legs flailing until he turned his own weapon on himself and fired.

And with that final shot of self-destruction, the battle was over. The acrid smell of spent cordite hung thick in the air; the Cherokee ponies were still rearing in fright at all the commotion. And three men lay dead in the yard, their blood staining the grass.

"This place hears me!" Touch the Sky declared, looking at Morningstar. "I take no joy in the death of these Cherokees. Their wives are widows now; their children have no father. I would gladly smear charcoal on my face to celebrate after killing a Pawnee. But these deaths here only leave me sad that these red men played the Indian turncoat for whiteskins."

The armory was located at the rear of the house on the ground floor, in a room which also doubled as Long's private library. The carbines were locked in wooden racks behind a heavy iron lock and chain. But the three Indians used fireplace pokers to snap the chain. They stowed the Spencers in gunny sacks provided by Morningstar. They also cleaned out the stores of powder and lead.

They left the dead in the front yard for Long to discover upon his return, grim and final notice that this fight was going all the way. The Cherokees could arm themselves for the inevitable battle with Mankiller's Indian hard cases.

However, Touch the Sky's elation was short-lived. That night he sneaked into the settlement of Great Bend. Under cover of a cloud-banked sky, he checked for messages from Kristen under the pile of bricks in the Steeles' back yard.

He found one. And it told him that tomorrow she was being sent away forever.

Kristen had also warned Touch the Sky in her note not to come around the house anymore because her father had found out they were meeting. But the knowledge that she was leaving for good forced Touch the Sky to admit that he wanted to see her. Once they had loved each other so much. And when that love was suddenly made impossible by her father's hatred, it left a permanent ache like an important promise left unfulfilled.

Touch the Sky knew in his heart that his love belonged to Honey Eater, that his place was with the Cheyenne people. But Kristen held a special place, too, especially since she had suffered greatly for her loyalty to him and for her steadfast concern for the red man. Hadn't Jack Morningstar, to whom bitterness and cynicism were no strangers, praised Kristen's kindness toward his dying wife? If Steele was punishing her like this, Touch the Sky had to at least find out if anything could possibly be done for her.

Touch the Sky crouched in the shadow of the rickety storage shed, unsure what to do as he looked toward the house. Kristen's window was aglow with lamplight, though he saw no sign of her.

What to do? How close, he wondered, was Hiram watching her? And then he started to worry. What if Steele, whose dangerous rage could rival Black Elk's, had hurt his daughter?

Touch the Sky made up his mind. He had to take a chance and find out.

He glanced carefully around the shadow-mottled yard and slipped up to one back corner of the house. He shot quickly up to the front of the house and looked across the street. A bored-looking man in a floppy-brim hat stood in the shadows, smoking a cigarette and watching the house.

But Touch the Sky felt little threat from the man. The Cheyenne stuck close to the house and made his way back to Kristen's window. He fished for a pebble and tossed it up. It clinked against the glass. He waited, but there was no sign of Kristen.

He tossed another pebble, and another. Perhaps she wasn't in her room. He arched his neck and saw that the sash was open a few inches. It would be a great risk, but he could go up and wait for her.

Again he moved to the front of the house and checked on the guard across the street. The man had knelt out of the wind to build himself another cigarette. Touch the Sky dismissed him as a threat and returned to the window.

Another pebble. No response.

His shaman sense was back, a vague tingling deep in his bones. It warned of trouble, but that same sense told him to face the trouble, that it might be like the crisis stage of a fever and best put behind him.

He gripped the lightning rod and pulled himself up hand over hand. He reached the sill, then peeked over. The room appeared empty. Touch the Sky slid the sash up wider and hauled himself over the sill.

The vague tingling in his bones became a cold, numb certainty in his skin. He looked to his right and stared into the twin bores of a scattergun.

"Welcome to the Steele residence," Hiram Steele said. "Most people wait until they're invited."

The fear Touch the Sky felt upon spotting the weapon now gave way to a cold contempt. This frontier bully had driven the Cheyenne's adopted white parents out of the mercantile business and had tried to destroy their mustang ranch as well.

"Kristen couldn't be here to entertain you," Steele said. "She sends her regrets."

Steele's scornful laugh was brash and loud. His man outside had watched Kristen hide her note for the Cheyenne. Steele had read it, then left it there, guessing it would lure the Indian. He had guessed right.

"You're a dead man, you son of a bitch," Steele said. "Do you realize you just broke into a white man's house? Ain't no court in the country will try a white man for killing a blanket Indian who broke into his house, especially his daughter's bedroom."

"You're a coward, Steele. A criminal coward. You hire out thugs to do your dirty work, like these Cherokee hard cases you arm to terrorize the reservation. But it doesn't matter now if you kill me. It's too late. Three of your hired guns are already dead, and we just got every last weapon out of Long's armory. Your policemen are soon going to be doing the hurt dance. And after they're planted, you and Long are next."

Steele had turned pale when Touch the Sky mentioned the weapons. "You're a liar! A stinking, flea-bitten liar."

Touch the Sky laughed in his face. "Am I? Go ahead and kill me. But stand by for a blast if you do because my friend Little Horse is waiting for me to return. When the moccasin telegraph tells him you killed me, you won't find one place to hide from him. You remember Little Horse, Steele? He sent quite a few of your thugs across the Great Divide. And he's been waiting for a piece of your scalp—especially now that you've robbed our tribe with that shipment of shoddy trash."

"It's all he-bear talk," Steele said.

But Touch the Sky read the doubt in the man's cold, hard, flint-gray eyes. Now, thought Touch the Sky. It was time to act.

"And before you pull those triggers, Steele, let me ask you something. Do you remember a time when you wrote a certain letter to your partner Long? A letter you spilled ink all over and never posted? Maybe you were a little drunk when you wrote it. Maybe that's why you mentioned so many incriminating details of your illegal operations. Maybe that's also why you decided not to send it. You sure's hell said a lot of things in that letter, things that would get your ass skinned in the white-man's court. And, Steele, you signed it. It's got your wax seal on it."

Steele's face clouded. He didn't quite understand what this brazen young buck was driving at.

Now Touch the Sky shot his bolt. He quoted a line that he remembered from reading the letter so many times. " 'This Great Bend Reservation is our nut to crack, Long. We'll get rich off these godless savages and let the Indian lovers in Congress take the heat for it.' "

These words jogged Steele's memory, and blood rushed into his face.

"I came into your house a while back and found that letter," Touch the Sky lied. "Little Horse has it now. If anything happens to me, he will take it to our cavalry friend Tom Riley. Riley hates you with a strong passion. He'll make it the mission of his life to see you burn.

"The same thing happens if you do one damn thing to hurt Kristen for this. I swear it! She'll be getting out from under your roof as soon as she can anyway. You just leave her be."

Steele's face showed he was defeated, though he still held the gun on Touch the Sky. On the frontier, men winked at those who swindled Indians. Back east, however, the newspapers railed against such activities. If he was ever named by a prominent writer, the Indian Bureau would drop him like a bad habit. Even worse, some men became public examples and were harshly prosecuted. He could even be ordered to pay all his illegal profits back.

The Cheyenne watched all this play on Steele's face. He backed to the window and lowered himself down, expecting a load of buckshot to tear off his face at any moment.

Instead, he slipped off into the black folds of night. Elation tingled in his blood. The immediate threat from Long or Steele was effectively hobbled. However, the Cheyenne also cursed his own carelessness. He had lied about giving the letter to Little Horse; he had had it with him all along. Had Steele thought to search him, Touch the Sky would be dead by now.

As he made his way closer to Pawnee Creek and his hobbled pony, Jack Morningstar's words reverberated inside his skull. *Mankiller makes his own law. We'll have to take him and his police on in battle before it's over.*

Chapter Fourteen

Armed now for a fair fight, the Cherokees nonetheless tried the peace road one last time.

Morningstar and some of the other skilled tradesmen had formed a temporary council of headmen. They ousted Red Jacket as chief and voted to send a message to Long, Steele, Mankiller, and Red Jacket to surrender, negotiate in good faith for change, and all future bloodshed could be avoided.

Red Jacket, a wily survivor who changed politics with the wind, immediately capitulated in a statement about his love for Indian self-determination. Long, too, was in favor of appeasement. However, it was Hiram Steele and Mankiller who prevailed. And neither man was willing to negotiate a point. For by now Steele had thought it all over and realized that the incriminating letter could never be turned over if both Cheyennes were killed, for one of them was carrying it. Only if they left this place alive could that letter be used against him.

At Steele's insistence, Long wired an emergency request for troops from Fort Hays, citing an armed uprising by hostile Indians. Mankiller and his deputies, in the meantime, turned their reinforced police headquarters into a bastion. Food, water, and ammunition were stockpiled. Their plan was to wait there for the pony soldiers to arrive from Fort Hays, then lead the fight to disarm the rebels.

But Touch the Sky and his comrades knew—thanks to the moccasin telegraph—about the request for troops. And thus they also knew they had to move first before they arrived. Surrounding the police and holding them would not be enough. They would be safe once the army arrived. And they could not be left in a position to ever again terrorize the reservation. The Cherokee council had agreed on this point unanimously.

The decision was unpleasant but also unavoidable. A bloody battle loomed.

Touch the Sky and Little Horse studied the police headquarters, a long, low building made of thick cottonwood logs and loopholed for rifles. Its site had been chosen with the thought of armed rebellion in mind. It was located on high ground, a lone rise in the middle of a vast expanse of open grass. At one end of the building, hunkering on the least exposed flank, was a smaller, windowless stone building with a heavy iron lock on the door.

This, Morningstar explained, was the main powder cache for the reservation.

"A lot more in there than we got from Long's place," he said. The three friends were hidden in a tree line at the bottom of the rise, getting the lay of the land.

Touch the Sky and Little Horse traded uneasy glances. This was not a promising scenario for a battle. That rise was steep, by plains standards, and anyone riding or running up toward the headquarters would be a low, easy, dangerously vulnerable target. Morningstar estimated that as many as 17 or 18 braves were holed up there— a formidable fighting force, especially on high ground.

"We will need a diversion," Touch the Sky said.

"What type of diversion?" Morningstar asked.

Touch the Sky shook his head, still unsure on that point.

"Something," he insisted, "or the battle will be a slaughter, and we will be the slaughtered."

Time was critical. Troops at Fort Hays were combat ready and could be dispatched immediately. Within three sleeps, Touch the Sky knew, the reservation would be swarming with bluecoats. The place had to be ready for them, with the real criminals out of power and a new system in place. This final battle had to also break Steele and Long.

The new council met in the skilled tradesmen's lodge to select men for the raid. The building overflowed with volunteers. Only braves with 18 winters or more behind them were selected. The warriors were issued weapons and divided into battle groups. Because Touch the Sky, Little Horse, Jack Morningstar, Captain Bill, and Otto had already ridden on one mission together, they would form the spearhead group. Due to the steep rise, this would not be a mounted battle— a good thing, since sound horses were scarce.

The confrontation was set to begin at sunrise. Braves broke into their battle groups to make sure each warrior understood how to crimp a cartridge in a carbine and prime the seven-shot cylinder. Old men who had fought in the Creek Wars back east, or against whiteskins, took the young warriors aside to share advice with them.

"Brother," Little Horse said, the lodge buzzing all around them, "have you given more thought to this diversion you mentioned?"

"I have, brother."

Touch the Sky caught Jack Morningstar's attention and waved him over. "How much black powder do we have?"

"Not so much. Enough to ration out maybe eight or ten shots per man."

Touch the Sky nodded. He handed Morningstar a chamois pouch. "Put out the word. Every brave going into battle is to measure out one hundred grains of powder—enough for one shot. Each is to put it in this pouch."

By now Morningstar's respect for the Cheyennes was complete. He accepted the pouch.

"Sure I'll do it," he said. "But what's it for?"

159

"A diversion," Touch the Sky said evasively, adding a nervy little smile.

An hour before sunrise, the attackers gathered in a cedar copse well below the police headquarters. The rise could be seen even in the predawn gloom, a huge, black mass against the lighter gray of the sky.

Touch the Sky and his group moved among the warriors, calming the younger and more nervous ones, checking weapons and equipment. Again and again, Morningstar and the other Cherokee leaders repeated a Sioux battle slogan adopted by the Cheyenne: *One bullet, one enemy.*

"Here," Morningstar said, handing Touch the Sky the pouch, now puffy from the load of black powder within. "What do you plan on doing with it?"

"Keep your eyes open, Cherokee, and you'll find out."

Little Horse knew his friend well, and he had already guessed what Touch the Sky had in mind. His guess was confirmed when he saw Touch the Sky, in the light of a small fire, fashioning several exploding arrows. These crude explosives, a Cheyenne invention, were made by tying a primer cap to the edge of an arrow point. Then a little pouch filled with gunpowder was tied over the arrow point. With luck, on impact the primer cap would ignite the powder, causing a small explosion and sometimes a fire. They were good detonators for larger explosives. Touch the Sky and Little Horse had used them before with varying success. They did not always work.

For this reason, he handed Little Horse three exploding arrows.

"Place these in your quiver, brother, and guard them closely. When I tie this pouch of powder to the door of that armory, wait for me to clear out. Then shoot the pouch with an exploding arrow. With luck, that will set off the powder inside."

Little Horse didn't like this plan. For one thing, Touch the Sky would have to wait until daylight before he covered that open, uphill expanse on foot. Otherwise, Little Horse could not see to shoot it right away. And if not detonated immediately, it would be discovered and removed.

"Buck," Little Horse said, "you always claim the best sport for yourself. Let me run that powder up the hill."

Touch the Sky shook his head. Little Horse had been permanently slowed down when his right kneecap was shattered aboard the land-grabber Wes Munro's keelboat. Now he walked with a distinct limp.

"You are a better shot than I with a bow, brother."

This was true and Little Horse fell silent. The battle plan was repeated one final time for all the warriors. First would come a heavy barrage of fire arrows. These would force some of the policemen outside to quell the flames. Then the Cherokees below were to fire only carefully timed staggered volleys—one battle group at a time to conserve ammunition.

It was during this stage, while their enemies

were distracted by the fire arrows, that Touch the Sky would make his run for the door of the armory. If they succeeded in blowing it and detonating the powder within, a massed charge was to occur close on the heels of the explosion.

If they couldn't blow up that armory, Touch the Sky knew the battle might still be won. But the price would be bloody; that hill would be littered with dead Cherokees—and perhaps a pair of Cheyennes.

It was Jack Morningstar, the Acting Chief of the Cherokee Nation, who spoke the final words.

"The men on top that hill know they face hard justice if they surrender. So don't expect them to. They've murdered and beaten too many of us, stolen too much from us. It's going to be a fierce and bloody battle."

Then he surprised Touch the Sky by shouting out, "Cowards to the rear!"

It was an old Cherokee battle ritual to inspire courage in the final moment before battle. The two visiting Cheyennes were visibly impressed when, to the last man, the Cherokees raised their weapons at the ready and took two steps forward.

Their sister the sun abruptly set the eastern sky on fire. With each battle group in position, the first fire arrows were unleashed.

They flew through the pale gray light and thwacked hard into the cottonwood building. Soon the building was bright with tiny fires. Green cottonwood did not catch fire easily, yet once it did, it flared up quickly. One or two of the fires were serious enough to draw a few policemen outside.

Mankiller's deputies suffered no lack of ammunition. While the men were sent outside to smother the flames, at least a dozen rifles spat muzzle fire out the loopholed wall.

A deadly hail of bullets shot through the trees all around the attackers. Touch the Sky heard a Cherokee attacker cry out as he was wounded. But the Cheyenne was busy working his way around to the far side of the rise. He made sure Little Horse was in place, exploding arrows at the ready.

Then, while the second battle group opened up with covering fire, Touch the Sky raised his Sharps in front of his chest at a high port. He broke from cover and began the longest run of his life.

At first his heart swelled with surprised elation as he realized he was drawing no fire! Perhaps all the defenders were distracted to the front.

But then someone must have spotted him. For a heartbeat later—about one-third way up the hill—he ran into a deadly hail of lead.

Dirt fountained up from the ground all around his feet, bullets buzzed past his ears so close they sounded like angry hornets. He cut to the left, feinted hard right, and zigzagged in a crazy pattern so he wasn't easy to draw a bead on. But the closer he got, the more intense the fire he drew. A bullet grazed his left arm so close that it cut through the protective band of leather around his wrist; another creased his inner thigh and left a blood gutter. But screaming a defiant war cry, he finally hit the top and dived headlong for the shelter of the little stone armory.

Now he worked quickly, knowing time was the key. If he hugged the armory close and stayed on the west side, he couldn't easily be hit from the building nearby. He had nearly tied the pouch of black powder into place when the door of the police barracks banged open and two men darted out.

Touch the Sky picked up his Sharps, hit the ground rolling, came up, and snapped off a round. It punched into one deputy's chest and slammed him back inside. The second fired at Touch the Sky and missed, then levered his carbine and fired again. Below, Little Horse—armed with a carbine—broke out from behind cover and fired. The second policeman sprawled in the dirt, blood blossoming from his skull.

Touch the Sky finished securing the pouch, then frantically signaled to Little Horse. He didn't waste time running. He simply leaped downhill from the doorway and then rolled hard to get out of blast range.

Desperately, reloading his Sharps and covering that barracks door, he watched Little Horse string his bow below. The first exploding arrow had good range and detonated properly. But unfortunately it missed the pouch by inches. The little fire it started went out quickly.

Steady brother, Touch the Sky thought as Little Horse aimed his second arrow. It was a powerful shot and struck the pouch, but the primer failed to detonate.

One arrow left. Little Horse aimed and fired. The arrow thumped into the chamois pouch, and an eyeblink later the pouch exploded. Only a few moments later, the stores inside ignited and a huge fireball flashed up from the hill. Giant chunks of rock flew like cannonballs; the police headquarters lost half of its roof, most of one wall. Screams filled the interior.

Shouting battle cries, the Cherokees below began their assault. But the battle was over. The policemen staggering out of the building, many bloody or burned, were throwing down their weapons and waving white cloths in surrender.

Touch the Sky covered them while his companions raced to join him. But though he anxiously studied the faces of the emerging survivors, the one he hoped to see most never appeared.

Dead, maybe?

Then, below, Captain Bill shouted and pointed to the far side of the hill. Touch the Sky looked where he pointed and saw a huge bear of a man just then disappearing into the trees. Somehow, in the chaos of the battle, the wily Mankiller had made his escape.

By the time the troops arrived from Fort Hays, they found the Great Bend Cherokee Reservation all secure from the top down.

As Touch the Sky had predicted, this final show of strength had taken all the fight out of Ephraim Long—a man with no stomach for hard fighting. He resigned his position, effective upon the arrival of a new, reform-minded agent selected by the Quakers instead of the Indian Bureau.

The new Cherokee council sentenced the crooked Red Chief to permanent banishment from the Cherokee Nation. Jack Morningstar accepted the position of permanent tribal chief. And most important, the dreaded police force was disbanded in favor of a more honest system of unarmed constables and an all-Indian court.

Hiram Steele was badly frightened by this sudden and drastic turn of events on the reservation. With his ally Long out of the picture, he began to worry anew about that incriminating letter in Matthew Hanchon's possession. He began hasty deliveries of long-overdue goods—serviceable goods this time, not the shoddy substitutes.

But he also sent word to the two Cheyennes, an especially welcome message. He had already made arrangements to make restitution to the Cheyenne people, too. The pack train would be on its way to the Powder River camp within the next few days.

Still, Touch the Sky knew better than to celebrate this as yet another victory. For among the former policemen now serving time in the reservation jail, one face was missing.

Both Cheyennes knew that Mankiller was still out there somewhere, waiting to kill them.

Chapter Fifteen

Triumphant, but tired, Touch the Sky and Little Horse made their final ride to the hidden camp on Pawnee Creek.

For the assault on the police building, they had brought only their weapons. Now they were returning to pack their sleeping robes and other gear for the long ride back to their own hunting grounds.

"You heard Morningstar, brother," Little Horse said. "The hair-face businessmen promise that our tribe's contract goods will be on their way by the time we reach camp. Do you believe this thing?"

Touch the Sky thought about it, then nodded. "This time, yes. I am not fool enough to believe Hiram Steele has felt a change in his heart. Only, he looks to his past and knows the hair-face soldiers already have his name in their books as a troublemaker. Thanks to Tom Riley, he was investigated in Bighorn Falls. He is doing this now only because he fears to lose money.

"Count upon it, buck. When the sting from his present fear wears off, he will prowl his usual grounds. We have not seen the last of him or his insane greed."

"Straight words, Cheyenne. But at least for now the Cherokees are no longer eating putrid meat."

The question nagging at both bucks was so constant, neither had to voice it. Where was Mankiller? Had he done the wise thing and left the reservation for good?

Neither Cheyenne believed that. Mankiller was not one who lived for the wise choice. He was very much like Hiram Steele in one respect. He could not brook defeat, and these two Cheyennes had so far defeated him.

For this reason, they approached the cave with even more caution than usual. First they studied the area from the tops of tall cottonwoods before they even neared the dense thicket that covered the entrance to the cave. As they approached, leading their ponies at a walk, they stopped again and again so sharp-eared Little Horse could listen closely.

Touch the Sky watched his calico mustang closely, alert for any signs of nervousness. Likewise, he studied the birds in the area for the briefest signs of alarm. His eyes swept the surrounding growth, scoured the ground, and constantly watched their back trail.

Nothing amiss. Nothing. Yet every nerve in his body felt the death chill on it.

For the final approach they maintained absolute silence, communicating only with signs. Employing a scouting trick Black Elk had taught them, the two braves stood back to back and revolved slowly, thus double scanning the terrain.

Still nothing amiss. They hobbled their ponies. Little Horse held his scattergun close, all four revolving barrels loaded. Knowing his rifle was clumsy at close range, Touch the Sky had opted for his knife. He held it in his right hand, low and close to his side. If forced to use it, he would stab low and upward, the hardest thrust to block.

They dropped to a crouch, approached on hands and knees at intervals of about six feet. Still nothing amiss. They were so quiet that two squirrels playing near the cave entrance still hadn't heard them.

The Cheyennes exchanged a glance. If squirrels were playing that close and a thrush was singing on a branch just above the cave, Mankiller mustn't be near.

Little Horse nodded, some of the tension easing from his face.

A moment later, fear caught them by the throat and they glimpsed the face of the Wendigo. Little Horse had veered slightly left to avoid a muddy swale. Abruptly, a powerful grip enveloped his left arm and he was jerked right up off the ground—up into the treetops. It happened in an eyeblink, the sapling snare was tripped when his hand came down.

Not only did the sudden, powerful snap of the tree unbending pull Little Horse's shoulder painfully out of socket, it made him drop his shotgun. If their plight had not been utterly desperate, he would have looked comical dangling so far off the ground, legs flailing.

But their plight was desperate, for those squirrels at play meant nothing. The moment Little Horse was jerked up from the ground, Mankiller lunged from the cave and leaped on Touch the Sky.

It was too quick to comprehend. Touch the Sky still hadn't grasped what was happening to Little Horse. Now the air was thumped from his chest and he was driven back hard by Mankiller's weight and sudden, jarring kick to the back as he whammed into a tree. The double impact, front and back, was like being caught in the cross kick of two powerful mules. Touch the Sky saw a bright orange burst inside his skull; then his world was nothing but pain.

Touch the Sky had dropped his knife when he was slammed into the tree. Now, his eyes big and bright with eager triumph, Mankiller circled his victim's neck with those huge, powerful hands.

Touch the Sky's head, too, had knocked hard into the tree. He teetered on the brink of awareness—enough consciousness left to be aware that, incredibly, his body was suffering even more pain.

Touch the Sky had been choked before, but this was different. The blood flow and air were both stopped immediately, and the viselike power of the grip defied belief. Mankiller, those eyes never once blinking as they bored into him, picked him up off the ground as he throttled him.

Touch the Sky had no strength to fight this bear, though every instinct in his body urged him to struggle to the last breath and beyond. So he did, though his efforts were pathetic and useless. Death was coming for him on incredibly swift wings; the world was closing down to darkness and raw pain.

He had no breath for his death song, but his final thoughts were for Honey Eater and Little Horse and Arrow Keeper, and when Arrow Keeper's face passed before his mind's dying eye, the words from the old shaman's disturbing medicine dream came to Touch the Sky. *Be prepared to die before you are dead.*

And then Touch the Sky understood.

There were a few more heartbeats of struggle and awareness left in him. But instead, he pretended to die. He suddenly slumped heavily and went slack, perfectly feigning death while actually on the threshold.

Mankiller was disappointed, even in his elation. He had expected more of a fight from this formidable-appearing Cheyenne foe. Instead, he turned out to be nearly as fragile as a woman. Perhaps the other one would provide more entertainment.

Mankiller threw the dead Cheyenne down in disgust.

A few eyeblinks later, cold obsidian slid between his fourth and fifth rib and pierced his heart as the supposedly dead Cheyenne leaped up from the ground and stabbed him in one smooth, fluid movement.

Touch the Sky was so weak from his ordeal and the effort that he could not get out of the way when Mankiller's dead body fell on him. For a moment Little Horse was sure both of them were dead. Then he heard his friend roar in disgust as he squirmed out from under their tormentor.

And despite his own incredible pain, Little Horse felt his face go numb with shock when his brother staggered to his feet and looked upward. Already Touch the Sky's neck had swollen so huge it looked like he had no chin.

"Brother," Little Horse said through teeth clenched in pain, "are you alive or a thing of smoke?"

Touch the Sky's voice was weak, but miraculously, still there. "A thing of smoke would not be able to cut you down. You had best not send me over too quickly."

The two friends reported Mankiller's death to Jack Morningstar and requested permission to remain for two more sleeps, recovering enough to make the long ride north and west to the upcountry of the Powder. The grateful Cherokee Council made sure they were well equipped for the journey. Before they rode out, they were also informed that they both had the status of voting headmen for any Cherokee Council meeting— one of the highest honors and marks of friendship an Indian could bestow on a red man from another tribe.

But despite their many important victories, that ride home was difficult for both of them. Because, in their absence, their many enemies had surely been at work against them. Touch the Sky knew important changes loomed. Arrow Keeper lay seriously ill, if not already dead. Black Elk's jealousy had festered so long it was a deadly poison. And the power-hungry Wolf Who Hunts Smiling could not wait much longer before killing the one man who blocked the path of his ambition.

Yes, this fight at Great Bend was behind them, a glorious victory to be proud of. But old Arrow Keeper was right. For a Cheyenne, life meant being a warrior, and the end of one battle marked only the beginning of the next.

CHEYENNE

Double Edition:
Pathfinder/ Buffalo Hiders
JUDD COLE

Pathfinder. Touch the Sky never forgot the kindness of the settlers, and tried to help them whenever possible. But an old friend's request to negotiate a treaty between the Cheyenne and gold miners brings the young brave face-to-face with a cunning warrior. If Touch the Sky can't defeat his new enemy, the territory will never again be safe for pioneers.

And in the same action-packed volume...

Buffalo Hiders. Once, mighty herds of buffalo provided the Cheyenne with food, clothing and skins for shelter. Then the white hunters appeared and the slaughter began. Still, few herds remain, and Touch the Sky swears he will protect them. But two hundred veteran mountain men and Indian killers are bent on wiping out the remaining buffalo—and anyone who stands in their way.

___4413-7 $4.99 US/$5.99 CAN

Dorchester Publishing Co., Inc.
P.O. Box 6640
Wayne, PA 19087-8640

CHEYENNE

JUDD COLE

Follow the adventures of Touch the Sky as he searches for a world he can call his own!

#3: Renegade Justice. When his adopted white parents fall victim to a gang of ruthless outlaws, Touch the Sky swears to save them—even if it means losing the trust he has risked his life to win from the Cheyenne.
_3385-2 $3.50 US/$4.50 CAN

#4: Vision Quest. While seeking a mystical sign from the Great Spirit, Touch the Sky is relentlessly pursued by his enemies. But the young brave will battle any peril that stands between him and the vision of his destiny.
_3411-5 $3.50 US/$4.50 CAN

WHITE APACHE
DOUBLE EDITION
By Jake McMasters
Save $$$!

They left him for dead, he'd see them in hell!

Warrior Born. Everyone in the Arizona Territory is out for Clay Taggart's scalp. He can handle the wealthy S.O.B. who paid to see him swing; he can even dodge the bluecoats who are ordered to gun him down. It isn't until the leader of the Apache warriors who saved him turns against Clay that he fears for his life. But the White Apache isn't about to let anyone send him to Boot Hill.

And in the same action-packed volume...

Quick Killer. For every enemy Taggart leaves to feed the desert scavengers, another–like the bloodthirsty army scout Quick Killer–wants to send him to hell. Quick Killer is half-Indian, all trouble, and more than a match for the White Apache. If Taggart doesn't kill the scout first, his own carcass will be feeding the vultures.

__4231-2 $4.99 US/$5.99 CAN